JOY, PA

YELLOW SHOE FICTION

Michael Griffith, Series Editor

PA

A NOVEL

STEVEN SHERRILL

East Baton Rouge Parish Library
Baton Rouge, Louisiana

LOUISIANA STATE UNIVERSITY PRESS   BATON ROUGE

Published by Louisiana State University Press
Copyright © 2015 by Steven Sherrill
Manufactured in the United States of America
LSU Press Paperback Original
First printing

Designer: Barbara Neely Bourgoyne
Typeface: Sina Nova

Library of Congress Cataloging-in-Publication Data
Sherrill, Steven, 1961–
    Joy, PA : a novel / Steven Sherrill.
       pages ; cm. — (Yellow shoe fiction)
    "LSU Press paperback original."
    ISBN 978-0-8071-5956-9 (pbk. : alk. paper) — ISBN 978-0-8071-5957-6 (pdf) —
ISBN 978-0-8071-5958-3 (epub) — ISBN 978-0-8071-5959-0 (mobi) 1. Dysfunctional
families—Fiction. 2. Domestic fiction. I. Title.
    PS3569.H4349J69 2015
    813'.54—dc23
                                                              2014026204

Dedicated to Harold Camping
Born: July 19, 1921
Died: December 15, 2013

JOY, PA

One. Two. Three. Four. Five. Six. Seven. Eight. Nine. Ten. Eleven. Twelve. Thirteen. Fourteen. Fifteen. Sixteen. Seventeen.

This is how many times we stab her.

DAY 1

∀

"Willie. Get up. Kneel down. Put your hands like this."

Abigail Augenbaugh pulls the covers back, takes the boy's thighs, turns his reluctant body. He's almost too big.

"No, Mama." He curls tight. Tries to cover himself.

"Get up, Willie. There's not much time. The man says we have to pray. We have to beseech the Lord."

Abigail Augenbaugh wants nothing more than to beseech the Lord. But she doesn't know how to beseech. Abigail Augenbaugh tries anyway.

She positions the boy by the Spiderman bed, kneels there with him. Puts her hand on the back of his neck and lets a lifetime, generations even, of living in Joy, PA, living in the unrelenting shadow of Scald Mountain, press down upon him.

"Pray like this," she says.

"OK, Mama. I'll do it, Mama."

She's behind me. Pressing down. I'll do it. I will. I'll pray, like she says. Like the man says. I want to go to Heaven too. Mama is going to Heaven. The man is taking Mama. I don't want to stay behind.

"Tell me what to do, Mama. Show me how."

I talk and talk, but she can't hear me.

"Mama?

"Mama?

"I want to go with you. To Heaven, Mama. Please! Can you hear me?"

∀

There are words in Abigail's mouth. Words in her ears. But the bells take over. Three churches stand within sight of the house, and at the end of the block the courthouse clock tower rises into a tepid May night. Its moonish, glowing face looms over the street. Could be beautiful. The bells take over. There is a minute hand hanging limp, for years, and a dagger-ish hour hand that drags like the tongue of a stroke victim. There are three churches, and their denominational bell clappers argue over the exactitude of the hours. It's hard to know what time it is.

But the man says, *Soon*. The man on the radio says three days.

Abigail Augenbaugh prays. There are words in her mouth and ears. The boy prays too. Or maybe he doesn't. The bells take over. They stop. They ring forever.

"Did you pray, Willie? The man says we have to beseech the Lord. Did you beseech?"

"I did, Mama. I beseeched."

Abigail Augenbaugh tucks the boy in. It's an awkward, unfamiliar gesture. She's done all that she can do now. It's too late for the other things, the unfulfilled dreams. No scrapbooking courses at the community college, where she might meet new friends, maybe even begin hosting Pampered Chef and Ooh-La-La Lingerie parties at the house. No birthday parties for all the kids at Slinky Action Zone. Too late. Too late.

Abigail crosses the cramped hallway, closes her bedroom door, looks out the window, across the street, through a high wrought-iron fence, to where the town's oldest cemetery climbs the town's steepest hill. She tries to imagine the dead rising up from their graves. They will. The man says so. She tries to imagine Joy destroyed by the wave of earthquakes and fire that will sweep across the planet soon. She tries to imagine the absence. Abigail's mind is not up to the task. She takes the calendar from the top of her dresser—the calendar she got free from the Humane Society—steadies her hand, and makes a jagged X.

Three days remaining before the Rapture. Judgment Day. Or is it the *Apocalypse*? Abigail feels unprepared. The man on the radio says, from the mouth of God Himself comes the knowledge, that as the dinner hour marches in longitudinal increments around the globe the earth will shake and crack open. The True Believers will be caught up with the Lord. As for the rest, she can't bear to think of what will happen to those billions of people not fortunate enough to have been *chosen* by God.

Abigail Augenbaugh wants to be among those, the chosen. She'll do whatever it takes.

The boy prayed. Abigail made sure of it. Is there more to be done? The man on the radio says all come, wrecked and wicked, from the womb. There are no guarantees. The boy prayed. Abby was there.

There is a husband, in the basement. He never prays. Abigail is certain. Her husband lives in the basement. Abigail knows he's there, knows he's alive, because he curses and talks. There was a time when she would go down to him. There was a time when she wanted to. No more. There is no more time. The boy prayed. That's what is important.

Abigail wants to go back to the boy. To her son. Across the hall. She doesn't.

Three days.

Pray. Pray without ceasing.

Abigail Augenbaugh, overcome, retches. Vomits into a small trash can, wipes her mouth, lies back on the bed, waits for the dizziness to pass. Waits for a message. A sign. Waits for it all to be over.

"I did, Mama. I beseeched."

I take my lie to bed. I hold it tight. The lie throbs against my chest. Bores into my skin. Mama's in her bedroom. She's listening to the radio. She's crying. I'm hungry. I'm sick. My lie makes me sick. I didn't pray. I didn't beseech the Lord. Mama is going to Heaven without us. Mama will look down, from way up there, in Heaven. She'll see us, me and Daddy, down here. We'll look up, look for her face. Mama. She'll be in Heaven.

I'm hungry. Sick. I want to try again. I want to pray with Mama and beseech the Lord.

I go to her door. I go quietly. No one can hear me move. I am Ghost Boy. I am Stealth. I go to the door. Her door is closed. I squat there, against it. I hear everything.

I tremble, and I'm sure that many other people are trembling when we think that we're only a few days from that tremendous Day of Judgment that the world has been waiting for thirteen thousand years, knowing that someday, someday, there would be an end. All mankind knows that deep in their heart because everyone is created in the image of God and has the Law of God written on their heart, that they're sinners intuitively; they know they have to answer to God for their sins; they know there's finally going to come a time of reckoning, and it's all pointing to near the end of time. In your rebellion you have not become a child of God ... you are left behind ... you are sentenced to the rest of the Judgment ... you will die, and millions of people will probably die that very first day because of the stupendous earthquakes that will be all over the world in that twenty-four-hour period.

The man talks of the graves opening up, and his voice is sonorous and wet. The man talks of untold suffering, of cataclysmic destruction, of unprecedented death, and his phlegmy, grandfatherly confidence comforts Abigail. But she is confused. How will the bodies of all the unsaved dead fit on the surface of the earth? What will all those bodies and bones look like? Will they wander around, befuddled? Baffled by their awakening? Will they speak? Moan? Stink?

Abigail sobs quietly. She hears the boy, Willie, outside the bedroom door. She hears his breath. He breathes his whole ten years of living in and out with every lungful. The boy would've been eleven years old next month. Abigail tries to come to terms with all the life he's going to miss. Maybe it's not such a bad thing. She knows she ought to go to the door, to let the boy, her son, in, to take him in bed, put her arms around him, tell him all about Heaven. Pretend, for his sake. Or believe, even. Abby doesn't know the difference. She knows only what she is told. What the man on the radio tells.

We'll worship and serve the Lord, all day, all night, forever.

She ought to stroke his head, to kiss his cheek, to calm his fears. But that is not the kind of mother Abigail Augenbaugh knows how to be. They prayed together. She made sure of that much. They'll pray together tomorrow, and pray again the next day, as the Rapture draws nigh. That's the best she can do. She'll do as the man on the radio instructs. To come broken and contrite, to beseech the merciful and compassionate God. Abigail turns away from the sounds of Willie at the door, turns up the volume.

Sometimes I get calls asking about after Judgment Day begins, what about these buildings here and what about that, and what about that? They're not listening. When Judgment Day comes, there's not going to be buildings. Everything's going to be flattened; there's going to be a huge, huge earthquake; it's not going to be business as usual at all, not at all. It is the end of the world. Even the mountains will be cast down and the land removed out of its place. It's going to be super, super horror. The true believers will see it all. We don't know just how it's going to work out. God doesn't give us all the details. Then everything's going to be annihilated and never be remembered again. And the whole business of what happened on earth will be gone. It will never, never come to anybody's memory again. It will be totally gone.

I lied. God knows it. God knows everything. Beginning and end. God will take Mama, will leave me and Daddy here. Mama is crying. The man on the radio talks about the Bible coming straight from the lips of holy God. It must've been like comic-book talk. Big white bubbles full of words, falling out of Heaven. Crushing everything. How big are God's lips? Does God have teeth? Does he have old-man breath? The man on the radio talks about the graves opening up. There is a graveyard across the street. I see it from my bedroom window. The man talks about dead people coming up out of the ground. About live people flying up to Heaven. I lied. I did not beseech, and now Mama will fly up to Heaven, and I'll stay behind and the dead people will come after me.

Mama is in the bed crying. We prayed. I lied to her. I have to be strong. I have to pray again. By myself. I'll beseech the Lord. I wish I knew how. I open my mouth to try, but my words are not like prayers. They spill off my tongue like ball bearings. They clatter across the floor. They roll under the radiators. I don't want Mama to hear. I have to be strong. I have to be brave. I go to the laundry hamper. I dump it out. I dig through the dirty clothes, find my Spiderman pajamas. I don't care how they smell. I don't care how old they are. I change. I push my legs and arms through the tight holes. I have to be strong. Brave.

I go downstairs. By myself. I open the basement door. Daddy's there. I'm not allowed in. He's down there on the couch, swimming in the blue-green TV light. Words and sounds gurgle up into my ears, but I don't understand them. I want to go down into his blue-green light. I want to curl up against Daddy and tell him about my lie. I am not allowed in. My lie burns in my belly. I shut the door. I open the refrigerator. I swim in the yellow light. I swim in the emptiness. In the cabinet I find a handful of cereal in the bottom of a box. I choke it down. I have to be brave. Strong.

I hear something. I hear everything. It's outside. I go outside. Through the front door. I pass right through the wood and glass. I hear the neighbors. The stupid little girl laughs from the second floor. I go between the houses. They stand close. I am a knife blade between them. I am not scared. It's dark outside. I am outside. I see the light in their kitchen. I stand on the trash can and look in the window. I see their supper table. I can almost reach in and take the salt shaker. It's shaped like a donkey. I hear bathwater running. I hear the girl laugh overhead. Like she's in Heaven. Stupid girl. My foot slips. I fall. The trash can tips; its aluminum lid rattles on the sidewalk. I am brave. I am strong. I hear the quiet in the house. I hear the back door slam open. I press my body against the foundation of the house. Feel the cool cinderblocks thorough my Spider-man shirt. I become darkness. I become night. I will not be captured. Any second, I can blaze, become the mighty Fist of Destruction. I will not be taken alive. I will pound them all into a bloody mess. I wait. My lie pulses deep inside me.

I hear the man shout as he goes back into the house.

"Goddamn raccoons!"

I am strong. I am brave. I see the Happy Meal bags spilling from the trash can. Like answers to a prayer. Inside, I find some French fries, slick with ketchup, and a piece of cheeseburger wadded up in a napkin. I find a juice box. Like answers to a prayer. I take it. I take it all, sit on the front steps of my own dark house. I look up and down the sidewalk, the street, at all the old houses. Over the roofs, the dark hump of the mountain blocks most of the moon. I can smell the paper mill, like rotten eggs. I can hear the wheels of train cars screaming. Screaming. Just like every other night. The man on the radio says it'll all be gone in two days. I eat and drink slowly, taking the tiniest bites possible, the tiniest sips possible. I can make the meal last forever if I try.

You hear the boy stomping around upstairs. Always stomping around upstairs. Where the hell is the wife? Somewhere in the house, but you can't say for sure where. She's been disappearing for years. By now the woman is nearly transparent. She ought to keep the boy quiet. She knows better.

You turn the TV volume all the way up because you like to hear the solid thwack of the tee shots and the little pop when the putter strikes the ball. You can only watch so much porn. You can only play so much video golf. But you can't stop either.

Where the hell is the wife? The boy? You can't remember when you last saw them. But you know they're up there, stomping around in the night. You ought to go up there. You ought to get your fat ass off the couch, take it upstairs and straighten things out. But you don't. Man up!

What the fuck. You don't.

You sit on the couch. You lie on the couch. You jab at the remote, switching back and forth between the Masters Historic Edition and *Ass Parade*. Heaven lies somewhere between the twelfth hole at Augusta and those white panties. You do this all night. Every night.

Outside, a tractor-trailer Jake-brakes its way down Scald Mountain; the diesel scream rips open the quiet. The quiet is what gets to you. You're grateful for the truck, but then it's gone. Inside, every goddamn lunatic notion that squeaks into existence takes hold of your mind and lights it up like a pinball machine. Tilt. Tilt. Tilt. They tell you to take the pills, so you take the pills. Half a dozen pills, three times a day, every day. They tell you the pills will stop the thoughts from ricocheting around your brain. They tell you the pills will help you sleep. They tell you the pills will make you happier. Or, at least, not so mad. They lie. They don't tell you the pills will make you fat, will stop you up so that you only shit once a week if you're lucky, will shrivel your dick and pinch the head off the tick that is your sex drive. They don't tell you that the sleep you get isn't quite sleep. It's like trying to swim in a big vat of molasses. You don't sleep at night. Too risky. Too quiet. So you lie on the old couch you dragged to the basement, you lie there fat, constipated, exhausted, impotent, barely able to move.

You got the three-year-old Xbox from the boy. He cried. You took it anyway. Man up! Don't be such a pussy. You might have stolen the PGA Tour game, the Masters Historic Edition. You can't remember. You watch porn, the same tired DVDs again and again. You mute the movies so you don't have to listen to them talk. Moan. The moans embarrass you. Sometimes the wife comes to the basement to do laundry. You turn up the volume when she comes down. Deeper, big boy. Stick it in! You haven't seen her in a long time. You haven't seen anybody in a long time. You don't care. Not enough, anyway. You lie on the couch and watch porn. Hopefully. You can't sleep. You don't sleep on an old couch in the basement of a rented house. You don't own anything real. Anything except your club. Big Bertha. You keep Big Bertha under the couch where you can reach her. You've had her for years. Long before you enlisted. Long before you got married. You keep Big Bertha polished—with her graphite shaft and titanium head—and within reach. You can't concentrate. Polishing the club helps you concentrate.

There is a boy upstairs. The boy is your son. The word swells in your mouth. Clots on your tongue. You don't remember how or when you brought the couch down. There are no windows in the basement. The cement floor and cinderblock walls hold in the damp cool air, and keep out the desert.

I want my birthday. I don't want the world to end.

From the lips of God. From the belly of the earth.

I heard him say it. I heard him say it. I lied to Mama. I lied to the man on the radio. I lied to God. I don't want a Rapture. I want my birthday. I'll be eleven. I'll ask for a new Game Boy.

Abigail Augenbaugh prays herself to sleep. The woman is exhausted. There are no dreams, for better or worse. Neither memory nor prophesy can conquer her fatigue. She doesn't dream of the pale wash of light on her bedroom wall, from the streetlamps around the graveyard, light that gets sliced into thinner and thinner strips as she closes the blinds. She doesn't dream of what's beyond those blinds: row after cramped row, street after narrow street, of two-story plank houses—some over a century old; the courthouse at one end of the block and at the other the Presbyterian steeple and its derelict manse. She doesn't dream of the weedy yards or sagging front porches, or the faded plethora of tattered American flags hanging from rusty brackets or roped to banisters, left over from the fervently marketed *War on Terror*. Not tonight.

Abigail Augenbaugh does not dream the whittled history of Joy, PA, the only town she has ever known. Abigail sleeps, and Joy continues its plodding industry despite the impending Apocalypse. The paper mill—its stink of sulfur filling the town—keeps churning out envelopes in three sizes. The tired third-shift employees at Allegheny Candy continue packing chocolate crosses and Last Suppers, Easter Bunnies and Santa Clauses into cellophane-wrapped boxes. Farther down the hill, at the foot of Scald Mountain, the railroad tracks and the Little Juniata River carry nothing of value into or out of town.

Nor does she dream of her own ragged and hollow few decades on the planet, an endless plodding toward—what?—nothing. Abigail Augenbaugh perches along the edge of the hand-me-down double bed—her side, despite the fact that her husband, Burns, hasn't slept there in years—trying even in sleep to hold on to the Bible teacher's syrupy, bitter promises—*Apart from Salvation, we are worms and maggots. The lamb shall lead them to living fountains of waters. In just a few days, God's elect, two hundred million people, will join the wedding feast, will be married to the Lord Jesus Christ. Will be forever the Lamb's wife. Throughout eternity.* But the torpor will not be denied. The boy prayed with her. She's done all she can. She sleeps.

The world somersaults. I can't move. I can't get off the floor. My feet are trapped in the WrestleMania quilt. There is thunder and lightning. There is screaming. And, as if coming down from Heaven itself, that song. *Bip bop bop.* The Mario Bros. theme song. *Bip bop bop, ticka ticka . . .* It's everywhere at once. I can't escape. I wear my Spiderman pajamas. I am brave. Nothing can hurt me. My bed shakes. The windows rattle. The thunder comes from the lips of holy God. I creep to the window, peel back the WrestleMania curtain. I am brave. My heart will not explode. I take a deep breath and peek out. There is fire in the sky. Black birds the size of cars sweep the sky, carrying away people in their talons. I look across the street, I see the graveyard. I see the ground split, peel, and roll away. I see the dead—all the dead—stand up in their trenches. They wipe the mud from their empty eye sockets, crawl out of their graves. I see the dead—all the dead—stumble and trip and begin to roll down the steep hill. I see the dead—flinging their dead arms, kicking their dead legs, screaming their dead screams—begin to pile up higher and higher beneath my window. Thunder. Lightning. That music. Faster and faster. Louder and louder. I am brave. The dead reach up for me. I am brave. Blood pours from the open graves, floods the street. *Bip bop bop… ticka ticka.* Blood pours beneath my bedroom door. I am brave. I wear my Spiderman pajamas. The dead reach up. I can't stop them. I am brave. My heart will not explode. The blood soaks my feet, soaks my legs. I am brave. I scream, but there is no sound. I kick, I hit, but my arms and legs refuse to move. The dead pile up and roll into my bedroom window. The blood soaks my pajama bottoms. Thunder. Lightning. I am brave. The dead crawl across my floor, reach up to me. I am in my bed. I am brave. Thunder. Lightning. The hands of the dead take hold of my ankles, my wrists and I wake up. And I wake up. Wake up. And I wake up with my lie.

They're all out to fuck you over. And they're all in it together. You've got to keep that in mind. You've got to keep your eyes open. You've got your basement. You've got the Xbox and the porn. You've got Big Bertha. But the whole night lays itself out before you. The whole night. You've got the pills. Will they last? What if they don't? The basement walls, are they substantial enough to withstand whatever comes? Whatever comes. Are you substantial enough? You try to remember the last time you talked to another human. You can't talk to the wife. What would you say? *Dumb bitch. I'm sorry.*

Dumb bitch. I'm sorry. I am. Sorry.

They're all in it together. Together. You try to remember. It may be that you've never had a real conversation. Ever. You used to see people talking, at the mall, in the grocery—watched their faces, their bodies—and you could tell that something passed between them. Back and forth. How does that happen?

Maybe it was the pharmacist? The one with the accent and the sexy mole on her bottom lip. When did you get your prescription filled? Last month? Two months ago? You watched her count out the pills and tried to imagine her little tits. She said something about the Pirates game, and you wanted to jump over the counter. But you're too fat. Your hair is too dirty. Your breath, foul. The pharmacist with the mole and small tits talked about baseball.

"Titties," you said.

It was the best you could do. The pharmacist backed away from the counter and asked if you were experiencing any side effects. You're fat. You sweat constantly. You can't sleep. You're constipated. You're impotent. There's a nest of yellow jackets where your brain used to be, a snapping turtle in your belly.

"No," you said.

Back in the basement, you stripped and tried to imagine her face onto the bodies in *Big Round Behinds*. Nothing. You stayed naked and struggled with Augusta's twelfth hole.

How long ago was that?

How'd she get back in your brain?

Where are your pills?

Where's the goddamn phone?

You want to call the pharmacy. You want to talk to the pharmacist with the mole and the small tits. You might tell her that the desert sand bubbles up from the floor drain in your basement. Sometimes the pills can stop it. You might tell her what actually happened. Over there. You might make up a better story. You might tell her that the boy is always stomping around upstairs, but that you've never beaten him. You might tell her that the last time you remember seeing your wife she was making biscuits. Canned biscuits, not homemade. You came upstairs—can't remember why—just as she peeled the foil away and whacked the cardboard tube against the edge of the counter. The airy pop was too much for you. Like ordnance in the distance. You slammed the door and almost tripped on the stairs back down to your couch. You might tell the pharmacist this. Or you might ask what color panties she's wearing.

But it's the middle of the night. It'll be dark for hours. The pharmacy is closed. The pharmacist with the mole and the little tits is not there. She's somewhere else. The wife and the boy are sleeping. You hear the sand pumping through the sewer lines. Soon it'll start filling the basement. They tell you to take the goddamn pills, so you take the goddamn pills. You tell them, just give me a blowjob and a bullet. That's all you need. But nobody listens.

You pick up Big Bertha and lie on the couch. This is your life. A minute, a few seconds of clarity, then the thought-bombs explode in your head. It wasn't always this way. But even back then, even before the Army, you had no real options.

You bought Big Bertha with your own money, money earned mowing the greens and fairways at Scald Mountain Country Club the summer before high school. "I'm thinking about joining the golf team, Daddy," you said. It took you a while to say it. Years. He laughed at you. There was no way you'd tell him about the Golf Course Management program over at the community college. You knew well enough how Daddy felt about the community college. "Goddamn liberals!" He laughed. At you. He didn't have a choice. You forgot all about joining the team, forgot all about the associate's degree. For a while afterwards, you snuck out to the driving range to hit a bucket of balls. Then you gave that up too. In the middle of eleventh grade, you dropped out.

You never told anybody. You never told anybody that it felt like, even if you did your best, you didn't deserve anything good. Joining teams and going to college and hoping for a different kind of life, that was for the boys whose fathers belonged to the country club. Those boys got the pretty girlfriends and the blowjobs. Those boys went to college. You didn't deserve any of that. You deserved, if you were lucky, a job at the paper mill, like your daddy. Or work in the train yard, moving boxcars all day, every day. You deserved, at the very best, a lucky accident that would earn you a disability check every month. You'd learn to take something like pride in your misery and you'd defend it to the goddamn end. One thing was certain, nobody was going to let you get too big for your britches.

You never told anybody that you thought these things. You'd tell that pharmacist, with the mole and the titties, next time you saw her. You sure as hell couldn't tell the wife. You remember, when you got back from the Army, that bitch nurse at the VA insisting that you join her group. *Therapy,* she called it.

You keep the pill bottles in an old tackle box, along with a fillet knife and a little pistol you bought for your wife—protection from Muslim terrorists—just before you were deployed. You never liked fishing, not a single one of the hundreds of times you went. Alone. With your own father. The woman, the wife, is afraid of the gun. Stupid. Bitch. At the bottom of the tackle box, beneath the bottles, and a handful of loose bullets, you find her business card, the nurse from the VA hospital. You don't know what the pharmacist likes. You find the card is oil-stained, the 800 number worn nearly off. You've held this card before, trying to weigh its worth.

HELP AVAILABLE 24 HOURS A DAY.

You read it again.

HELP AVAILABLE 24 HOURS A DAY.

You've read it many times, over the years.

Bullshit.

You decide, for the moment, that it's all bullshit. What do they know about your life? What kind of help could they possibly offer? Some nights are better than others. This is a bad night. Bullshit or no, you call anyway. Some nights are better than others. This is a bad night. It's like a tape loop. You take a deep breath and jab at the number pad. After three rings, a flat, sexless voice answers your call.

"You have reached—" the voice says.

"Please listen carefully," it says.

You are already doubtful of the outcome.

"Press one if you are having thoughts of harming yourself. Press two for behavioral health. Press three for—"

You slam the receiver against the concrete-block wall. The phone shatters and lands, gutted, at your feet, both the battery and tiny speaker dangling from wires.

"What do I press?" you say aloud. "What do I press if I want to come down there and jab your eyeballs with a toothpick?"

Sand clots your mouth.

"What do I press if I want to shove a funnel down your throat and—"

It's not like you'd *really* do these things, right?

"What do I press if sometimes I want to push a wheelbarrow full of dynamite right through your front door and blow us all to Hell?"

It's the *Hell* part you're not sure of. Could things be any worse?

What do you press just to shut it all up?

How do you stop the pressing, the nothingness that crushes you minute by minute, day in, day out?

You try to remember if there is another phone upstairs. You don't know what time it is, but you're sure to have hours before sunrise, before you feel safe enough to sleep.

You go to the Xbox. The Xbox is your salvation. Help is available twenty-four hours a day. There are more than twenty-four hours in the Hell of your days. In your basement, your hole, there is no *time*. And time is running out. You tee up on the first hole. In there, the sky is always blue blue blue. Everything is beautiful. The azaleas. The magnolia trees. In the distance, the green shimmers like a jewel, its mustard-yellow pin flag flutters in an unreal wind. Everybody awaits your next move. Ready to cheer. The crowd hushes just before you swing.

The curtain is closed. My pajamas are wet. My sheets, my Wrestle-Mania sheets are soaked. I can smell the paper mill. My pee. I pull the earphones out; the Mario song leaves my head. I hear a train. *Bip bop bop, ticka ticka.* I peed my pants. I want my birthday. I don't want Mama to go with Jesus without me. It's dark. I'm wet. I don't want to leave my room. I don't want to leave my bed. I'm wet, but I don't care. I wish. I wish I could stop it. I am brave. And strong. If I were braver, if I were stronger, maybe I *could* do something. I could stop the world from ending, somehow. Daddy would be so proud. I'd be a hero. Everybody would love me. Everybody would call out my name.

"That's him! That's the boy who stopped the Apocalypse! That's Willie!"

DAY 2

⋈

One. Two. Three. Four. Five. Six. Seven. Eight. Nine. Ten. Eleven. Twelve. Thirteen. Fourteen. Fifteen. Sixteen. Seventeen. Eighteen. Nineteen. Twenty. Twenty-one.

This is how many times we stab her.

Abigail Augenbaugh wakes into a troublingly beautiful May morning. She looks out the window. A light shroud of fog climbs up from the foot of Scald Mountain; it greens by the minute. Dew, gathered on the silky caterpillar nests in the branches of the ash trees and box elders, sparkles in deceptive beauty. The daylilies in all their orange fury; the rhododendron and laurel unfurled to greet the sun; the yellow bells' unkempt splay: these all lay claim to her sight. A garbage truck passes; a city bus goes by in the other direction. Both vehicles are stunning and glorious in their filth. Abigail Augenbaugh almost yields to the beauty.

How does it happen that a day so close to the end of the world can be so regular and so magnificent? Abby looks at her calendar. The calendar is from AMVETS. A smiling young black woman in a perfect uniform graces the May page. *Donate Now*, the text reads. A lopsided red circle marks a midmonth day. Abigail made the circle. She thinks it's a reminder about Burns's medication. It doesn't matter. Abigail prayed with her boy last night. There are too many hard days to count, stacked up behind that pending date, that empty box at the end of the week. Tonight she'll pray with the boy again. She is doing her part. She is helping the boy prepare for what's to come. Abigail doesn't have anyone, didn't ever have anyone to help her prepare. She prayed with the boy last night. There is solace in that, and a little balm for a lifetime of maternal shortcomings. She never had anyone to show her the way. She prayed with the boy last night. Tonight she'll make another mark. Today she'll go to work and hand out tracts. She'll do God's work. Like the man says.

A sudden chill makes Abigail shiver in her thin nightgown. She folds her arms across her breasts, tiptoes into the hall, pauses at Willie's closed bedroom door. Barely touches the knob.

"Mama!" the boy calls out.

She opens the door, and the smells of sweat and urine and preteen boy wash over her. She prayed with him last night. They beseeched the Lord together. These smells, they don't matter anymore.

"I don't want to go to school today, Mama."

"Are you sick, honey?" The curtains are drawn, the blinds shut, but she can make out the boy's hump-shape tight against the wall in the bed.

He doesn't answer right away. He shifts beneath the WrestleMania blanket.

"Yes," he says. "I mean, no. I don't want to go to school. I want to stay home. I want to get ready. To be ready."

For what, he doesn't say, but Abigail knows what the boy means. She crosses the room, stands by the bedside, almost sits. Abigail reaches out, touches the blanket covering the body of her son. He flinches at the touch.

"Everything is all right," Abigail Augenbaugh says. "It'll all be over soon."

She backs out of the room, watching, feeling motherly. When she reaches the door the boy calls out again.

"Mama! Are you still there?"

"Yes, Willie," she says.

"Stay, Mama," he says. "Stay home with me today. We can pray some more. We can beseech."

Abigail pauses.

Abigail pauses.

Abigail pauses.

Abigail closes the door gently.

Abigail has work to do. God's work.

Abigail works as a boxer at the Slinky factory. All day long she drops jiggly coils of metal or Day-Glo plastic into colorful little square cardboard boxes. She stacks those boxes neatly into larger, thicker shipping boxes, then sends the whole shebang down the conveyor to the loading dock. The toy has been losing relevance for years. The company tries to make up for that loss by trumping up the *historic* value, the cultural importance of their outdated product—to both their aging employees and the toy-buying world at large. Once a year, the junior- and senior-high kids get a tour of the factory. There is a Slinky float in the Joy Christmas parade, the Fourth of July parade, the Veterans Day parade, the Thanksgiving parade. Sometimes there is a Slinky Queen on the float, sometimes not. Abigail has always wanted to ride the Slinky float. In Abby's secret place, she wears the cloak and crown of the Slinky Queen. All the boys liked the Slinky Queen. The Slinky Queen rules Joy, PA, with beneficence and love. And love. And everybody in Joy, PA, loves the Slinky Queen. In her secret place, her deepest mind, Abigail Augenbaugh waves to her adoring townspeople from atop the Slinky Throne.

But none of it matters anymore.

She puts on her official Slinky Employee Smock and goes quietly downstairs.

It's daylight, and though the basement door is closed, she knows Burns is asleep on the couch. She knows the opening credits of that golf game are looping on the television. She hears the irregular little bursts of polite and fake applause.

Burns is asleep. Burns does not work. Burns hasn't worked regularly since coming back from Iraq. He tried, for a week, stocking shelves at Surplus City. But that was years ago. Now, her husband lies on a couch in the damp basement, growing heavier and paler, playing video golf and watching those disgusting movies. When she can't hear the sounds of the golf game, Abigail won't go into the basement, not even if all the laundry in the house is dirty. She used to go down. He used to come up. The man on the radio says it doesn't matter.

Abigail spreads a thin layer of margarine on a piece of white bread, sits at the table waiting for the coffee to brew. There was a time, a while ago, when the pride Abby felt she had to show for Burns's military service (a mandate handed down from on high, a decree enforced by by the uberpatriotic television commercials, the billboards, and the hundreds and hundreds of tattered little American flags scattered throughout the town) outweighed any disappointment or embarrassment she felt over the real, daily, relentless aftermath of his experience. But disappointment and shame are powerful foes that have won nearly every battle in Abigail's life. She has no idea what Burns thinks or how he feels, about anything. He takes all those pills. He rages. She used to wish he had a job. Then she wished he'd just come out of the basement. The husband. The man on the radio comes to her every night.

None of it matters, now. In just a few days, nothing will matter.

Abigail follows the nothingness into her brain, stares vacantly at the wall until heavy footsteps on the front stoop and the rattle of the mailbox startles her. Abby drops her buttered bread. It lands face-down on the floor.

The Slinky clock over the sink reads 8:15. Abigail wipes the mess from the floor, parts the curtain on the front door, looks furtively up and down the sidewalk, then quickly snatches the mail and rebolts the lock.

Bills. A cancellation notice from the phone company. Something official-looking from the VA hospital. They keep sending things. They pry. They make promises. They want to know things about Burns. Abigail opens the trash and shoves all the mail beneath the discarded bread and paper towels. None of it matters.

She looks at the clock. 8:45. Time for work. Time to box Slinkys. Where did that half hour go? Where does any of it go? All that time in a life. Abigail wonders if once she gets to Heaven with Jesus she'll understand things better. Abigail worries that she won't be any smarter in Heaven.

She laces up her thick-soled work shoes. She loops the Slinky Employee lanyard around her neck, turns the photo in so that it faces the smock. What Abigail feels about her job cannot be called *hate* only because she cannot conceive of deserving the luxury of hatred. Years and years of demeaning, mindless jobs have rendered Abigail numb and obedient. Sheeplike. She moves through the routine of her days without expectation, without hope, unseeing and unseen, unquestioning and unconsidered. Like her mother. Like her grandmother. Until now. Until the man on the radio. Until the coming Judgment.

Abigail takes her worry and her empty coffee cup to the empty sink.

Abigail doesn't understand strong women, women who stand up straight and speak loudly enough to be heard, women who get ahead in the world. She fears them. When the three sharp knocks at the door penetrate Abigail's muddlement, she has no choice but to drop the cup. It shatters in the porcelain sink. Abigail sucks in a sharp breath and falls to her knees.

She's done this before. This hiding. This cowering. Instinct will not be denied.

Three more knocks, louder this time.

"Hello," a woman's voice calls through the door. "Mrs. Augenbaugh?"

Abigail doesn't recognize the voice.

The caller, no doubt, heard the cup shatter.

Abigail crawls across the kitchen floor, her own kitchen floor, to the window. She slips a trembling finger between the blinds and peeks out. She sees a long gray skirt, pattern-less, pressed and neat. Thin legs. A delicate butterfly tattoo, one blue wing draping the anklebone, disappears into a shoe that, though scuffed, is nicer than any Abigail has ever owned.

"Mrs. Augenbaugh?"

The voice is quieter. As if the speaker knows Abigail is close.

"My name is Carole. Carole Onkst. I'm the guidance counselor at the middle school. Mrs. Augenbaugh, I want to talk to you about William."

William? Hearing her son's actual name called confuses Abigail for a moment. Her knees hurt. She tightens her focus onto the worn flecked linoleum, and into the pain. She can hear the clock ticking in the other room. She'll be late for work.

"We can help, Mrs. Augenbaugh."

Willie. The woman is talking about the boy. Her son. But it's too late. The man on the radio says so. Abigail Augenbaugh thinks to give the woman a Rapture tract. It would explain everything. The tract. Abigail loves the word. She got it from the man on the radio. She trusts him. Carole Onkst, the guidance counselor, would read the tract, would understand, would come inside, would kneel there on the floor with Abby, and pray. And pray.

But Abigail doesn't move. She doesn't even pray. She waits. She listens. She hears the screen door open, hears a faint scratching sound, hears Carole Onkst speak softly, just on the other side of the curtain.

"I'll come back later," she says. "I'll come back again. Call, if you need to. Anytime."

Then nothing.

Abigail wonders what it would mean to open the door, to allow Carole Onkst in, maybe even to allow Carole Onkst to talk to Willie. To take Willie. To take the boy, her son, Willie, William, out of that house, away from the day. Would it make any difference? Would it help? Would it save the boy from the Judgment to come?

"Wait—" Abigail Augenbaugh says. Whispers. Is it too late? "Wait." It's all happening too fast. Is she doing the right thing? "Wait."

But when Abigail is finally able to stand and open the curtain, Carole Onkst is gone. There is no sign of her presence. Maybe she was never there. Maybe Satan was trying to tempt Abby. To take her boy. To sway her commitment. Satan is everywhere, and he is powerful. The man on the radio says so. Then Abby sees the business card tucked into the door-jamb. The sign.

Carole Onkst has scribbled something on the back of the card, but Abigail Augenbaugh can't bring herself to read it. She crumples against the door and tries to breathe. Is it too late? It is too late. Is it too late?

I tried to tell her.

I wanted to tell her.

"I lied, Mama."

That's what I wanted to say.

It's hot. I am wet. I look on the floor. There are no dead people. I get up and look out the window. There are no dead people. There is a woman. She's alive. I've seen her before. From school. I'm not going back. Ever.

The woman knocks, then backs off the porch. Looks up. I drop to the floor. I'm not going back. I lied to Mama. She knocks again. I peel back the curtain. I could jump. Easily. I could land on her head. Break her stupid neck. She should mind her own business. I could kill her. I killed her once already. At school. No, but I planned it. There in her office. With her stupid pictures of her stupid family on her stupid desk. With her stupid soft nice voice. Stupid soft nice eyes. I killed her. No. I planned to. Then I saw the tattoo. A butterfly. I wish I had a tattoo. I wish Mama had a tattoo. My papaw has tattoos. He's dead. We went to the nurse-home just before he died. The tattoos on his arms were all shriveled up. Skulls and snakes. Papaw didn't talk to me. He coughed a lot. Mama made me dump out the pus basin. She took me for ice cream afterwards. She cried on the way. I kept thinking about all the stuff that came out of Papaw's lungs. I wonder if his grave will open up too. I wonder if he'll talk to me.

I hear a car door slam, an engine crank. I look out, watch her drive down the road. I am not going back. Ever. My mattress is wet. I flip it. I am strong. Powerful. If I wanted to, I could turn the house upside down. The whole house. If I wanted to.

∀

Abigail rises. There is work to be done. God's work. And Slinky work.

The boy is upstairs. The man is in the basement. She can't change either of these facts.

There is work to be done.

Abigail Augenbaugh hates being late, hates punching the ancient time clock after everyone else. The solitary *chunk*—that claims to mark the legitimacy of her day—reverberates throughout the entire Slinky plant, and it seems as if everybody watches Abigail make her ponderous way along the back (windowless) wall, down to the employee locker room, and back up past the supervisor's fluorescent-lit office to her place on the packing line.

But that scrutiny, that burden, is almost bearable. Less bearable is that when running late, Abigail is sure to encounter her next-door neighbors. The Augenbaughs park their decrepit Chevy Celebrity on a cracked slab of concrete abutting the alley, behind the house. There must've been a shed or garage on the slab sometime in the past. No more. Sometime in the past, Burns had a valid license and did most of the driving. No more.

Last month, Abigail stopped paying the insurance. Now, she drives the uninsured Celebrity to and from the Slinky plant, Monday through

Friday. Abby prays that her luck (and the engine, and the transmission) will hold for the remaining few days. So far, these prayers have been answered. There is hope.

The Celebrity is parked in the alley, just through her small weedy rectangle of backyard. If Abigail went out her back door—across the unheated mudroom and down the two cement steps—she could hurry through the crabgrass and to her car without having to see, or talk to, Tim or Tina DeFonzie. But for Abigail to be able to leave the house through her back door, she'd have either to go back in time and change the past or overhaul her way of dealing with the present.

Six months prior, after a night of freezing rain, Willie slipped on the ice. The boy caught himself by hanging onto the mudroom's screen door, which pulled the top hinge from its frame. Abigail couldn't ask Burns to fix the door, nor could she call the landlord, so the screen door hung askew all winter and spring, and jammed so that the back entrance was unusable. The week before Easter, already preparing for the coming Rapture, Abigail propped her old ironing board in front of that door, thinking she might like to press her good skirt. She wanted to look her best for the Lord. But the ironing board became an easy place to deposit the recycling bins. Then, things for the yard sale she planned to have someday. Then, bags of trash. By this May morning, a few days before the Rapture, the mudroom is packed, floor to ceiling, wall to wall. Abigail Augenbaugh has no choice but to leave her house through the front door. She cannot reverse the clock and catch Willie before he falls. She cannot rescind that moment of hopefulness—in which she longed to look nice—that led her to set up the ironing board.

The man and the boy are in the house. The Lord is on his way. There is nothing Abby can do to make a difference.

Abigail stuffs her purse full of Are You Ready? Rapture tracts, closes the front door, quietly, and ducks into the narrow passage between her house and the DeFonzies'.

The whole house.

I'll tear down the whole goddamn house.

I will.

I'm just about to do it when I hear the front door.

"Mama," I say. She's walking between the houses. I will her to stay.

"Don't go, Mama. Wait. Wait for me."

If she paused long enough, Abby could easily put her hands out and touch both houses. It's cool there, between the homes. Always in shadow. And peaceful in fits and starts. Abigail regularly hears Tina rattling pots and pans in the kitchen, cooking dinner for her husband and kids. She hears the girl giggling and playing games in her bedroom. She hears the boy screaming in the tub. She hears Tim urinating. More. He disgusts her. He fascinates her. Those times when Abigail is sitting on her toilet and realizes he is right across the way, just over a thin transom of emptiness, close enough to reach out and touch, that realization makes her stomach heave, her heart clutch. Abigail wants only to stave off the wickedness from within, the wickedness from without, until the Lord swoops down and scoops her up into his arms, his Heaven.

Abigail hears Tim and Tina fight. She hears them, what, fornicate. There's no other word: *Fornicate* holds the necessary judgment. Abigail always tries to pee quietly. And she and Burns haven't argued, or anything else, in years. Once Burns saw her linger at the window, saw Tim DeFonzie lifting weights in the backyard. Glistening. Golden. They fought, Abigail and Burns. They may or may not have fornicated.

There is no pause this morning as Abigail rushes through the still shaft of emptiness and into the already blaring sunlight. Hurrying.

"Hey," Tim DeFonzie says from his weight bench.

The neighbor works, part-time, at Joy Plaque & Trophy. He works, full-time and shirtless, doing bench presses and squats and dumbbell curls in the makeshift gym he set up beneath a blue plastic tarp in the backyard. Through the DeFonzie mudroom window Abigail sees a shelf full of trophies from lifting competitions. The miniature figures atop each trophy—faux-gold and perfectly featureless—are obscenely greedy in capturing the morning sunlight. She wouldn't put it past Tim DeFonzie to have stolen some of them from work. He is a Catholic, after all.

"You had a visitor," Tim says. He settles the barbell into its rack and sits up. "Some lady in a suit knocked on your door."

There is substance to his chest and shoulders, girth to his arms, lean definition everywhere else. And the tattoo on his chest. The Sacred Heart. Crimson and dripping. Wrapped in thorns. A halo of flame. But Abigail Augenbaugh will not look. She will not. She knows, too, that buried in the sweaty thatch of black hair raging up what are surely his high-school gym shorts, all the way up to his throat, and dangling from a heavy chain around his neck, is a thick gold crucifix, with the suffering Savior rendered in exquisite detail. But Abigail refuses to look. She looks at her own feet, the sensible shoes. She looks across the DeFonzie yard to the Virgin Mary statue, sheltered in a sky-blue grotto Tim made by cutting a bathtub in half with a torch.

Abigail fingers the latch on her purse. She ought to just reach in, get a tract, and shove it in Tim DeFonzie's face. She ought to look him in the eye. She ought to.

"Hey Abigail," someone says. It's Tina. She leans out of her back door, half-hidden by the screen.

Abigail Augenbaugh knows that Tina DeFonzie wears "lingerie." That she has a tattoo as well. On her shoulder. Some words, and a child's face. The tattoo is a near-photographic likeness of their other son, the boy who drowned last summer. Or was it two summers ago?

Abigail knows the DeFonzies send their living children to Catholic school, and that the pending Rapture is going to leave them behind. Tim DeFonzie scratches roughly at his inner thigh, then contorts to stretch some specific muscle group. Still, Abigail refuses to look. She opens and closes, then opens and closes again, the flap of her purse.

"If she comes back, I'll tell her you moved," Tim says, smiling.

Abigail hurries to the Celebrity, pretending to unlock the door despite the fact that the lock hasn't worked since they bought the car. The rectangular hole in the middle of the dashboard, where the radio was before Burns pawned it, gapes like a mouth. Vein-like wires spill from within. Just before starting the engine, she hears it speak. Or maybe it's Tina.

"You want potted meat for lunch, Timmy?"

No!
No!
No!
I hate them.
I hate everybody.
I'll run. I'll catch her. I'll run all the way to Slinky.

I go downstairs. She's gone. Stupid. Stupid. Stupid woman. I find her card. It says her name. Out loud. I hear it speak. I eat the card. I am hungry. I eat the card. I eat her stupid name. I choke. I swallow. I eat the card. I am still hungry. I remember her name. I want my mama. I'll run and catch her. I'll run until I find her. I will. I'll run over the stupid neighbors. I'll run over anybody that gets in my way. I'll run so fast. So fast. The roads will melt under my feet. When I get there, I'll tell her about my lie. She'll put cool rags on my feet. She'll kiss me. She'll forgive me. We'll start over.

∀

Abigail parks the Celebrity in the gravel lot along the side wall of the Slinky plant. She walks, head down and stoop-shouldered, beneath the rusted awning and through the windowless employee door. For years, for decades, she has made this same walk. She walks into the single-story, aluminum-sided behemoth of a building that all but consumes a flat parcel of land pinched between the Little Juniata River and the eroding base of an unnamed, laurel-choked ridge that rises several hundred feet above the roofline.

She tries to leave her struggles, her worries, at the door. *Slinky* is about fun.

The railroad track and a narrow access road share the slender space along the front of the property. At the south end of the factory three chemical storage tanks rise over the roof; their blunt oxidized domes nudge at the sky. On the remaining land to the north, just beyond the loading docks, a salvage yard with its mountainous heaps of rusting metal, the prehistoric cranes that roam there chewing deep oily ruts with their rattling steel caterpillar tracks, commands the earth. For all Abigail ever knew, the Slinkys she spent her days boxing had former incarnations as Pontiacs, Schwinns, and Frigidaires.

Way back when Slinky was all the rage, the factory expanded, biting farther into the cliff to make room for increased production. Now, every so often, a chunk of the crumbling scarp will fall and half-bury the patio and a couple unstable picnic tables—used mostly by smokers—wedged between the rear of the building and the wall of earth. So far, no one has been killed.

Abigail enters.

Abigail pauses with her time card at the mouth of the punch clock. It feels like an eternity. All of it. Her pause. The years stacked upon years she's punched that very same clock. It was not the plan. It was never the plan. To spend so much of her life clocking in and out at the Slinky plant. The length of the day stretching out before her. And the few days left until, until real eternity begins.

Abigail puts her purse in the break-room locker, then tries to sneak past the supervisor's office window.

"Mrs. Augenbaugh," he says.

I'll run all the way. Except that when I get to the door I hear the stupid neighbors.

I hate them. I hate them all. I hate everybody. I go back to the kitchen. I am quiet. Daddy sleeps during the day. There are little clots of paper in my teeth. I want to tell Daddy about them. He's in the basement. I want to ask him about the end of the world. Is he going with us? Is he going with Mama? To Heaven. I hear no sound, but I know he's there. I'm not going to school today. I'm never going to school again. I'm hungry. I have to catch Mama. The cereal box is empty. There's some jelly in the fridge, one stale cracker in the cabinet. I hear the stupid neighbors slam their back door. The woman yells for them to hurry. Daddy calls her *slut*. She has a tattoo. I like her tattoo. I wish I had a tattoo. She waved at me, one time. One time, she gave me chewing gum. Slut. The man walks down the sidewalk out of sight. His wadded shirt hangs out of his back pocket. He's an asshole. Daddy calls him *asshole.* I am strong. I can run him over, if I want to. I can destroy him. Stupid asshole. Stupid Jesus tattoo. They have kids. Stupid kids. One time we found a dead rabbit. We put it in a shoebox. We prayed. It stayed dead.

I smell pee. It's mine. I am strong and brave. My pajamas are mostly dry. I get a cup of water from the sink. I look out my window, into the stupid neighbors' window. I see their kitchen table, where they sit and hold hands and pray before they eat. Stupid dead rabbit. I wonder if they know about the end of the world. I am happy that their world is almost over. I see their kitchen table and the plates from breakfast. I see a couple slices of bacon. Some scrambled egg. I see half a glass of milk. In a flash, I know exactly what to do. I am a genius.

∀

She tries to focus on Mr. Jinx. On his mouth. But nothing like words registers in her ears. The man is somewhere between forty and sixty years old, Abby can't tell. He's been the packaging supervisor for as long as she can remember. Mr. Jinx follows rules, and she likes that about him. Abigail stands in his office doorway. The conveyor belt rattles hurriedly behind her. The box-and-tape machine beats a syncopated rhythm: schkkk-chick-chicka. Schkkk-chick-chicka. Schkkk-chick-chicka. A forklift sputters by—with its insipid safety beep—leaving a stinking diesel cloud behind. Somewhere amid cacophony the radio plays, barely audible. Tuesdays and Thursdays the radio plays contemporary country. The other days, AM Top Ten. Abigail cocks her ear, but can't tell what day it is.

Abigail wants to get to work. She wants to box the Slinkys. There is order and predictability in the job.

"You ought to be ashamed," he says.

At least that's what Abigail thinks he says.

Mr. Jinx has an oversized pie-shaped face. A big, wide forehead—capped by a fringe of short, kinked, spiderweb-thin hair—looms over his watery eyes, those bugged out by thyroid problems. Mr. Jinx's nose hangs like an upturned spade, a shovel about to excavate his little, lipless ditch of mouth. Mr. Jinx follows rules.

Mr. Jinx's skin, all that can be seen, is freckled. Rust-colored splotches tinged with a pale green, some as big as fifty-cent pieces, others small as a tick. It's like he's draped in camouflage and paisley. Until his mouth opens and a small shadowy hole breaks the pattern, Abby gets lost in his face. She moves a step farther into Mr. Jinx's office.

"I worked with your pap at the paper mill. Uncles too. Worked with your mama over at Gospel Hill Chocolates. You ought to be ashamed, acting like this. Acting a fool."

"Yes sir," Abigail says, sincerely, though she has no idea what Mr. Jinx is talking about. It is very likely that the packaging supervisor knows more about Abigail's family than she herself does.

Abigail is a good worker. She does as she's told. People say things about Mr. Jinx; there've always been rumors. And people make fun of him. Other people. Not Abigail.

Mr. Jinx opens his desk drawer, reaches in, comes out with a stack of pamphlets. No, not pamphlets. Abigail sees that what he holds pinched between his thick freckled thumb and forefinger is a stack of her Rapture tracts. She can make out the twin humps of the Mosaic tablets drawn on the front page. From the few visible letters, Abby knows the title is "Does God Love Me?" But she doesn't remember leaving a whole stack of these anywhere. The day before, she left a couple tracts in the employee bathroom, on the back of the toilet, but that was all. And the color of the print isn't quite right.

Mr. Jinx splays the stack on the desk, fans them like a deck of cards, plucks one out and hands it to Abigail. Right away she sees the problem. They're not official Rapture tracts. Not real. There's no text inside, and the folds are careless and crooked. But that isn't the worst. On the front, someone has made two additions to the Ten Commandments. One written with a draftsman's precision; the other in a childish scrawl; both gross and obscene and involving Mr. Jinx. Someone, some wicked Slinky employee, no doubt got hold of a real Rapture tract, made the blasphemous alterations. Someone with access to the Xerox machine.

"What do you know about these?" Mr. Jinx asks.

Abigail's face burns with shame. Her whole body heats up. She doesn't know where to fix the violation. Where is the highest degree of *wrong*? Who is to blame? All she can do is shake her head. No. Nothing. No.

"Mrs. Augenbaugh."

Mr. Jinx pauses for a long time. Something new hangs in the balance. Abigail's stomach heaves. Bile stings the back of her throat.

"I know you didn't do this," he finally says. "But you have to keep your mind on the work, Mrs. Augenbaugh. On the job. Or we'll find someone who can."

Abigail hears the *we*, and it registers. It goes without saying that there is, and always has been, some group of *others* keeping tabs, pulling strings, opening and—more often—closing doors of opportunity. Abigail is afraid of all of them. Mr. Jinx rakes the false tracts back into his open desk drawer. The boss man looks at her. She can't tell if he is sneering or smiling. Abigail backs toward the door.

"Pull yourself together, Mrs. Augenbaugh. Stop all this foolishness before it's too late."

Too late. Abigail works to reconcile the phrase.

"You know the Fourth of July parade is coming soon. Be here before you know it—"

Mr. Jinx flicks the tip of his tongue back and forth across his teeth. Abigail can't remember ever seeing him do this. The man talks and talks. Abby loses focus.

"Slinky Queen," he says.

"No promises," he says.

"—a good word," he says.

Abigail goes to her station. Over the staging table she can see directly into Mr. Jinx's office. His freckled face, seen through the wire mesh in the safety glass, looks like a monstrous jigsaw puzzle come to life. Abigail confronts the mountain of stiff brown shipping boxes. She flips the switch to begin the endless regurgitation of Slinkys and the colorful boxes that will contain them.

I'll eat just a little. I'll build my strength. I'll go find Mama, and we'll pray at Slinky. I'll eat just a few bites. I am brave. I know what to do. I suck a tiny piece of paper from between my teeth, spit it out, cross the skinny walk to the neighbors' house with lightning speed. I put my hand on the knob of their back door. I command the door to be unlocked. I turn the knob. The door opens. I am powerful. Superhuman. I go inside. I look in the garbage. It's full of empty cat food cans and eggshells. I know these people. I know their secrets. I saw them. I saw them do it one time. The sex. I sit at the table. I eat everything they left behind. I am still hungry. I go to the refrigerator, chug all the milk, and put the empty jug back on the shelf. Chug all the Sunny D, put the empty jug back. I don't mean to. I decide to stay a while. I don't mean to. I do mean to. I am a dangerous criminal. I do what I want. I know these people. Their secrets. She talked to me. One time. Something stupid. "If anything ever—" she said. "All you have to do—" she said. These people. In their stupid living room, I turn on the TV, sit on the couch and flip channels. The stupid white cat jumps into my lap. I take the cat to the front door and throw it out onto the porch.

Abigail works through the morning break. She thinks about the adulterated Rapture tracts in Mr. Jinx's desk drawer. She thinks about the legitimate Rapture tracts, the real Rapture tracts in her purse. It is her responsibility, as a True Believer, to distribute them. To get *the word* out. The man on the radio told her so. Abigail wants to go to Heaven. But Mr. Jinx talked about the parade, about the Slinky Queen. Abigail wants to go to Heaven. In Heaven everything will be different. But what about the Slinky Queen? There is very little time left. The man on the radio says only two million people will go to Heaven and spend eternity as the bride of the Lamb. The others, billions of them, won't. They'll die. They'll be shamed by God. Abigail spends much of the morning trying to understand the man's message. She can't. She has no concept of *millions*, and less of *billions*. Her notions of eternity have sadly human limitations. What does it mean to be the bride of Christ? How will it differ from being the bride of Burns Augenbaugh?

All morning long, Abigail boxes. She boxes the endless conveyor of Slinkys. She boxes the details of her life. Her husband. The boy they made, with preparation. No real decisions. No choice. She boxes her doubt. She boxes her shame. Her fleeting moments of hope. She boxes her thoughts about the coming Judgment. But they all come back. It all comes back, again and again. Joy, PA, Abigail's whole world, is an endless conveyor of predictable uncertainty.

Was there ever an alternative? Abigail can't remember. The details she remembers from childhood are not her own. They come from the lives of the Joy, PA, elite. The sons and daughters of local royalty. The Yoder boys, heirs to the Yoder Gravel & Stone empire. They were legendary. Luminescent in their glory. Even the crippled one, Danny Yoder, who broke his neck—naked and drunk at a keg party—diving into Yoder's Quarry. Even he *shone*. Made even more heroic by his handicap. Abigail remembers a kid, not the name, not the gender, only that the kid came from railroad money, only that the kid choked to death on a thick white disc of hard-boiled egg one Easter. Abigail remembers that Bonner Chocolates girl who handed out chocolate penises and vaginas one Valentine's Day. The school was rife with scandal and rumors for weeks, months, years.

Abigail's father had a running joke. "Yeah, Abby went to college." Then, after a pregnant pause, he'd make her explain that her first job was washing dishes in the campus cafeteria. Abigail got the joke, and the joke got her.

Those children of Scald Mountain Country Club members—who spend their days wearing suits and ties, and doing things Abby cannot begin to imagine—where are they now? How are such children raised?

Mr. Jinx said something about the parade and about the Slinky Queen. Didn't he? Abigail imagines herself up on the Slinky float, imagines herself into the Queen's regalia. She looks down from her throne into the faces of the people lining the streets to see her. The throng. Sees there the Yoder faces, the Bonner faces. All the rest. Abigail waves, reaches out. And the gesture is full of love. Understanding. Forgiveness.

Stupid cat. It runs into the street. I close the door. It's not my fault. I don't mean to but I go upstairs. I do mean to. I've never been in this stupid house, but I know where every room is. I go upstairs. There is a Slinky on the stairs. I crush it under my powerful foot. There are pictures on the walls. The stupid little boy's room, I don't even bother with. I look in the parents' room. Maybe there are jewels. I'll steal all the gold and diamonds. I open the laundry hamper instead. I see the mother's dirty panties at the top of the pile. I pick them up. My pecker gets hard in a flash. Pushes against my Spiderman pajamas. My friend Travis told me about this.

I hate everybody but Travis. I wish Travis was here. I wish Travis was still here. Travis lived on the corner. He had superpowers. Travis's house had plywood in some of the windows. Travis had a BB gun. Me and Travis used to shoot carp and turtles in the pond. One time me and Travis set a turtle on fire. We stole hairspray and a lighter from Mama's bathroom cabinet. It was like a blowtorch. One time me and Travis shot Mr. Sprankle's dog. Mr. Sprankle lives across the street. Travis's daddy whipped him and smashed the BB gun around a telephone pole. Travis's dad whipped me too. That was before my daddy stayed in the basement so much. I was scared my daddy would whip me too. I wanted my daddy to beat up Travis's daddy. My daddy didn't do anything. When we shot that dog, you could hear it yelp all up and down the block.

Travis taught me everything. He showed me what to do. He called his The Beast. Me too. I unleash my beast. There's some yellow stuff and a little poop stain in the underwear. I jam the panties to my face. My beast roars. But I can't spooge like Travis. Travis spooged better than anybody. I've never spooged. Not yet. If the world ends in two days, I'll never know what it feels like.

"Goddamnit," I say, like Travis taught me.

I can feel my heartbeat through my beast. I stuff the underwear into my mouth and pee into the hamper. The head of my pecker burns. The beast won't sleep. I put the panties back and close the lid.

Abigail knows, because she's seen pictures, that there is geography and architecture beyond her cramped enclave of Allegheny Mountains. Land, buildings, and people that look different from anything she has ever known. Something beyond the shadow of Scald Mountain.

Heaven, maybe.

She went, just once, to the Joy Public Library. The stacks and stacks of books and movies and newspapers written about people with other kinds of lives overwhelmed Abigail. Terrified her. There is nothing worth exploring, much less documenting, in an Augenbaugh life. She'd gone to the library on a (terrified) whim after overhearing Darnell Younce, the Slinky Quality Control Checker, talk about a recent Oprah Winfrey show dedicated to self-help books. Darnell Younce joked about a book called *The Joy of Sex* for so long that it gave Abigail nightmares.

Abigail's daddy said Oprah Winfrey was in bed with the Democrats, the communists, and Satan. Abigail's daddy was always mad. Abigail's mama thought what Abigail's daddy told her to think. Abigail, influenced by her daddy, thought Darnell was a know-it-all bitch, probably a dyke (who actually did complete a couple semesters at the community college), but she couldn't help watching that loud mouth open and shut. And she couldn't help hearing every syllable that tumbled out. Abigail was confused by the words *self-help*. Nevertheless, she rode the rare wave (small swell, actually) of naïve, gullible (not quite hopeful) curiosity all the way into the library parking lot after work that day. But as soon as she stepped through the door, into the hushed, musty, overly organized space, Abby knew she was in over her head. She hurried to the restroom, wasted enough time there to make the visit seem legitimate, then hurried back out to the Celebrity. Back home, where the misery was snug and familiar, much like the packaging room at the plant. Abigail packs boxes all day long. She had her King James Bible. It's all the book she needs. The man said so.

Abigail understands the parameters of her job, so it doesn't terrify her. She has even come to semi-peaceful terms with Mitch and Andy, whom she knows mostly by their tattooed sinewy forearms. Mitch and Andy load the trucks that back up to the dock. Abigail packs and tapes the boxes, then nudges them down a short conveyor belt, where they roll through a curtain of thick rubber slats. Mitch and Andy smell of meat. More often than not, Andy or Mitch will reach in and yank the box out of sight before it reaches its destination. The boys—she thinks of them as boys—are rowdy and rambunctious. Goofy, even. They laugh all day. Andy and Mitch smell of meat. Abigail doesn't mind, their laughter or their smells.

Every time Mitch or Andy parts the rubber curtain to reach inside of Abigail's space with their dark arms—full of dragons and skulls, snakes and naked women—every time, a jagged shaft of sunlight and a diesel-y draft of air come with them. Sometimes they tease Abigail. Sometimes they give her things, scoot strange little gifts up the conveyor belt where only she can receive them. Once, in an empty Slinky box, she found the bleached-white skull and beak of a crow, and a single black feather. Another time came some pages from a porn magazine, wrapped around a sparkplug and held in place with rubber bands. There was some handwriting that Abby refused to read. Later, in another box, a long coil of honeysuckle vine in full bloom. She hides all the gifts from Mr. Jinx. But she keeps them.

All day the boys laugh and talk. Abigail occasionally thinks she hears her name. She eventually decides that they are just comfortable in their maleness. Basically good-natured and not much of a real threat, Abigail decides.

Andy and Mitch both ride muddy, unmuffled dirt bikes to work, load trucks all day, talk loudly and constantly about beer and "poon," then ride away together at the end of their shift. Sometimes after work, while she sits in the Celebrity in the Slinky parking lot, watching those boys ride away—first one wheelies, then the other—something Doppler about the sounds of the high-pitched engines bouncing off the cliffs makes Abigail think of her husband, Burns, on the couch in the basement, getting fatter and further away. And of Willie, her son—William—who more and more seems to have come from some other womb.

Mitch and Andy, no matter the weather or season, always eat lunch in the smoking area: two unpainted picnic tables crowded onto a concrete slab and sheltered by a pitched aluminum roof held up by skinny metal poles. Over the years, various people and/or things have come into contact with the posts, so the roof sits askew over the slab, sags at one end, and lists toward the mountain, toward the triptych of metal tanks and their rickety ladders. Andy and Mitch like it there. Mitch and Andy smell of meat. Jerky. The boys make jerky—beef, venison, turkey—in the cramped kitchen of their trailer. The boys are building a nice little black-market business selling at work, local bars, flea markets. The boys regularly bring free samples when they're trying new recipes.

"Hey, girl," Mitch says, waving a shriveled stick of jerky in Abby's face. "Pineapple teriyaki."

Abigail shakes her head no. Smiles, sort of. She sits at the picnic table. It is May, and the cherry and Bradford pear trees that grow up the side of the mountain are all in bloom, and it is beautiful, despite the caterpillar infestation. Despite, even, the coming Judgment. The end of the world. Abigail isn't hungry. She sits at the end of a table occupied already by Darnell Younce (who operates the dye injection unit for the plastic Slinkys) and her archrival, Sue Grebb (who runs the extruder and cut-off saw for the metal toys). Something pings off the aluminum roof. A bug maybe. Or a pebble. Everybody looks up. Everybody looks down.

"How 'bout them tent worms?" Darnell eventually says, with too much enthusiasm. "I had to scrape them off my windshield this—"

"They're not *worms*," Sue interrupted. "They're caterpillars."

"What they are is *nasty*. I ain't never seen so many. It's like something right out of the Bible. Like that Moses movie with Cha—"

"I've seen lots of bad years," Sue interrupted. "And you wouldn't know Moses if he came up and bit you on the titty."

Rumor has it that Darnell is studying to be a masseuse, or a yoga teacher. Something carnal. Something wicked. Abigail clutches her purse, stuffed with tracts, a little tighter. Sue, squat and round, doesn't put up with the other woman's nonsense.

"Sit yourself down, hon," Sue says to Abigail, brushing a spot on the bench, then jokes. "Let me get these worms off."

Abigail does as she is told and, powerless against both women, is grateful that Sue spoke first. She feels safer with Sue. Abby slips into a moment of silence, a break in the perpetual argument between her coworkers. The space closes quickly around her. Abigail has no idea what they're debating. She doesn't really care. Will she miss this when the Rapture comes? Abigail tugs at the zipper on her purse. She is distracted, running several unlikely narratives in her head, when she hears the sound.

At first Abby thinks it's a bird, several birds, spring robins made crazy by the urge to mate. To rut? Every May day they splatter themselves against the windshields and grilles of unwitting drivers, the feathers and viscera stunning in their beauty, humbling in their urgency. But it's not birds making those noises.

It's Andy, sitting at the other table, with a harmonica. Abigail comes into focus. She sees Mitch pull a ridiculously small guitar out of a backpack.

"That boy's been whacking that silly little guitar all week," Darnell says. "Getting pretty good, too."

"It's a ukulele," Sue says. "Don't you know nothing? Them boys got the devil in them."

Abigail hears the boys seek then find the right pitch, and begin to play and sing. She recognizes the tune immediately, but not the words. It's a hymn, a song Abby grew up hearing. Grew up singing. "Just a Closer Walk with Thee." But Mitch and Andy have changed the words. Abigail scoots a few inches closer to Sue and cocks her ear.

"Just a closer walk with Jinx," Andy sings. "Let us find him on his knees."

Sue throws a carrot stick that bounces off Mitch's forehead. He smiles and keeps strumming.

"Sweeeeetly blowing—"

Sue passes judgment on the situation and dismisses them by loudly changing the subject. She turns to Abigail and bellows, "We miss you down at church, hon. When you coming back?"

I go to the stupid little girl's room. It smells like stupid little girl. Like bubblegum shampoo. There's a goldfish, almost as big as my beast, in a bowl on her dresser. There is a plastic bottle of bubblegum shampoo. I open it. I smell it. I don't mean to, but I take a drink. They think they're perfect, these stupid people. The perfect family. The goldfish is fat and slow. I reach into the bowl and catch him easily. I put him in her pajama drawer. All of a sudden I feel dizzy. The bed is not made. I sit on the edge. Her stupid Elmo doll lies on the pillow. All of a sudden I feel sick to my stomach. I puke, sitting on the edge of the stupid little girl's bed. All down the front of my Spiderman pajamas and onto her floor. It looks like milk and Sunny D. I see chunks of scrambled egg and bacon. Little pukey balls of chewed paper. I take off my pajamas, ball them up, put them in the stupid little girl's dresser drawer. I pull out something of hers. It's a Disney princess nightgown. Too small for me, but I don't care. I force it over my head. It rips some when I wrench my arms through the armholes. The stupid princess nightgown hangs down to my bellybutton. I'm naked below. I am dizzy. I am cold. I am so tired. The world ends tomorrow. I never got to spooge. I lied. I didn't beseech. I lie down in the stupid little girl's bed. I cover up. I hear the fish flopping around in the dresser drawer. I am so tired. So tired.

The instant Sue Grebb asks her question, a midday wind peels down off the mountain and blows through the shelter, carrying with it, like a reluctant avalanche, hundreds of tiny white petals from the pear trees.

For the briefest moment, they're all blinded.

Church? Abigail thinks.

I am the Human Lightning Bolt. Everything I touch explodes. Sparks fill the sky. People are screaming all around. Maybe I'll save their lives. Maybe I won't. I smell burning flesh. I hear the shrieks and cries of my victims. Nothing can stop me. I am strong and brave. I hear the screaming. The screaming. I open my eyes. Where am I? This is not my room. There is no fire. But there is screaming.

It's that stupid little girl. She's standing in the doorway screaming and pointing at me. I could destroy her. Somebody is running up the stairs. I pull the blanket over my head. I close my eyes. I make it all go away. I make the world stop spinning. Everything stops.

Everything except the person yanking back the covers.

"Lord-god-almighty!" the mother shrieks.

I could strike her down. But I don't. I close my eyes tighter. I feel the air on my skin. I am naked except for the stupid princess gown. The stupid little girl screams and screams.

"Danita!" the stupid mother screams. "Go downstairs now!"

She's by the bed. I can hear her breathe. I can hear her heartbeat. I can smell her, the ladyness of her.

"Get up!"

I look at her. My gaze burns the flesh from her face. It smolders. It stinks.

"Get up! Get out!"

She grabs my arm, pulls hard. I am a rock. I do not budge. I press my face into the stupid princess pillow. I make it all go away. I think she hits me. I don't know. I feel no pain. I am all powerful. I curl into a ball. My pecker pushes out from the back of my legs. I create a force field. She can't hurt me. Nothing can hurt me.

Satan is in the pulpits. All of them. The man on the radio says so. The Devil himself has come into the churches. All of them. It is part of God's plan. Something to do with the *salvation program*. The man says so.

The man says that the True Believers should flee from the churches.

It's too late, Abigail thinks.

"It's too late," Abigail says out loud.

"What?" Darnell asks.

The wind blows the flower petals down from the hillside. The wind swirls beneath the picnic shelter, picks up ashes and stench from the overflowing bucket of sand and cigarette butts at the edge of the concrete slab, pulls with it the mechanical stink from the salvage yard, envelops the lunching Slinky employees. But what chokes Abigail at the close of that noon hour, what stings her eyes and clogs her nostrils, is a sense of loss. Not the niggling ever-present dread that has run, uncatchable, through her veins every day of her life. Nor the feeling of loss that accompanies birthdays: a surly monster that grows bigger and more horrific by the year. What rolls down the mountain that day, what nearly bowls Abigail

Augenbaugh over, is a moment of awareness, a moment of clarity, in which she sees clearly Sue Grebb, Darnell Younce, Mitch and Andy, even Mr. Jinx; sees her small life as it is, confined to a few streets, a couple decaying blocks, of Joy, PA—the town itself pinched in by a few ragged humps of the Alleghenies; sees Burns and Willie, and knows that she knows them even less than she knows her coworkers; sees them as they are: the two strangers she shares her house with. Abigail sees all this—with no understanding of how she got there—with the absolute certainty that in a few days she will lose everything. These are her people, like them or not. This is her place. And by the end of the week, they'll be dead or dying, and Joy—along with every other town and city and village in the world—will be destroyed. Heaven.

In that crystallized, rarefied, instant, sitting at the picnic table, about to go back inside and box Slinkys for the rest of the day, Abigail quakes inside. In her soul. Her soul. That thing, that place, the man on the radio rants so fervently about.

What if the boy, what if his prayers weren't enough? What if? Burns, the man, her husband, is lost. Abby knows that. She has let go. She released Burns to his own demons a long time ago. But the boy. Willie. Her son. She birthed him. She bathed him. She fed him. What if the promise of spending eternity as the bride of Christ, eternally worshiping the Lord, the destroyer, isn't enough? What if it doesn't fill the vacuum inside Abigail? A sense of urgency rifles her veins and slams and slams against her ribcage.

Can she bear the few remaining hours of her shift before rushing home to pray with Willie? What if she simply left? What if she just clocked out, hung up her smock, and drove home? To be with, to pray with, to beseech the Lord with, her son. But the fine details of the fantasy are beyond Abigail's imagination. Even in the face of the coming Rapture, the act of quitting her job is too scary. She tries and tries to envision herself rising from the table and walking away. But the act will not take shape in her mind.

What can she do?

More than her "Christian duty" or out of concern for her coworkers' souls, it is fear of being alone (even up there) that stirs Abigail's hand, that makes it reach deep into her purse and extract a stack of Rapture tracts. Before she can change her mind, Abby juts one into Darnell's face.

It's too late, Abigail thinks. "It's too late," Abigail says.

Darnell takes the offering, studies it, reads the title aloud.

"Judgment Day Is Almost Here—"

Darnell smiles, shakes her head gently.

"I think your god abandoned this old sodomite a long time ago," she says.

Mitch and Andy laugh. They leave the table, together.

Abigail turns away.

"It's too late," she says again. Takes all her courage to do so.

"Abigail," Sue Grebb begins to speak, but Darnell interrupts.

"*Too late* is nothing but a state of mind, girlfriend."

Darnell stands, moves up close behind Abigail, lays a hand on both shoulders.

"You'll be back here tomorrow. The next day. Next year. Same as the rest of us."

Abigail tries not to tremble. Tries not to weep.

Darnell gently, tenderly, pulls the loose strands of hair over Abigail's left ear, tucks them, and traces a fingertip down Abby's cheek. Darnell bends close. Whispers. The words roar in Abigail's head.

"Go home. Make a nice dinner for your family. Give your husband a blowjob. Take the boy to play Goony Golf. Then call me if that's not enough."

Darnell traces her tongue along the rim of Abigail's ear then eases the tip inside.

Nothing can hurt me. My force field is strong. She screams. They scream. "Danita, get the hell out of here! Anthony, go! Go now!"

I feel her over me. I feel her breath on my shoulder.

"What are you doing here? Why are you in Danita's bed? Why—"

She has so many questions. I stop listening. I squeeze my eyes tight. I am a superhero. I am The Rock. I will not budge. I hear nothing. I see nothing. I feel nothing.

She pokes at me with her finger. Her thick red nail digs into my skin. I don't mean to, but I bleed a little. I feel nothing. I feel nothing.

"I'm calling the police! I'm calling your damn mama! What are you doing in here? I tried! I tried to be nice. I did. What are you wearing? Danita's nightgown?"

The yelling doesn't stop. I can lie here forever. I do lie here forever. Stupid girl. Stupid mother. How long will she stay? I am strong. I can outlast her. She talks nonstop. Is she talking to me? I hear the door slam downstairs. She yanks and yanks. The bedspread gives way. My beast roars. Slays them all. They beg for more.

"TINA!"

The voice gets louder as it climbs the stairs. Like it's spilling out of a giant bullhorn. I am strong. I am The Rock. I will not budge. I fuse my stone body with the stupid girl's bed. There is a hand on my leg. There is a hand at my elbow.

"Goddamnit boy!"

"Tim, don't—"

There is the stink of grease and oil and rutted earth. There is the peal of wind that brings the flower petals down the mountainside. There is the schkkk-chick-chicka, schkkk-chick-chicka, schkkk-chick-chicka of the box-and-tape machine. There is the wet tip of Darnell Younce's tongue burning inside Abigail's ear canal. There is laughing. Someone is laughing. There is the slamming door. There is the song. What is it?

"Moooooon Riverrrr—"

Who's singing? Why?

"Mooooon Riverrrrr—"

There is Mr. Jinx, bright red in the face and yelling. And pointing. And yelling.

"I'm sorry," Abigail says.

But no. It's not Abigail that Mr. Jinx points at. Yells at.

"He stinks! He stinks like puke! Why are you here, boy? What are you trying to pull?"

"What the hell?"

He yanks hard. I land on the floor.

"Tim! You'll hurt him."

I keep my eyes closed. He tries to make me stand. He tries to make me sit.

"This is sick," he yells. "Disgusting. Danita! GO DOWNSTAIRS RIGHT NOW!"

"Should I call the police?" the stupid woman asks. I could destroy her with a flick of my wrist.

"Get me a knife!" the stupid man says.

"What are you gonna—?"

"Just get me a damn knife. Do it! Now!"

There is crying. I don't think it's me. She goes away. Comes back. My eyes are shut tight.

"Tim? Don't hurt—"

I feel something cold against my skin, pressing into my collarbone.

"Goddamnit! The little bastard pissed on me!" he says.

She screams. There is crying. I don't think it's me.

I feel the knife. I am brave. I will die like a warrior. I feel the blade slip under the cloth of my superhero cape. No, it's the princess nightgown. Will it protect me? I feel the stupid man's grip tighten on my elbow. I feel a sharp jerk at my neck. I wait for the blood. I wait for the pain. Nothing comes. I feel the blade at the other side of my neck. I feel the yank. I feel the air against my now naked body. The stupid man cut the nightgown away.

"Put this in the trash," he says.

"Should I call the police?" she says.

"No, Tina! Just throw the damn gown away!"

"What are we going to do?" she asks.

What could they do? I am all-powerful. I can crush the whole house to smithereens if I want to. I hunch into my nakedness and hold tight to myself. It's the only way I can protect them from certain death.

"I'm taking him home," the stupid man says. He grabs me by the hair and lifts.

"Put a towel around him or—"

"No!"

I blaze. I scorch the walls as we pass. Light bulbs explode in their sockets. My agony is glorious. I don't mean to, but I decide to let them live. For just a little longer.

You swing. And swing. And swing.

It might be sleep. Or it might be a sandstorm. You can't tell.

Are you in the barracks? No. You must be in the basement, in Joy.

Is it sleep, or is it thunder and hail? You can't tell.

You taped the windows. You moved the washing machine across the floor to cover the drain, but sometimes the sand still bubbles up and drowns you. What's that goddamn noise? That pounding in your head? No, not this time. Not inside your head. Outside your head. You are on the couch in the basement. Tiger Woods stands always ready on the tee box. A breeze stirs the magnolias. What's that pounding?

You grab for something. It's Big Bertha. That pounding comes from upstairs. You react. You react without thinking. You charge up the plank stairs. Maybe you were trained to do so. Maybe not. Maybe you are afraid.

You nearly knock the kitchen door off its hinges. The fat titanium head of Big Bertha looms overhead. That pounding. Your heart is pounding. You are out of breath. Your head is pounding. You are dizzy. There is pounding inside you and outside you. The front door. Someone is beating at your front door.

Who the fuck! You think you say. You will not go without a fight. Your hand grips Big Bertha's shaft. Tightly. Your nails dig into your palms. Four little sickles of blood.

You raise the club and open the door.

∀

"Moooooon River!" Mitch strums the ukulele and sings from high on the ladder of the center storage tank. Andy clings, half a dozen rungs higher, singing along, his pants and underwear to his knees, wiggling his bare backside for all to see.

Everybody looks up.

Everybody listens.

Everybody sees the bolt give way, the ladder cant away from the tank.

The boys could die. Right then. Right there. And all present would bear witness. Or the boys could sprout wings on their way down to earth and fly up and up and up. And all present would bear witness.

The ladder creaks and jostles one more time, then is still. Still. The danger has passed. Clearly, the Lord has spared them.

"Mooooon River—"

"You boys get down here right now!"

It hurts. He hurts me, the stupid man who drags me by the hair all the way downstairs and up onto my porch. It hurts, but I am brave. I will not walk. It hurts, the way my bare feet drag across the sidewalk. There is blood. I decide so. I'm sure of it. My heart bangs against my ribs, and then the man bangs on my door. He holds me by the hair and hits the door. He just keeps hitting and won't stop.

«

You know who he is. You know who they both are.

You stand in your doorway, fat, sweating, heaving for breath, with Big Bertha raised and ready. The sun blinds you, but you see him. He stands there with his goddamn hairy chest and the gold chain and the tattoos and the muscles, and he's got your boy. Your boy is naked. And his bitch of a wife is screaming through the window screen.

"Watch out, Timmy! Oh my God! He's got a gun!"

Stupid bitch.

You know the boy is yours. You don't know why he's naked. You don't know what time it is, or what day. It is day, though. Sunlight. You should be sleeping. Or trying to. But the bastard woke you up pounding on the door. And now this.

The boy is trembling. The boy is your son. You look at him. You look at the man. You look inside your own sorry ass for some scrap of fatherhood. Something to motivate you to protect him. The boy. Your son. The man has him by the hair. You can see his scalp. His toes are bloody. You try to focus. You find the man's eyes. They're locked onto you. You know he's aware of Bertha.

"Be quiet, Tina," he says.

Can you take him?

"What?" This you say aloud. The syllable deafens you.

"What!" the man yells. "Yeah! What? What the hell is this little pervert doing in my house? In my daughter's room? In my daughter's bed?"

You hear the courthouse clock strike its bell. Once, twice, three, four, five, six, seven, eight, nine, ten, eleven ... will it ever stop?

I open my eyes. I have to. The stupid man loosens his grip. I almost fall. I taste puke in my mouth. I might be crying. I don't mean to. I am body and not body. That woman keeps yelling. She might be crying. I could just reach over and crush her jaw. I don't. I decide to stay. In my body. Not body. I look at Daddy. Daddy is fat. He used to be skinny. Daddy's skin is the color of milk on the kitchen floor. He's breathing hard. I want him to hit the stupid man. I want Daddy to beat them all until there is nothing more to beat. Daddy can do it. Daddy is a soldier. Daddy is a hero. I will beseech Daddy. No other.

∀

Everybody laughs.

No. Not everybody. Mr. Jinx doesn't laugh. Abigail Augenbaugh doesn't laugh.

Why won't they listen? Why don't they care?

It's too late.

No. What if it's not too late?

Schkkk-chick-chicka, schkkk-chick-chicka, schkkk-chick-chicka.

What if she goes home and does what Darnell says? Does that thing? Does those things?

Mr. Jinx isn't laughing. Mr. Jinx is not laughing.

Everybody else goes inside. She sits, sweeping flower petals off the picnic table. Abigail Augenbaugh hears the zipper close on Andy's pants. Hears the boys clamber down the ladder.

Abigail wonders if Mr. Jinx will be in Heaven with her. Probably so.

Schkkk-chick-chicka, schkkk-chick-chicka, schkkk-chick-chicka.

"Look, Mr. Augenbaugh."

The man says your name.

"Burns," he says. "I, I really appreciate what you did, serving the country and all."

You've heard this nonsense before. Big Bertha twitches in your hands.

"And I'm sorry for—for whatever it is that's happening now—"

The boy is yours. You ought to do something.

"Come inside, Timmy," his wife says. "Before something happens."

You should be the one to do the *something*.

She has a round ass that jiggles when she carries groceries or kids down the sidewalk. You remember it. You don't remember.

You will not do anything. You wish things were different. Things used to be different. They did. Maybe they didn't.

"Take your boy inside, Burns. Clean him up. Put some clothes on him, for godsake."

He lets the boy go. On his knees, the boy slips between you and the doorframe. You think he crawls into the kitchen. The man leans close to you. Too close. Closer than anyone has ever come. Ever. He speaks. It's whispering. It's wet and hot and smells of vitamins.

"I'm going to tell you this one time," he says.

You feel sweat trickle down the crack of your ass.

"I'm calling Family Services. I'm not going to call the police, this time. But if he sets foot in *my* house again, if he comes sniffing around my girl, I don't care what happened to you over there, I'm gonna beat both of you."

You should do something. You notice a smudge on the heel of Big Bertha's head. You wipe it off with the hem of your shirt. You should do something. You step inside and close the door.

≠

The boy goes inside. I am the boy. I crawl through the door. The boy's bleeding feet leave two ragged bloody tracks across the floor. I am the boy. Those are my feet. My blood. I go inside. Inside is the Rapture. The boy's filthy living room contains the entire Apocalypse. The earthquakes. The firestorms. The tidal waves. The Rapture stinks of puke. And bubblegum shampoo. He sees everything. He sees the beginning. He sees the end. All the lies he's ever told. Everything he's ever killed. I see the boy in the distance. In that perfect moment. That glass moment. I see through the walls. I see through the bodies. Through Scald Mountain and the river. I see through space, black as coal. I see the boy coming toward me, from far far away. It's too late for the boy. I tell him so. We decide that we will not beseech anymore. Ever.

∀

Mr. Jinx holds the door for Abigail, but steps outside and closes it before the boys get there. Abigail has struggled, from the beginning, trying to understand who gets into Heaven, who gets left behind, and *why*. The man on the radio says all that is "God's business." He says "what right do we have to question holy God?" He says "Almighty God is merciful and awesome," and those who don't agree will soon be "under his terrible wrath."

Abigail's heart thumps as she makes her way through the plant. She wishes she was braver. Or brave at all. She wants to go home. But she has work to do. God's work. God's work? The Slinky production line fires up, drowns out the radio. She hurries through the break-room door to find

Darnell standing—her back to Abby—at the bank of employee cubbies. And Darnell has four legs. It must be the heat, Abigail thinks, or the stress. Abigail blinks, trying to come to terms with the vision. She does. It's not a hallucination. It's not a monster from the Book of Revelation. It's Karl, the walleyed boy whose sole job is to sweep the floors. Darnell has him pressed up against the cubbies, her chest to his back. Abigail knows without seeing that Darnell's hand is in Karl's pants.

Abigail fumbles for the door. Drops her purse. Everything spills onto the floor. Darnell and Karl both laugh. Both kneel to help Abigail collect her stuff. Abigail refuses to look at either one. Karl picks up the extra-large bottle of extra-strength Tums; rattles the few remaining tablets, and hands the bottle to Abby. Darnell gathers the Rapture tracts, neatens the stack, but hesitates before returning them.

"Do you really believe all this nonsense, girl?" Darnell asks, thumbing the pamphlets like a deck of cards.

Abigail reaches for her things. Darnell pulls back.

"Do you?" she asks again.

Abigail shakes her head. No. Abigail shakes her head *no*.

Abigail has denied the Lord.

"I have to go home," Abby mumbles.

Darnell jams the tracts back into the purse, wipes her hands together and holds them palms-out toward Abigail.

"Jinx will have your ass if you leave," she says, finally.

Karl slips out without speaking. Darnell follows. Abigail stumbles into the bathroom, collapses onto the toilet. Her hands shake so she can barely get the stall door locked.

Abigail denied the Lord. What should she do?

She hears the man's voice in her head.

Pray for mercy, he says. Pray and pray and pray for forgiveness.

Abigail leans forward, presses her face into her hands, her forehead against the graffiti-filled door, and begins.

You've never beat the boy. Not once. Not even that time he drilled holes in all the bathroom walls. You should've beaten him then, but you didn't. You never beat the boy. You look around the kitchen. The boy is not there. You should do something. Who the hell does he think he is? That asshole neighbor.

Maybe you should beat the neighbor. He's out there, in his backyard. You can hear the barbell clink into its rack. Where's your wife? The kitchen is a fucking pigsty. Maybe you should beat the wife. You never have. Not yet. You see the plastic tub of Metamucil on the counter. You rear back with Bertha. You swing as hard as you can. The white tub shatters on impact; the explosion of grainy orange powder coats everything.

You're not cleaning the mess up. Where's the wife? The boy? He may be upstairs. You haven't been upstairs in you don't know how long. The first human you see in months, and it has to be that asshole next door. You go into the basement. Back to the couch. You should be sleeping. Daytime is when you sleep. You turn on the Xbox. You can't concentrate. What if that asshole calls Child Welfare? You turn on the porn. You stare at an enormous white ass. The hairy cunt, staggeringly beautiful. For a second, you think you might be getting a hard-on. But you just have to piss. You piss in the utility sink.

They tell you to take pills. You need a pill now. A battalion of tiny sand-niggers storms around your brain. Your vision blurs. Where's the boy? You think you have a boy? Was that your boy, naked? You need a pill. Pills. You find the bottles. Some colors are missing. The bottle is empty. Is that thunder? Lightning? You realize the storm is in your head. You imagine the smell of ozone. You wish you could sleep. You wish you could get hard.

You dump the tackle box on top of the washing machine. Pill bottles and bullets clatter against the lid. You notice that the bullets look like big pills. If you could just talk to somebody, to the right person. You have no idea who the right person is. No one comes to mind. One person comes to mind. The pharmacist with the mole on her lip and the little tits. She's always there. You look for the phone. You remember smashing it last night. There may be a telephone upstairs, up in her bedroom. Weren't you just upstairs? No. You don't think so.

Wasps live in my mouth. I smell like motor oil and dirt. I smell like nothing. Absence.

My toes bleed. I hear Daddy downstairs, slamming things. I dig through the hamper, find my Captain America pajamas. Dung beetles roll their cargo through my veins. The ichneumon fly breeds in my nose. I am the assassin bug. I find my video game under my mattress. I find a shoe. I wish I had a cape. There is one day left. I go out into it, changed. I will find Mama. I need to make a plan. I look for the boy. I feel him, close.

You have Big Bertha. You need your pills. Where is the boy? Where is the wife? You haven't seen them in weeks. Why did you break the phone? You just need to call in the prescription. You can talk to the woman with the tits and the mole. You can tell her what you need. The drugstore is a few blocks away. Can you walk that far? You think so. Do you have the prescription? You'll take the empty bottles. You think that's all you need.

Do you have any money? You check the pockets of your sagging sweatpants. Empty. You try to pull them up over your gut. How long have you been fat? The stupid pills you have to swallow turn to fat inside you. Clog you. Shrivel you. You don't know the last time the sweats got washed. What else could you wear? You know what to wear.

You drag your crumpled uniform from beneath the couch. You put it on sometimes when the nights get really bad. It doesn't fit. The pants won't zip, nor button, but the belt works fine. Your fat arms and shoulders make the jacket splay open. But your name is there, on the pocket. She'll see it. She'll talk to you. Where's the boy? You bet he'd like to see you in uniform. You told him all kinds of bullshit about your time over there. What choice did you have? You can't find the hat. You wish you had a hat. You haven't washed your hair in months. Or more. You remember a hat. It's a golf hat. You ordered it from the Masters course in Georgia. You got it as a birthday present for yourself years ago. It's in pretty good shape. Where's the boy? He should see you in uniform. He'd be proud. You never beat him. The boy.

You put the golf hat on. You fill your pockets with pill bottles. You get the number from the phone book. No paper; you write it on your palm, digging hard with the ballpoint pen. You find fifty cents in a pocket. You pick up the little pistol, then put it back down. You pick up Big Bertha, shoulder her, take some deep breaths, and climb the stairs.

The man on the radio talks in great detail about God's plans for Judgment Day. His plans for the end of the world. The man on the radio talks in great detail about God's Program of Salvation for the True Believers. Abigail imagines a vast office with rows and rows of neat desks and efficient secretaries in immaculate white blouses. Abigail Augenbaugh wonders if she could ever be one of God's secretaries.

But she can't get the image of Andy's naked buttocks out of her mind. She can't get the exquisite burn of Darnell's tongue out of her ear.

Abby wishes she could beseech God. It's what the man on the radio says to do. But, she doesn't know what the word means, so she's not sure how to do it. She thinks about kneeling. Maybe she has to kneel in order to beseech. But the bathroom floor is sticky and filthy. She wonders if kneeling matters.

Abigail stands, turns, and kneels, snugging her knees against both sides of the toilet. She presses her hands together, laces her fingers, props her elbows on the lid, and makes an attempt.

"Beseech," she says, hesitantly. Then, "Lord Jesus."

Abigail thinks and prays, and makes some plans of her own.

I go past Travis's empty lot. I duck into the alley. I wish Travis was here. Me and Travis found all the secret escape routes. If he was here, Travis would help me make a plan. Empty garages line the alley. I swoop from garage to garage. Nobody can see me. I move like lightning. I wear one black slipper. I wish I had a cape. Something moves at the edge of my vision. I slam myself against a garage wall. I am The Chameleon. I become the gray boards. I look out, with my super vision, and see three, four, five black balloons, almost deflated, float by, bouncing slowly along the pavement. Five black balloons. Their gold ribbons, knotted, drag along a torn piece of paper. It reads *Happy*. I wait until it passes the back doors of the Dollar Store and the kitchen of Main Moon. I run fast. An old Chinese man sits on a bucket and smokes, out back of Main Moon. I move so fast he doesn't even see me.

I have to make a plan. There is revenge. There is world destruction. There are only a few days left. Does he know? Daddy? About the end of the world? Daddy could stop it if he tried. Daddy is a soldier. A hero. I could help him. Does he know? Daddy? About the boy? The boy will help. The boy will be here soon.

I know all the escape routes. I am The Creeper. Mole Boy. I know all the secret ways. I will not be captured. I need to make a plan and I know where to go. It's our hideout. I run the alleys. I run the weedy path through the golf course. Me and Travis used to collect golf balls and throw them at the turtles and frogs in the pond. Me and Travis liked the pond. It was at the bottom of a hill. We had to run behind the apartment complex to get there. Sometimes girls would lie out on blankets, listen to stupid music, and tan. *Rich bitches,* Travis would say. *I got just what they need.* We hid behind the dumpster. Travis taught me to watch between their legs. Travis closed his eyes every time he spooged. Once I closed my eyes, grunted, said, *I did it, Travis.* He said, *Dumb fuck.* He said, *Lying little bastard.* He said, *You pissed all over your foot.*

I run past the dumpster. I don't even look for girls. I run all the way to the river. There's a train trestle; a single track, held up by three concrete pylons, crosses the water into Joy. Travis showed me this. Twice a day, once in each direction, a line of diesel locomotives pulls boxcars, hoppers, flatcars, and tankers up the mountain, or down the mountain. Travis showed me this. The railroad ties are open to the water below. He walked out to the first pylon. *Come on, pussy,* he said. I followed. *Look down,* he said. I did.

There, between the ties and below the tracks, the top of the concrete pylon was flat and clear. A square space the size of a breakfast table. *Climb down,* Travis said. I didn't. *Pussy,* he said. I did. I slipped between the sticky wooden railroad ties. Standing, my head and shoulders rose just above the level of the tracks. I had to hunch.

69

I felt the train before I heard it. The rails jittered. The whole pylon buzzed. I started to climb out. *Where you going, pussy?* Travis laughed. He stood over me, straddling the tracks. I hunched. I squatted, my head almost bumping the track. I sat with my back against the concrete support, my legs hung over the base. The muddy river churned below me. *Don't move, pussy,* Travis said. I almost couldn't hear him for the roar of the oncoming train. Then he was screaming at me from the bank. *Come on, you dumb bastard! Run! Run! Run!*

I saw the lead locomotive come into sight. I almost shit myself. I climbed up from the top of the pylon, out from between the railroad ties. I tripped and almost fell into the river. I can't swim too good. I might have been crying. We hid in the bushes on the riverbank until the whole train passed. It might've taken fifteen minutes, maybe half an hour. The train was long. Travis laughed. After the train passed, me and Travis both went back out on the bridge and climbed between the tracks to the top of the pylon. Travis said there wouldn't be another train until suppertime. I trust Travis. We sat there. We spit in the river. We made plans. We busted bottles. It was our hideout. Our secret. We stole things from Travis's mom, Travis's dad. A Bic lighter with naked boobs and a butt. No head. A twelve-gauge shotgun shell. A tampon. Other stuff. We kept our secrets in a coffee can. We went there every day that summer before Travis left. We timed it right. Between the trains.

Now, Travis is gone. I'm by myself. The boy is coming. But the boy is almost here. The boy will be here soon. I don't know what time it is. I don't care. I will make a plan. Plans for us. For us all. I run by the golf course, past the dumpster, and to the river. I walk the ties without looking down. I might have even closed my eyes. I am Stealth Man. My body is pure movement. I slip between the railroad ties and lie flat on the cement pad. I wish I had a cape. I smell the river. I smell the creosote. I pull the Game Boy from my waistband. I turn it on and the Mario sound track fills the tiny space. I wish Travis was here. He knows about the end of the world, I'm sure. Travis knows everything. I want to tell Travis about the boy. What would Travis do? What would Travis do?

But Travis isn't here, and he isn't coming back. I have to do this mission alone. I might not survive. I am not afraid. A milk jug and a pie pan float by in the river. I'm hungry. I eat the hunger. I can see planks of blue sky above me, between the ties. My feet are hot. The sweat stings my scraped toes. I take off the black shoe. I need to think. I need my Mario Bros. I lie back on the concrete. I feel the vibration almost immediately. My whole spine tingles. It's the train. I can feel it coming my way. Crawling along my backbone. I will not move. I know this. We decide not to move, no matter what happens.

The drugstore is just down the street. You haven't been out of the house in god knows how long. God knows. Fucker. You can't see over the stubby mountains, the sumac, the crumbling rock-faces. You don't recognize anything. And you've seen it all before. You've never been able to see over the mountains. Why should it be different now? God knows. Fucker. Sometimes, a thick July sky will blur everything, turn it all gray, and you can pretend there is a horizon to look out at. Sometimes snow clouds will roll over Scald Mountain and blanket your whole world. You've felt like a prisoner all your life. You never knew how to say so. Your daddy would've laughed at you. By the time you joined the Army and got some distance, your vision was already, and permanently, shortsighted.

You come out of your house, and Scald Mountain shoves you back against the door. The paper mill stinks. The drugstore is just down the street. Just past the post office. You cut through the alley. The ragweed and Queen Anne's lace blooming. The alley ends at Joy Plaque & Trophy. You know the asshole neighbor isn't at work, but you keep your head down and hurry past anyway. You ought to talk to the boy about what happened today. You won't. The boy is your son. Sometimes you know this.

You thought maybe you could walk all the way to the drugstore, go right up to the pharmacist and get your prescription filled. Now you're not sure. People are looking at you, at your uniform. You know the post office is always busy. Always people coming and going, looking official, or important, or at least focused. You know there's always a line at the pharmacist's window. Old people with their oxygen bottles and diapers wanting to talk and talk and talk, and get their free blood-pressure checkups; other people so fat and pasty (angry tattoos sprawling across their ham-sized calves) you can't tell how old they are, what sex they are, driving their motorized scooters up and down the narrow aisles.

There is no way you can walk through all that, or wait through all that. Not even with Big Bertha at your side. You decide to call the prescription in. You have fifty cents. You know there is a phone booth outside Joy Books, on Penn Street. First it was The Joy BookNook. Then it was Joy Book & Video. Then it was Joy Adult Shoppe. (You remember all this, but you can't remember the last time you ate.) Now the roof is caving in, and there are knee-high weeds along the rear wall.

It's an actual phone booth, with a door, hinged in the middle, that hangs and squeaks when you force it shut. There is graffiti on every surface, bottles and cans and wrappers on the floor. A bunch of idiotic Jesus tracts, each more faded than the next. You try to imagine the fool who keeps refreshing the supply. You have no imagination.

You pick up the telephone, hear a dial tone, feel genuine relief. You dig the quarters out of your pocket. Look at your palm. Your sweaty palm. Fuck. Is that a 4 or a 9? You have no choice but to pick a number and dial. You hear the ringing at the other end. You only have fifty cents.

"Thank you for calling Joy Drugs."

You almost speak. You almost shout. But then you realize the voice is recorded. It's telling you to do things. To wait, to listen. To push specific numbers to get specific results. The words are moving too fast. You can't figure out what to do. What do you push if you want to talk to the pharmacist with the tits and the mole?

It's hot in the phone booth. The air is stagnant. There is a wasp nest up in the corner. The wasps stand at attention like perfect soldiers. The recorded voice stops. The courthouse bell fills the moment of silence. The wasps twitch and shuffle on their nest.

"May I help you?" a voice on the phone asks. You hear impatience in the tone. What should you do? You do the only thing you can think of.

"There's a bomb!" you say. "You've got ten minutes!" you say.

Then you hang up. You're dizzy, and your breath refuses to satisfy your lungs. There is no bomb. You've done this before, but you can't remember when. You turn to open the phone booth door. The door will not open. You are a fatass blob. Your flesh fills the booth. You pull and pull at the sticky handle, but the door is jammed in its track. It's hot. You can't breathe. You hear a siren in the distance. You hear a train whistle. You bring Bertha up, try to swing her, but there is no room. Her titanium head bounces off the safety glass. You feel a wasp land on your golf hat, another on your forearm. You can't tell if it stings you. You kick at the bottom of the door. Trash swirls at your feet. You keep kicking.

I lie with my back on the concrete pillar. It feels like the whole world is vibrating. Is it the Rapture? Is it the boy? Is it the train? We don't mean to, but we decide it's the train. The closer the train gets, the more I feel it. I am drawing the train's power into my body. Through my skin, into my bones. I am growing stronger and stronger. Diesel fuel pumps through my veins. I could bite the steel rails in half. I could lift the rails from their ties and hold them up as the locomotive charges over my head. Our head. We could lift our powerful head between the ties and stop the oncoming train with the muscles of my neck alone. I dig my nails into the concrete. Everything shakes and trembles. This must be what the earthquake will feel like. The earthquake that ends the world. I hear a rattle and clacking. I look to see my Game Boy. It vibrated off my chest. It's vibrating across the top of the pylon. It's about to fall into the muddy river. I leap. Quick as lightning, I come to the rescue.

The rest of the day goes wherever it is that days go, without any more, or any less, divine intervention. Abigail may or may not have spent it in the toilet stall, with the pubic hairs and the graffiti, by turns praying, reading rereading the Rapture tracts. She cannot remember.

No? She denied the Lord. Her own word grows thick and bitter in Abby's mouth. It burns a hole in her consciousness, and that hole fills up with guilt. She denied the Lord. She is a bad witness. She is a bad employee. She is a bad wife. She is a bad mother. Is she a bad mother? Is she a bad witness? Is she a bad employee? She is a bad wife. She is a bad mother. She is a bad witness. She is bad. Is she? She is.

Is it too late?

It's not too late.

She's got a plan. Abigail Augenbaugh has her own plan.

She'll stop by the store on the way home. She'll get some pizza bites, and big bottle of real Coke. She'll make a nice dinner. They'll have some good family time. They'll turn on Froggy 99, the classic rock station. Even better, she'll call up that Carole Onkst woman, that guidance counselor. She'll invite her over for pizza bites. They'll talk. Really talk. They'll figure stuff out. Then, when Carole Onkst, the guidance counselor, leaves, and the boy, their son, Willie, is tucked into bed, Abby will do that thing Darnell mentioned. Whatever happens tomorrow, the next day, or the next, will be OK.

And you kick and you stomp, and you whack the glass with Bertha, and the wasps orbit your head, inside and out, and you are about to die. Then you hear a voice.

"Hey?"

Is it a real voice? A human voice?

"You all right in there?"

You are struck by the absurdity of the question, but can't respond. It's a dude in a suit. He pushes at the center of the phone booth, and it opens. He steps back. You and the wasps escape. There's a stain on his tie. A green pen in his pocket. You see him look at your uniform. You raise Big Bertha high. The dude in the suit scrambles away, trips on a parking space curb, falls on his ass. That's when you see his sneakers.

"Hey, man," the dude says. He's got his hands up. You feel a little sick because you like the fear you see in his eyes.

"I'm just trying to help, brother. Can I, do you—"

You hurry away, leave him there on his ass. You see a crowd gathered in front of Joy Drug. Crowds make you anxious. Then you remember the bomb threat. This is your crowd. For just a second, you are the master of these fools. Then you can't remember why you made the bomb threat.

You look at the people, clumped together or standing alone, some nervous as ants, some giggling stupidly. You look and see that every single eye of every person—every asshole man, every stupid woman, every filthy kid—all the eyes there stare right at you. Shoot you full of judgmental holes. You blink. You look again. Now you see that every piti-ful human in sight is blind, all their eyeballs either plucked or thick with cataracts, either black pits or moon-white nickels. Then you remember the pharmacist. You look for her. She's standing alone by the Joy Drug sign at the front edge of the lot. A bank of fancy grasses surrounds the sign, the green blades, the yellow and red blades, rising up and spilling over at different heights behind her. Standing there like that, in her pure-white pharmacist's smock, she looks like a fucking angel. Why is she there? Why are they all gathered outside Joy Drug?

Then you remember the bomb threat. You tighten your grip on Bertha, take a deep breath, and veer off the sidewalk. They look at you, at your uniform. You haven't always been this way. Confused. Afraid of most things. Pissed off at the rest. You weren't like this before you went over there. You did it for them, the bastards. All of them. And none of them care. You did it for him. You did it for her. You did it for the greedy ass-holes who look down on the town from Scald Mountain Country Club. You did it for the faggy professors at the community college. You did it for the chunky son of a bitch selling hotdogs and spouting left-wing nonsense in front of the courthouse. You did it for the anorexic with the store-bought tan, the bleached hair, the fake boobs as big as the heads of the two dirty kids she drags by the hand across the parking lot, cursing and making threats. "We're going to Walmart!" she says.

You did it for her, the pharmacist.

It's hard to breathe. Sweat drips in your eyes. There is a golf ball stuck in your throat. But you force yourself through the throng. They part. They're afraid of you. In awe. You're a hero. A war hero. You make your way to the sign, the heavenly vision among the grasses. You bring Big Bertha to your side. She watches you approach. You need the pills. You want her attention. You'll accept her fear. The fearmonger holds the power. You walk right up to her. You've got things to say. Important things. You know she'll understand. She eases back closer to the grass. Maybe you stepped too close. You don't know. You take a step too. Closer.

It's just you and her. You open your mouth to speak. The golf ball falls out and rolls to a stop by her beautiful white shoes. You open your mouth again, and a cartoon thought bubble rises into the space over your heads. It's just the two of you. The war hero and his angel. You fill that space with all the important things you want to say. You tell her you tried. For a whole month, you went to their fucked-up meetings, sat in their fucked-up folding chairs, washed over by their fucked-up florescent lights, with all the other fuck-ups.

You tell her you admire people who can pretend it all away. You admire the ones who can lock into something, an idea, a hobby even, and hang on, pretending so hard it's the be-all end-all that they forget they're pretending. You don't tell her how much you admire the ones who can just check out and leave it all behind.

You tell her how sometimes, when you're in the basement on the couch, the whole world feels like it's a desert, it's all Iraq. Sand right outside your window. Sand in the yard. Sand up over the mountains and beyond. It's cool and damp in the basement. You tape around the windows and door. You know with the slightest crack, the sand will spill in, fill your basement, your sanctuary, and drown you.

You tell her about those rare rare moments when things make sense. When you realize that everybody you see, and everybody you don't see, has a whole life, whole histories, whole futures, and they're all different from yours. This makes you fear them. All of them. You confess to her that you don't understand how the world could be at once so vast and empty *and* suffocatingly cramped.

You tell her they caught your boy naked in the neighbors' house this morning. But what could you do about it? The boy is yours, but beyond ownership, there's nothing. What do you have to give the boy? What can you offer besides your rage? You tell her you have a wife. You think you do, anyway. You haven't seen her for months. Haven't fucked her in years. It's not that you don't want to, you say. You worry for a moment that the word *fucked* may offend her. You decide she understands that it was the only word you could use.

You tell her you take the pills like you're supposed to. You tell her the pills make you fat and constipated and impotent. Unable to sleep or eat. You tell her.

"Excuse me!" the voice says.

"Hey!" the same voice says.

You blink. Shake your head.

It's her, the pharmacist. "Can you back up, please?" she says.

You look down. You reach into your pockets, pull the pill bottles out, offer them to her. She doesn't respond. You see her nametag, pinned over her heart. Her fine little tit. You read the word Joy, but her name is blocked by a strand of hair. You reach out to move it.

"Hey!" she says.

You have more to say, too, but the lot fills with police cars and a fire truck so red it throbs. All the sirens wail, obliterating your words. Then you remember the bomb threat. The flashing lights ricochet inside your skull. Afraid of seizure, you close your eyes. You back away from the pharmacist. You turn. You see the sidewalk. You run. They're chasing you, even if they're not.

Abigail Augenbaugh clocks out. Abigail Augenbaugh digs through her purse, digs deep between and under the seats for change. Digs for quarters, dimes, pennies, wherewithal. Abigail comes up with three dollars and seventeen cents. It'll have to do.

It's loud.

I look up through the railroad ties. I see three long bars of sky. I hear the train. I feel the train. Everything shakes. I get to my knees. I take a breath. I squat. I don't know how close the train is. I feel it in all of my body. I am brave. I am invincible. I stand up between the ties. My head pokes up just above the track. I see the train. The engine is at the bridge. Maybe I could outrun it. I look down. The water around the concrete pylon seems electric. I could jump in the river. I can't swim. I could breathe in the water. I am The Amazing Gilled Man. I could dive to the bottom of the river and swim all the way to the ocean. I could rally all the sea creatures to my side, and we could stop the world from ending.

I can't swim. How close is the train? I can stop the train with my power ray. The power ray shoots from my eyes. I can destroy any target with my power ray. I can see through buildings and walls and clothes with my power ray. I can stop things. Trains, even. I take a breath. I stand. The face of the locomotive rears up. It blocks the sun. The wheels chew up everything else in sight. The air horn rips the world apart. I am deaf. I drop back to the top of the concrete. I curl up and close my eyes. Everything shudders. I can't tell where my body ends and the concrete begins.

You run. Even though you can't breathe, you run. You hold Bertha out in front, like a rifle. There may be footsteps behind you, or it may be your heartbeat. You run, and your flabby gut slaps back and forth. You almost touched her. You called in a bomb threat. You didn't get your pills.

You run toward your house. You see the neighbor kids on the sidewalk. Colored chalk is everywhere. They hear you first, your boots slamming against the cement, your wheezing breath loud and raucous. You run in a straight line. You will not be swayed. You see her, their mother. You'd like to bend her over. Bend over, you'd say. No apologies. But what then? She scoops them up, drags them to the stoop. You'd like to bend her over. But you don't stop. You don't even look. You run past, run up your own steps, through the door, through the house, into the kitchen. You slip. Your boot comes down on the linoleum and scoots right out from under you. You hit the floor hard. Maybe your head hits the table leg. Maybe you're bleeding. There is something sticky and orange all over the floor. It clings to your beige uniform. You remember smashing the bottle of Metamucil. You decide it's not so bad, lying there on the kitchen floor. You hear the traffic outside, the world is in motion, but inside your house it's peaceful. Those must be your legs, but from where you lie, from how you see, the drab tans of your pants could be mountains. The dirty floor a dry lakebed. You watch a thin trickle of blood make its way across the linoleum, mixing a little with the powdery medicine. It might be yours.

I am not dead. I did not die. I will not die. I am a magnet. I draw the power of the railroad into my body as it passes above me. I can see the thick axles. Sparks and sticky hydraulic fluid rains down on me. I open my mouth. I yell. The train eats my scream. No matter how loud I yell, the train is louder. I did not die. I am Loco-Moto. I stand up and become the train. I charge through town, destroying everything. No.

But the shadow passes. I look up, see sunlight. The train has passed. My ears ring. The train is still passing in my head. My body shakes from inside out. I look for my Game Boy. It's in my hand. My fingers cramp. I wait a minute, then climb up between the ties. Somebody at a loading dock is pointing at me. I see his mouth move, but I only hear the train. I could run him down, plow right through him, smash him to smithereens. I don't.

I run back behind the golf course. I see the boys. The boys play golf in the afternoons. Sometimes they hang around the pond to smoke and cuss. And beat people up. The boys are trouble. I let them live. For now. We decide it. Me and the boy. I run faster. I take the long way, past the dumpster. I run up the alley. I see the chair behind Main Moon, where the old man sat. He's gone. There's a plate on the chair. Most of an eggroll is on the plate, lying in a swirled pool of orange and yellow sauce. I run past. I stop. My stomach stops me. I am Stealth. No one can see me circle back and snatch the eggroll. I run. I cross the street so that I can see the neighbors' house. I hide under some yellow bushes, eating the eggroll, and watch until the stupid mother takes her stupid kids inside.

I fly into the house, slam the door behind me.

Abigail Augenbaugh prays. She prays the Celebrity into the lot of Dingus' Convenient. And there, inside the store, along the back wall to the freezer shielded by shelves of Utz pretzels and chips, Abby acts more decisively than ever before in her life.

Abigail opens the freezer door, picks up the "family size" box of pizza bites. It's $5.24. She can't remember if there is a tax. There must be. There's always a tax. Right? Abby takes a deep breath. It's not too late. She lifts the Slinky smock and tucks the box into the waist of her pants. Into the elastic of her panties. The box is so cold against her flesh, Abigail almost cries out. It is bigger than she'd expected. The smock is loose, but Abigail has to walk stiffly and erect. She rolls her shoulders in a little more than normal. The box hurts. It is May. It is late afternoon. It is not too late. Abigail picks a bottle of cola from the display. What has she become? What will she become?

There is one other customer at the register. An old man in cowboy boots and a camouflage cap. His nails are perfect. Abigail sucks in quick shallow breaths. The man looks back at her and winks. She turns her attention to the rack of lottery tickets. Powerball. Lotto. Mega Millions. Mustache Cash. Fat Wallet. Lucky in Love. What does it all mean? Abigail wants the man in line to leave. She wants to get home to her husband, her son, their special dinner. The man in the camo hat is telling the clerk a story, or a joke, about fish, or a donkey.

The man looks back at Abigail, again. Does he know? Can he tell?

"Let's buy this pretty girl a lottery ticket," the man says.

He pays, winks again, and leaves.

"Good luck, honey," he says.

Abigail plops into the seat of the Celebrity. The box of pizza bites crumples, splits along its bottom seam. Little square pockets of cold dough spill into Abby's underwear. The clerk might be watching. There's nothing she can do. Abigail pulls away from Dingus' Convenient, stops a block away in front of a defunct Family Dollar, fishes the pizza bites out of her panties, returns them to their box, and puts it into the plastic bag with the cola and lottery ticket. She is a good mother. She is a good wife. She has a plan.

"Daddy?" I say. Just one time. He's sleeping on the kitchen floor. I think there's blood, but I don't look too close. I go to the sink. The floor is sticky. I get some water and sit at the table. I flip on my Game Boy. He must be gathering his powers. He is gathering his powers. He's wearing his hero suit. I'm wearing my hero suit. When he wakes, I'll tell him about the boy. We're there together. Together we are unbeatable.

It might be yours. The blood.

Blessed. Is there any other way to say it?

Abigail pulls into the alley, and the sight of the DeFonzies in their backyard, this time, unlike all the other times, makes her happy. What has happened? What has she become? A good mother. A good wife. A good family. Like the DeFonzies. It is not too late. Even if the Judgment comes, just two short days from now.

Abigail parks. She'll go in the house. She'll start the oven. She'll go. Go down into the basement, help Burns off the couch and up the stairs. But first she'll say hi to the neighbors. Invite them over for pizza bites. Abby practices the sentence in her head.

Tim DeFonzie methodically raises and lowers a clanking barbell full of metal plates. Even from a distance, Abby sees his chest muscles bulge and stretch. Tina stands at the grill by the back door; smoke roils around her. The smell of charred meat reaches the alley. Abigail sees the daughter dancing around in the grass with a naked My-Size Barbie. She looks for the son but doesn't see him. The little DeFonzie boy often makes a game of running across the alley just in front of moving cars. More than once, Abigail has had to slam on the brakes.

Abby gets out of the Celebrity confidently. Won't they be surprised? she thinks.

When the DeFonzie son pops up from behind the Virgin Mary grotto, grinning maniacally and firing right at Abigail Augenbaugh with the largest squirt gun she's ever seen, she smiles.

The water jet hits Abby between the eyes, blinds her momentarily. She feels the stream soak the front of her Slinky smock.

"Anthony!" someone yells. "Cut that out!"

By the time Abigail's eyes stop stinging and she can see again, Tim DeFonzie stands, shirtless, in her path. And her nipples are hard. Abigail blushes, but it's OK. She doesn't know where to look. Without really meaning to, she watches a bead of sweat fall from the foot of the cross around Tim's neck, trip and spin down the hirsute ditch between his pectorals, through the thorns of the Sacred Heart tattoo, skirt the rim of his navel, and dissipate among the damp shorthairs sweeping the corrugated plain of his belly and disappearing beneath the waistband of his low-hanging gym shorts.

"Ohh," Abigail says, more croak than word. She folds her arms across her chest.

"Pizza bites," she says, showing Tim the bag.

"I told your husband," her neighbor says, "and I'm telling you. Keep that little per—keep that son of yours away from my house and my kids. Or else."

Abigail looks at his feet. Her feet. The smells from the grill make her salivate. She looks across the yard. My-Size Barbie straddles the Virgin Mary grotto, and the DeFonzie kids are running around and around them both. Abigail waits and waits for the "or else," but nothing comes. She stops. Time stops. Wind and waves and orbits cease. The lumbering cataclysm grinds to a halt.

"Pizza bites," she says, again.

Did something happen? Something happened while she was at work. Something changed. It would be easy to deny the boy here, as she'd denied the Lord earlier. *I don't have a son,* she could say. But there is Willie. The palpable fact of Willie. Willie is her son. Has Willie gotten into trouble? He couldn't have. Not after last night. Not after praying and beseeching. No. She has a plan. The nice dinner. The classic rock. Willie is a sweet boy. She knows he is. She thinks she knows so. She's going to call that woman. Carole. She has the whole night planned out.

"Time to eat!" Tina yells. She puts a platter of food on a picnic table made from a massive wire spool. Tim stands close. Maybe he wants to kiss me, Abigail thinks. Blessed day.

"Blowjob," Abby says. She doesn't mean to. But she can't take it back.

Tim DeFonzie doesn't respond. "You'll be getting a visit from Family Services," he says. "Any day now."

Any day now? It's too late. Is it? Abigail watches Tim walk away; the muscles of his back splay like wings.

Any day now, he whispers. *Any day now.*

"Hey!" someone says. "Hey!"

It's Tina, yelling.

≠

I'll save you, Mama. I'll save you. Mama. I put on my cape. I need nothing else. I gnash my teeth. I blister the wind. My terrible roar rips the day in half.

"Hey!" Tina DeFonzie yells, and they all turn to see the boy.

The boy runs, naked but for some thin fabric flapping behind him, down the sidewalk. Screaming. The boy is Abigail's son. The boy is Willie.

The little DeFonzie girl shrieks, rushes to her mother's side at the picnic table. Anthony hides behind the grotto, his weapon at the ready. Willie hurtles down the narrow walk, arms raised, palms together, as if diving. As if flying. The boy babbles, wails, runs without pause into the solid tattooed torso of Tim DeFonzie.

He would have bounced, except that Tim catches him by the neck.

Abigail Augenbaugh tenses, flushes, trembles. What to do?

There is the body's allegiance to the boy. She birthed him. She raised him. She prayed with him, just last night. Too, there is allegiance to her God. The man on the radio talks about it. There is Tim DeFonzie's horribly beautiful arm locked onto the boy's neck. Her boy. Flesh of her flesh. She ought to say, *Let him go.* She ought to say, *Who the hell do you think you are?* She ought to swing, kick, bite, scratch.

Abby is not capable of looking into Tim DeFonzie's eyes. She tries. She tries again. She looks to her son. His filthy, oil-flecked face. Looks into Willie's eyes. Looks for the boy who knelt with her last night. Abigail Augenbaugh cannot see that boy. He is not present in the raging eyes of the animal held tight in her neighbor's grasp.

Tim DeFonzie lets the boy go. The boy stumbles into Abigail Augenbaugh. She cannot embrace him. Her arms refuse to open wide.

"Family Services," Tim says, a stern finger jabbing for emphasis, then goes and sits at the table.

Abigail Augenbaugh is confused. She has to muddle through the moment, somehow. She has to. She steers the naked boy by his scrawny shoulders, along the sidewalk past the DeFonzies, Tina with her hand over the little girl's eyes, and past the platter of still-sizzling bratwurst and venison burgers, the plate of cheese and tomato slices, glorious in their geometries.

"Let's get you some supper," Abby says, so loudly that it startles the other children. "I've got pizza bites and Coke."

I saved you, Mama. Didn't I? Didn't I save you from him, Mama? You didn't save me. I saved you. You let him hurt me, didn't you? He hurt me. And you let him. Didn't you, Mama?

Supper. It's all she can think to do. It might be the last one before they join together at the foot of the Lamb, in eternal worship. Supper. It's what a good mother would do. A good wife. They'll listen to Froggy 99. They'll put Willie to bed, tuck him in together. Maybe she'll read him a Bible story. The one about Noah and the flood that drowns everything.

Or maybe the one where blind Samson brings the temple down and crushes all the Philistines. Abby wonders what a Philistine is. It's a good story. They'll put Willie to sleep. She and Burns. She'll surprise him with the lottery ticket. They'll scratch off the silvery box together. They'll win. Everything will change. It's hard to say. Abigail can't even imagine what they'll do. She and Burns. He'll be so happy. She'll surprise him. No end to the surprises. She'll unzip his pants. She'll do that thing. She really will.

Abigail leads Willie through the door and into the house. The home. Their home. She's ready. Everything will be different. She's ready.

Bip bop bop, ticka ticka.

The house, stifling airless and still, provides only a moment's respite for Abigail. She hears the Mario Bros. theme song coming from the kitchen. Then her eyes adjust to the lack of light, and she sees Burns on the kitchen floor.

Abigail wonders if he is dead. Wonders if he died playing Willie's game. *Bip bop bop, ticka ticka.* Burns *dead,* she thinks, and leans against the door. What about the pizza bites? What about the lottery ticket? It's a winner; Abigail knows it. Feels it. She has been bound to this man for a decade and a half, bound for the last few years by the immovable enormity of his absence. There is a person living in the basement and inhabiting something of the body and soul she knew as Burns. But barely, and rarely, does she recognize him. His living, breathing presence on the couch below has created a palpable vacuum in the rest of the house, a dense black hole of unknowing that threatens more and more to spill out, to suck in and consume the whole of Joy. But today was supposed to be different. Was going to be different. It's not too late. She is a good wife. She is a good mother. She is a True Believer.

Bip bop bop, ticka ticka.

There is no movement from the kitchen. No sound other than the Mario tune bopping along happily somewhere out of sight. Burns dead.

What would it mean? Who would protect the boy during the coming Judgment? What about the lottery ticket? The nice supper? The other plans? What about the boy? Damn it. God damn it. The boy, their son, Willie. Alone to face the Rapture. While she, among the elect, would be called up on that final day to spend eternity worshiping the merciful Lord, with Burns dead, there in the other room, Willie will have to face the horror all by himself. The weeping and wailing. The violent earthquakes. The rotting bodies. The starvation. The eternal dark.

Abigail Augenbaugh is confused. She is scared. She is conflicted. Angry. Ashamed.

"It's not my fault," she says.

"Mama," Willie says.

Bip bop bop, ticka ticka.

"I didn't mean to," she says.

"Mama," Willie says. "There's something wrong with Daddy."

Bip bop bop, ticka ticka.

"It's not my fault," she says. Again.

Maybe it's all a test. The Lord God likes to test his faithful flock.

"Mama," the boy says.

But she doesn't know what to do. She never knows what to do. Never.

The Lord works in mysterious ways. Abigail has heard the phrase for her whole life. Whole life. Don't question; don't ask.

Burns is in the other room. She sees his still legs. For all she can know, he is dead. The boy crouches by the front door, looking at her. Abigail's mind spins. Cannot find traction in the muck of her upbringing. With the few days left before the Rapture, what would she do? With the body? Without the body?

God likes to test. The man on the radio says so. Everybody says so. Abigail remembers a Bible story. Isaac on the rock, and Abraham with the knife raised high. God is somewhere in the wings. Goading. It was a test, everybody says so, but Abigail doesn't understand what it proves.

What would a good mother do? What would a good mother sacrifice? Abigail looks at the cowering boy, filthy and naked. Could she bring the knife down on him? Plunge the blade into his thin belly? Would this end his suffering? Would this be an adequate sacrifice to her God? Her neighbor said to expect a visit from Family Services. If they come, and find her dead family, they'll put Abby in jail. Will Jesus be able to find her in the cell? In the Bible story, Isaac is spared. The boy gets up from the cold hard stone, still loving his father. His father gets a gold star in history. The outcome in Joy, PA, would surely be different.

Bip bop bop, ticka ticka.

"Mama—"

Abigail takes Willie by the arm and practically staggers into the kitchen. It's not too late. Is it? Burns lies on the floor. Dead or not dead.

"Daddy's dead, honey," she says. It might be true. Have faith.

"You want some pizza bites, honey?" she asks.

She turns on the oven.

"Let me get you some pizza bites."

No. No. Daddy is not dead. She killed him. She didn't. Didn't. Didn't save me. She didn't help us. She abandoned me. She'll go up to Heaven. Without me. Us. She will never help us. I hate her. I hate her. I hate her. I hate her. I hate her. I hate her. I hate her. I hate her. We hate her. We hate her. She is nothing. She is the enemy. I will not crack. I will not give in to her torture. I am fire. I am rage. I am storm and flood. I hate her. I hate her. I hate her. I hate her. I. Hate. Her. No. No.

"Let's have some supper, honey," Abigail says. "Daddy is dead."

He must be. Dead. It is a test. It is *the* test.

"Everything will be all right," she says. "Soon. Soon. It'll all be over."

No.

Bip bop bop, ticka ticka.

"No," the boy says. "No."

"We have to beseech," Abigail says. "Like the man tells us. We have to."

"No," Willie says. "He's not. Not dead. Daddy. Daddy's not dead."

Willie stands, naked and accusing. Behold the boy.

"You did it!" he says. "It's your fault! Daddy is dead. Daddy is not dead."

Abigail Augenbaugh falls to her knees. Not to pray, but to look. At the body. At the man. At Burns. He lies, in his ill-fitting uniform, partly under the table, and clinging to the golf club. But he is breathing. Breathing. Alive. Alive despite the pinkish tendril of blood seeping from beneath his head and rooting its way through and coagulating in the orangey powder covering the floor. Alive. It is a test. Abigail passes the test. It's not too late.

I am hungry. I am not hungry. I am scared. I am not scared. I am dead. We are dead. I am not dead. We are dead. I remember the dream. Slinkys as big as dinosaurs. They chase me through town. Their giant wobbly footsteps. They eat everything. They eat me. I remember the dream. The dream is right now. I remember her. She is upstairs, looking out at me. She sits in a chair and laughs and laughs and laughs.

∀

Reprieve.

Blessing.

Mysterious ways.

She is with her family. They are all together. The husband, Burns, lies, breathing and bleeding quietly, on the kitchen floor. Willie, the boy, their son, sits at the table. So beautiful in his bruised nakedness. Abigail is there too. She is the mother. She is the wife. It is not too late. She is the mother. She is not an imposter. *The* imposter. She wants to tell somebody. She wants to call that woman, Carole Onkst, the guidance counselor. She looks around for the business card. Where is it? She has things to say. She is the wife, the mother. The daughter, too.

Abigail had a father. She remembers his legs. She squatted and played and waited beneath the folding table at the flea market. She remembered the La-Z-Boy recliner, the color of snuff, and her father yelling at the television all day and all night. The man died arguing with Oprah. His brain popped. Abby can't remember if she cried.

Abigail had a mother. She can't remember the face. She remembers judgment, and proclamations of sacrifice. Three times catch in the craw of the girl's memory. Three events. Three moments in which her mother became distinctly human. Once, when the girl was whipped at the laundromat. She saw the mother steal some quarters. She asked for one. She wanted a grape jawbreaker. The mother raged. Once, when she was whipped after Vacation Bible School for asking the mother if Jesus made the Hinnish twins retarded on purpose. And later, after age had ravaged both mind and body, every time she changed the woman's diapers.

"Mama."

"Mama!"

"Stop it, Mama. Stop."

Reprieve.

Blessing.

Mysterious ways.

There is a husband breathing. On the floor. And bleeding sweetly.

Once, for a whole month, as a girl, Abigail pretended she was getting married to a dentist. Even sent out engagement announcements. It was her greatest act of creativity. Once she pretended she was actually attending college, and not just washing dishes in the cafeteria. Once she followed the skinny boy with dirty fingernails around the mall, followed him through the hasty decision to join the Army, followed him out to his car, and pretended not to be embarrassed, terrified, and ignorant when he pulled her underwear down. There he is, on the floor.

Where is that card? That business card? Abigail Augenbaugh wants to call Carole Onkst.

Come over, she'll say. *We're doing good. Come over and have some supper. Things are good,* she'll say.

Abigail turns the oven on high.

Abigail cannot remember the last time they were all in the same room. Together. It had to be sometime before Burns took the TV downstairs.

Months and months ago. Now, here they are, three days before the end of the world, the Augenbaughs in their kitchen. *It's nice,* she thinks. It occurs to Abigail that she ought to thank the Lord for the opportunity. She does so. Abigail finds a baking sheet, dumps the pizza bites into a mound. There are pubic hairs stuck to the thawing dough.

I am bleeding. He is bleeding. She needs to bleed.

Daddy is a hero. I know it. The boy knows it.

I remember a car trip. Daddy came home from the Army. Mama drove. Daddy, the father, slept with his head against the window. Mama, the mother, listened to the radio. The man on the radio talked about Heaven. The road curved back and forth, up and down, through the mountains. I was carsick. The boy was carsick. So much fog. I was scared. The boy was scared.

"Look!" the mother said, at the top of the mountain.

The boy saw them, the whole line of windmills, their skinny white poles standing taller than anything the boy had ever seen. The three massive blades of their propellers chewing away at the sky. The boy, Willie, was scared.

"They'll cut my head off, Mama," he said.

"I don't want to go to Heaven," he said. "I want to stay here. Stay home."

How was your day, she asks her son. *How was school?*

I'm making us a nice supper, she says to Willie. *Pizza bites.*

Abigail thinks to change out of her Slinky smock. To put on something pretty. Something she'd wear to church, even. She'll make dinner. They'll sit together. When Burns wakes, she'll be sensitive, and not put him on the spot. She won't talk about unemployment or nightmares. She doesn't know yet what she'll talk about, but it'll be great. Maybe they'll all go for ice cream after.

Won't she be surprised? Carole Onkst. To see how well the Augenbaughs are doing. Abigail wishes she had time to wash the curtains and sweep the sidewalk. "I'll wear my brown dress," she says. "The one with the flower belt. The one I wore to Willie's baptism. Won't she be surprised?"

Abigail reaches out, puts her hand on Willie's shoulder. "We had pigs-in-the-blanket that day," she says.

Then Abby notices his bloody toes. She looks at her son. The naked boy. The oily smudges on his face and hands, the gritty detritus in his hair, the filthy hands and feet. So sweet. So beautiful. These things fill her with motherly love. Abigail's heart swells. She practically cries.

"Did you get a boo-boo, Willie? Honey?"

What happened next? I don't remember. I do remember.

The mother stopped the car in a gravel pull-off. She rolled down her window.

"Listen," she said.

And the boy heard. I heard.

The gigantic windmill blades turned in slow motion. Every time they swept past, the blades moaned. Called out. Cried. It was almost magical. Almost.

"I'm scared, Mama," I said.

"They'll cut my head off, Mama," he said. "I don't want to go."

Then Daddy woke up. Terrified. He yelled. He cussed. He put his fist through the windshield. After that, we went home.

"My poor baby," Abigail says.

She reaches to brush something from his hair, but Willie pulls away. The boy smells like fire. No. Something is burning. Is something burning? Abigail wants to ask what happened. How'd he get so dirty? So hurt? She doesn't. But she has to do something.

"I'll take care of you, Willie. I am the mother. You are the son."

Abigail goes upstairs.

I wish Daddy would wake up. Get up, Daddy. I wish Travis was here. Travis would know what to do. Travis knows everything. Travis knew about the girls who suntanned by the golf course. Travis knew about the secret hideout under the train. Me and Travis went to the pond, on the seventh hole, and threw rocks at the carp and turtles. Sometimes they chased us away, the men on mowers, the boys with golf clubs. Me and Travis made plans for revenge. The boy misses Travis. I miss Travis.

One time Travis stole a rifle from his daddy's closet. We took it to the pond. Revenge. It was hot, and the big fat carp floated at the surface gasping for air. They breathe, Travis said. Travis knew everything. Travis shot one of the carp. It rolled belly-up in the middle of the pond. The rest of the fish submerged, out of sight. Travis made me wade in, clothes and all, to get the dead fish.

Travis held the rifle. I held the dead fish. Its tail was slick. Blood dribbled from the bullet hole, onto my foot.

"Listen!" Travis said.

Travis knows everything. Of course I listen.

"Somebody's coming!" Travis said. "Run!"

We did.

She goes upstairs. Comes back with one of her old nightgowns.

"I got this," she says. "It's all I could find."

"Lift your arms," she says. "I'll take care of you."

The boy smells like fire. Why does the boy smell like fire?

Abigail fills a shallow bowl with warm water and soap. She takes the dishrag from the sink, kneels at Willie's feet. She cradles the boy's foot in her palm, holds it over the bowl, and with all the gentleness in the world, bathes the toes until the dried and crusted blood softens, drips and stains the water.

"Let's eat it," Travis said.

Travis had a pocketknife. We stabbed and sliced at the dead fish. The blade was too dull. The back door opened. It was Daddy. Run, I said. No. I didn't. I wanted to. Daddy wore his uniform. He wasn't fat. Not yet. He had something in his hand. It was a skinny knife in a leather sheath. Daddy took the fish from me and Travis. Daddy took the knife from its sheath. Daddy slid the thin blade along the spine and ribs of the carp. Daddy returned to the house, came back with a camp stove, a frying pan, some flour, salt, pepper, and lard. We cooked that dead fish, right there in the backyard. We ate it with our fingers.

I miss Travis. I miss Daddy.

Daddy is a war hero.

Me and Travis played Army. Travis always got shot. Low in the belly. I always doctored him. Travis had a birthmark, a big purple flower blooming across one cheek and over his forehead. Some boys made fun of it. I didn't. One time, in the hideout, I told Travis the birthmark was pretty. Travis almost threw me in the river. I cried. Travis moved. Bulldozers came, knocked his house down. Filled in the basement. Someone planted grass. It's like Travis was never there.

Sometimes the boy misses Travis more than he misses the father.

"I got us a lottery ticket," she says.

"We're gonna win," she says. "Let's go to Red Lobster. It's Daddy's favorite. We'll play Goony Golf. You'd like that."

Abigail is pleased with herself. If they could see her now, how carefully she washes her son's feet. If they could but witness the perfect love she pours out over the boy, they'd take back all the insults, all the hurtful, spite-filled, mean things that have held her back, kept her down, that have bound her forever to the millstone of fear and doubt. But they can't. Abigail knows that Jesus is watching. And that is enough.

Stop, I say. Don't touch me, I say.
I hate her.
I hate her. I will not look at her. She is the enemy. Daddy is the hero. I am a hero. She is not a hero. She works for the dark forces. The water stings. I am a prisoner of war. She is the torturer. I will not crack. The kitchen is my prison. The water stings. I grab the salt shaker. It's made of glass. It's shaped like a donkey. Daddy won it at the fair. I look down at her head. I could slam the salt shaker into her head. She is the enemy. She is stupid. She is ugly. She is evil. I hate her. Her ancient Chinese water torture is powerless against me. I eat hope. I spit fear. I am made of stone. I will not crack. I will drive the glass donkey through her skull. She is stupid. She is ugly. She is not my mother. Not our mother. I hate her. She smells like fire. No. There is smoke. It hurts. My foot. It bleeds. Stop, I say. Don't touch it, I say.

You dream. You dream yourself off of the couch. You dream yourself out of the basement. Out of the house. The house holds the woman, the boy. You dream yourself out of the desert. And back and back through time. You dream your own father. That asshole. That motherfucker. You dream yourself nine years old and camping in the spring. Early spring. Ice on the lake. You dream the dark woods and your own fear. You dream the cold. Dream the camp in a small meadow by a frozen lake, the men drinking beer. You dream your own drunkenness. Small mountains, overgrown by leafless trees, dotted with bare patches of rocky scree. You dream yourself at the bottom of a massive empty bowl.

They drank and drank, told jokes you didn't understand. You laughed anyway. You dream the near-dark, and yourself half in, half out of a pup tent. You dream the sound. Not thunder but just as big. An earthbound noise, like the crust of the earth itself cracking open, swelling up all around. As if from everywhere at once. Too big to have a source. Then, immediately, a wailing, a moan, a hungry, crazed geometry of noise.

You dream a boy leaping up, running to his father's tent. Nearly weeping from fear. The men all laughed. You dream it. Again and again. One of the men made up a story. About the sound. Said it was the growling belly of the giant valley troll. Said the troll guarded the lake. Said the troll had to be fed before it would let anybody fish the lake. Said the troll liked to eat little boys. Dream a sleeping father. A drunken father. A laughing father.

Again, the horrible sounds filled the bowl in which the boy lay.

The men all laughed and laughed. The father laughed too. The troll was hungry. The troll has to be fed in the morning. The boy, of course, was meant to be troll food.

"Such a pipsqueak," somebody said. "Swallow you up in one bite."

You dream your ignorance. You dream no way of knowing that the sounds were nothing more, or less, than spring thaw. The great slab of ice pulling away from the shoreline, undulating ever so slightly, amplified each and every crack. Dream the boy going back to his tent alone, awaiting his fate. All night long, the ice cracked and cried out in the dark. All night long, you try to ready yourself for death.

∀

Abigail's heart flutters. Pure hope churns in the pumping muscle. She is washing her boy's feet. Burns is breathing. She is cooking supper. There is a lottery ticket. Spring, in all its reckless fury, rages just outside the door, and Joy is drowning in fecund desolation. But in the Augenbaughs' kitchen, a miracle is happening. Abigail allows herself the luxury of a daydream. She and her husband and their son stand in the front yard, clean and smiling, and Jesus swoops down in a cloud, or maybe just his arms, wide as the county, scoop them up. Or maybe he rides a golden chariot. Abigail struggles with visualizing exactly what is supposed to happen, so she skips to the next part.

"It's not too late," she says.

Abigail and her husband and their son, rising up through the pollen-choked sky, holding hands, singing songs. High above the train yards and the mines. Above the stinking plumes of smoke from the paper mill. Up over the Alleghenies. Up where mountains and borders and boundaries become irrelevant. And they're wearing pure-white robes. But she wonders what happened to their clothes. Doesn't matter. Soon they'll be at the feet of God, worshiping. Forever. She wonders how long the trip will take. She wonders if her ears will pop.

You keep dreaming. You have nothing else to do. You didn't die that night. The valley troll spared your life. The father, the fucker, spared your life. You dream a car trip with him. Pittsburgh. Summer. Sweltering. You dream an air show. All the way there, the father talked about crashes. He wanted to see some crashes. You spent all afternoon looking up into a cloudless sky. There were no crashes. By suppertime you both had blistering sunburns on your faces.

You dream, later maybe, his disability checks. His Gideon membership. Once, on the way home from a doctor's appointment, he told you to stop at Walmart. He wanted to slip some Gideon pamphlets under the windshield wipers of the parked cars. He wanted you to help him. It was a windy day. Clouds charged across the sky. You stopped the car at the far end of the lot and he stepped out with a handful of *Good News*. You sat in the driver's seat, wanting a moment. You watch him cross in front of the car. Watch a gust of wind pick up a thin plastic Walmart bag, carry it, gaping open like a feral parachute, over the shoppers and their cars, bobbing and swirling, until it catches and covers the father's head. You watch the man, suddenly blind, terrified, confused, drop his pamphlets, began cursing and wildly swinging at the air.

You got out of the car. This isn't in the dream. You get out of the car. The old man is slumped to the macadam. You get out, take the plastic bag off the father's head, help him into the car only moments before a sudden downpour drenches everything in sight. You drive away, drive right over the forgotten *Good News* pamphlets quickly becoming a pulpy mess in the parking lot.

You dream another man. It might be you. Fucker. He had a plan. A criminal justice degree from the community college. Play a little golf on the team. Get hired at the prison.

Fucker. Getting too big for your britches. Everybody said so. Fucker. Dropout.

You dream smoke. You dream something on fire. You dream that girl, that day, at the mall. You dream you remember the X-rated aisle at Spencer's. She laughed. You got hard. You remember the Army recruiter by the Orange Julius, and the climbing wall that rose to the ceiling two stories up. Dropout. Fucker. You climbed that wall.

"Show your girl what you've got," he said. So you did. Back on the ground, he let you try on some GI body armor. "I don't let everybody do this," the sergeant said. "Wouldn't surprise me if you got over there and single-handedly kicked Hussein's ass," the sergeant said. "I'd kill the bastard," you said. "You're the man for the job," the sergeant said. "Sign right here," the sergeant said.

You had a fucking death-boner. You were invincible. You climbed that wall. You married that girl. You were bigger and stronger than anybody in Joy, PA. You ate ham and pineapple pizza, because it seemed exotic. You fucked her in the parking lot, in the car. Because it seemed exotic. You went to the desert. You missed Parenting Classes. You went to the desert. You dreamed yourself a Shower/Laundry and Clothing Repair Specialist. No. It's the goddamn truth. The bloody uniforms never stopped coming. Ever.

When she gets to Heaven Abigail is sure that Jesus will stroke her cheek and tell her what a good mother she was. Abigail will forget all about leaving Willie and Burns behind to face the Apocalypse. When she gets to Heaven. When she gets to Heaven.

Don't touch me.
I am invisible.
I am a mirror.
I am a stone.
I am air.
I am water.
I am nothing.

∀

There, in the darkening kitchen, with her bleeding son and her bleeding husband, on the cusp of a new day, on the outskirts of Heaven, Abigail manifests her Christian love. She lifts Willie's other foot over the bowl, draws the wet cloth slowly along the arch. He winces. What is it? Abigail sees the splinter. A poison arrow. A tiny wooden minnow swimming beneath the surface of his flesh. She holds the boy's foot firmly, presses the hard sickle of her thumbnail at the buried tip of the splinter and pushes.

Willie curses. Kicks. Kicks the bowl of water. Douses his slumbering father.

They hit you. They hit you hard, while you sleep. It might be a mortar. It might be suicide bomber. You are wet. It might be blood. Yours or anybody else's. There is smoke and fire. Your head throbs. You can't see. Where are you? You see legs. Bare feet. A kid's bare feet. You kick. You jump up, back to the wall. You have your weapon. You raise Big Bertha high and ready to swing. Someone calls your name. Someone calls you Daddy.

There is smoke. You are wet. *Daddy. Daddy.*

Burns. What? What the fuck? *Burns. Everything is OK. Daddy. Burns. I made supper. I got us a lottery ticket. Burns. Daddy.* You swing and swing, your back to the wall. You can't tell what you hit. If you hit. There is smoke. There is blood. There is always the blood.

Burns. What? *Daddy.* What the fuck? Who is talking? What do you want?

Then you see. Your vision clears a little. You wear your uniform. Your head throbs. Someone calls your name. Someone calls you Daddy. You're in a kitchen. It's your kitchen. In Joy, PA. The war and the desert are somewhere outside. You remember now. You went for the pills. You remember the bomb threat. You look across the room. A woman crouches by the door. It's your wife. You don't remember her. A boy sits at the table. You remember him from the morning, naked at the door with the asshole neighbor. He's your son. He is naked still.

You lower your weapon. The room spins. You sit at the table. The boy doesn't look at you. The wife gets up, says something about dinnertime. She sounds so happy you want to beat her with the club. You raise your club. You are the father. The husband. The hero. The man.

∀

The man on the radio says you can't know who is saved and who is not. Who is going to Heaven and isn't. He says, too, that you have to pray without ceasing for your family. And that maybe God, in his infinite mercy, will save them at the last minute.

Abigail knows.

Abigail looks out at the coming night. The chariot of the Lord is out there, somewhere, on its way. But night does what night does, draping its tattered blanket over Joy, PA, and everyone there. That the dark cowling is nothing more than mere orbital hocus-pocus is beyond Abigail. Abigail knows. She has prayed enough. Beseeched enough. When the Rapture comes (tomorrow? the next day?), they'll go into the yard together, hold hands, wait for Jesus.

Here we are, they'll say. *We're ready,* they'll say.

Abigail squats on the floor, leans against the counter and looks at her family. Burns stands over her with the golf club raised high. A jagged crescent of blood marks his pale forehead. She sees the welts, stings maybe, on the pasty, bloated flesh of his arms and neck. His uniform pants are unbuttoned; his belly strains against the belt. Poor suffering man.

Willie, her son, their son, a watery patina of blood smearing his sweet face.

Here we are, they'll say. *We're ready,* they'll say.

"Mama," somebody says.

Back when she went to church—back before the man on the radio told her to stay out of the churches, said God had put Satan, *installed* Satan, in all the pulpits—back then, she never asked Burns to go with her. Did they ever talk about it? Did they ever talk about the sacrament? The blood and body of Christ? Did they? Did they ever talk about judgment and forgiveness? Sin? Salvation? Abigail can't remember.

It's not too late. She can talk now. Pray now. It's not too late.

"Mama," somebody says. "Something's burning."

I am hungry. Something burns. It might be me. I am flame. I am hunger. I am flesh in the fires of Hell. I eat the man. I eat the woman. I eat myself.

Something is burning and the club is raised and she is squatting beneath you and all you want to do is bash her skull in and the boy is sitting at the table and what is he wearing and why is he bleeding and what is he eating and you look down at them and you look out of the window and you can't tell if it is day or night or summer or winter or if even you are awake or asleep or alive or dead.

Burning. The smoke. The stench.

It could be the souls of all the unsaved, the millions and billions of sinners, already smoldering. But no. Abigail Augenbaugh knows. Once again, Abigail is gifted a rare moment of clarity. A parcel of time so small as to be nonexistent on the clock face, but spanning from everlasting to everlasting in its scope. And what is it that Abigail knows in that fleeting instant? Much.

She knows that humans do what humans do. Regardless of consequence or promise of reward. She knows that Joy, PA, will scroll along on its mandated latitude, and the town's residents and what they do to and for each other are as irrelevant to the looping sun and the burlesque moon as are the outcomes of those actions. Night does what night does. Somewhere beyond that, the hurdy-gurdy universe careens indifferently. She knows the husband stands over her, ready to strike. She knows the boy, Willie, sits at the kitchen table. He's eating something. It is the lottery ticket. She can see it in the boy's teeth. She knows the smoke, the stink. The pizza bites. The supper is burning. Abigail lays her head on the boy's pale thigh, looks up at the husband. Awaits the blow.

Gone, the moment of knowing.

"Goddamn it, woman!"

You snap. You snap. The touch jolts, like a cattle prod. It knocks you from your seat. You stand over her, raise Big Bertha high. The boy cowers.

"What the fuck is wrong with you!"

"What the fuck is wrong with you!"

"What the fuck is wrong with you!"

One swing. Just one swing. Cave in her godforsaken skull. One swing. Where's the boy? He should watch you work. He should see this. He shouldn't see this.

"What's in the goddamn oven?"

You have to ask. She doesn't answer.

Gone. All. Man. Boy. Husband. Son. Hope. Family. This is a test. Abigail Augenbaugh knows it, finally. This is a test. Abigail Augenbaugh turns. Turns away. Turns in. Abigail's hands tremble as she pulls the tracts from her purse. She presses them between her palms. Abigail Augenbaugh turns her mind to God. To the wise guidance of the man on the radio. She kneels low. Beseeches with all her might. She cries out. She mouths his words: "Oh Lord God. I am a sinner. A sinner. Not worthy not worthy of your magnificent love."

《

"Get up, goddamn it! What's wrong with you? Where have you been? Where the hell do you go? Whoring? Is that it? You goddamn whore! You're fucking them all, aren't you?"

She babbles something about work, but you know she lies.

"Bullshit!"

There's never any money.

"You're fucking them all, aren't you? Everybody but me!"

Where's the boy? Your son. You have things to show him. Things to teach. She's on the floor, babbling.

"I'm not doing nothing, Burns," she says. You can barely hear it.

"Don't call me Burns!" you say. "Who are you? Who the fuck are you? Why are you here?"

"I'm your wife, Burns. We're married, Burns," she says.

But you don't believe it. This is not the woman you married. You're not even married. You're dead. You've been dead for years. You raise the club again. She's crying so hard she can't breathe. You say other things. Bad things.

"You don't mean that, Burns," she says. "I know you don't mean that stuff."

"Stop your goddamn blubbering," you say. "You sound like a goddamn goat. What are you doing down there! Get up! Get the fuck up!"

You are immense. You fill the room. You are pure power. You are pure. She curls into a ball. She gets smaller and smaller, like a bug. You stomp her out of existence.

∀

Abigail Augenbaugh sees it all now. Clearly. She is undeserving. The man on the radio says so. Says God says so. Says only God can save. Says God picks and chooses His elect. Says all we can do is beseech and pray without ceasing. *And maybe, maybe, maybe.*

Judgment Day is nigh. Abigail cannot help the man, the boy.

The man looms above her, raging. Ready to bring the full weight of his wrath down upon her weary body. Abigail presses her forehead to the cool linoleum. The floor is slick with blood and snot and water. The man, her husband, can kill her only if God wills it.

"Whore!" he says. "Bitch! Slut! I'm hungry! I'm hungry! I'm hungry."

Abigail looks at the man. There is utterance. Something about forgiveness.

There is jihad in your head. Explosions rattle your skull. Your teeth shatter, but you keep biting. She won't stop talking. Who is she? Why won't she shut her goddamn mouth?

"You don't know me! You don't know anything about me!"

She grovels on the floor. She won't stop talking.

"Who the fuck are you talking to?"

There is blood. Always the blood. There is sand. Jihad.

"You don't know. You don't know what I saw. You don't know what I did, what I had to do—"

"You did laundry, Burns," she said.

"Over there," she said. "You were in the Laundry Services Corps.

"You washed underwear, Burns."

Abigail Augenbaugh transgresses. Abigail Augenbaugh transcends. The boy at the table chokes on something. Gags and retches. The man above her readies his weapon. Abigail Augenbaugh awaits the blow.

The blow. The blunt force of fact. You cannot breathe. You cannot breathe. Sand clots your throat. But you will strike. You will. You will. You will strike with such force that all will feel your mighty wrath. The blow. The blow will kill you all. The blow.

∀

The blow.

The blow comes as a knock at the door.

The knock at the door stops the clock. Everything ceases.

Abigail looks up from her crouch. The man's eyes are black with rage. The mighty club, chocked midswing. The boy quakes in his cloak of fear.

The knock comes again. Abigail Augenbaugh could reach up, turn the knob, open the door. It might be Jesus himself on the stoop, His arms open wide. No. It might be Satan there, waiting. Tempting. No. Could it be Tim DeFonzie, shirtless and sweating? Tina DeFonzie? Mr. Jinx, maybe, with her Slinky cloak and Slinky crown? Or Darnell Younce with other sorts of promises? No. What if it's someone from the lottery, what if there are truckloads of money waiting outside the door? Or the man on the radio, come to comfort her, to pray with her, in these final hours? Or the police? That woman, that guidance counselor, that Carole Onkst? All Abigail has to do is open the door.

No. It is a test. The Day of Judgment is nigh. Abigail's entire life has been in preparation for this test. One unending study. All Abby has to do is open the door. That is all.

No. The Lord God alone provides, denies.

Abigail Augenbaugh crawls, quiet as a church mouse, under the kitchen table and wraps herself in prayer. In her world there is no room for hope outside of the church. The knock on her front door—interruption, intrusion, invitation—will go unanswered.

This is a test.

This is a test.

I bite and her head explodes. No. I bite and my head explodes. No. Someone is beating me. No. I am Lottery Man. I am the Savior. All kneel before me and pray. And weep. She is weeping. I am bloody. He kills her. No. I can't see. I can't hear. I can't breathe. See how my eyeballs pop out and bounce around at the end of the springs? Like Slinkys. I see yesterday. I see tomorrow. I am blind. It is the end of the world. The man on the radio says so. At the end of the world, all the dead Slinkys will chew up their coffins, chew through the earth, rise from their Slinky graves and wreak havoc. They're on their way. Already here. At the door. I hear them knocking.

You shit yourself. What else can you do?

The Beast is at the door. You had a wife. You couldn't keep her. You dream a pumpkin shell. You dream seven heads and ten horns. You dream the plagues—every last one—and the spring lamb. Who the fuck does she think she is?

Who is it?

Who's there?

Shhh. You are as silent as sand. As patient as death.

Sooner or later, fate passes over the Augenbaugh house. The absence deafens. Abigail waits and waits. The man in the room storms about for a bit, then he too departs. The boy? Abigail doesn't know about the boy. She didn't mean it. Didn't mean to say what she said. Didn't mean to do the things she did. All of them.

Burns, her husband, he didn't mean those things he said. Right? He can't help it. Right? He came back like that. Came back *that way*. Right? He can't help it. And she can't help him. Abigail knows it. The man on the radio says so. And the boy. And the boy. Judgment Day is nigh. Right?

You find yourself midswing. Where is the woman? The boy? Who was at the goddamn door? You swing and swing the club, knock everything off the counters. You think you see the boy run upstairs. You break dishes and cups, the salt and pepper shakers, a canister of flour, a canister of sugar, some coffee, and the pot. You beat at the cabinets and the stove and refrigerator until your arms are weak and too heavy to lift. If you were a real man, if you were the hero of the minute, you'd hit her. But you're not. You see the basement door. It's open. You'll be safe down there. Away from her, and the rest of the lunatic world.

There she is. Under the goddamn table. Still.

"Clean up this goddamn mess," you say.

You go downstairs. You shit yourself. You stink. Right? You go to your couch. You jab the remote until something comes on the television. It's a porn movie. There are four, maybe five guys, and one scrawny girl. You watch. You can't watch. You watch. Why did she say those things? You killed them all. The towelheads. She doesn't know what she's talking about. Who the fuck does she think she is? How can one girl take so many cocks? You can't watch. You do. You need the noise. You turn the volume up. She's crying upstairs, you think. Maybe it's the porn. You can't tell the difference. You turn the volume up even more, and still the crying. You keep turning the volume louder and louder, but you can't get the sound of crying out of your ears.

Because she wants to be a good wife, in these last days; because Burns, her husband, told her to, Abigail cleans what she can of the kitchen. Sweeps a little here. Wipes a little there. She is not angry. She is not angry. She focuses on the task at hand. Burns said to clean up the mess.

But soon Abigail Augenbaugh abandons the wrecked kitchen and, laboring under the heavy burden of her newfound truth, climbs the flight of stairs as if going to the gallows, the gutting scaffold, to await her Savior's return. The steps to the second floor seem ladder-like, higher and narrower than ever before. Not blood but lead courses through the veins and arteries in her legs. Each step is more difficult than the last. The treads and risers work against her. Abigail is light-headed. Dizzy. The dim bulb in the socket at the top of the stairs flickers. Pulses.

Abby climbs and climbs, for hours it seems, and by the time she reaches the landing it is all she can do to lie on the splintery hardwood floor and gasp for breath. The Rapture, her Rapture, is coming soon. She knows it. She has been chosen. She knows it. She needs only to hold on for a while longer.

It is not without pain or grief, however, that she anticipates leaving behind her family and everything she's ever known, to spend the rest of eternity worshiping at the foot of the Lamb. But abandonment in various forms is a familiar misery, a boon companion throughout her life.

She gets to her knees. Stands. Wills herself into the bedroom and closes the door. Her son is somewhere behind his own closed door, both his presence and his absence vying for command of her awareness.

Abigail Augenbaugh takes her pen in hand, finds the calendar. She wants to mark the day, to make the X, but her legs bounce and her hands shake with fear. She takes the calendar to the bed, lays it flat on the faded chenille spread, kneels. She presses the ballpoint into the box, but it takes both hands to inscribe the mark. Finished, Abigail has to lay her head on the bed. She thinks she might vomit. It is as if she has personally removed a day from every living creature on earth. As if she is responsible, solely or in part, for what will happen in just three short days.

Two more days. Two days left. Two days remaining. Two days to go. There is no best way to say it. Though she cannot reconcile the dichotomy, Abigail both longs for and fears the impending change. She can do what she has to, can abandon her damaged family, just like she abandoned the ravaged kitchen. She can leave behind the job at the Slinky plant. She can leave behind Joy, its coal-hearted mountains hollowed out, its pinched and polluted valleys. Leave behind all the unsaved. Those not chosen. But she needs help. Needs comforting and guidance. Prayer.

Abigail Augenbaugh lays her weary body down on the lumpy double bed, reaches across the vast expanse of what was her husband's side, and turns on the radio. The familiar voice, his voice, fills her ears, fills her bedroom, spills out of the window and down sidewalks and streets, flows under the bedroom door, down the stairs, into the basement.

She lies. I hate her. Daddy is a hero. Daddy is a killer. I hate her. Why did she say that about him? She lies. I want to break something. I have to break something. I open my dresser drawers. I open my closet. I want to break her teeth for the things she said. Daddy is a hero. Daddy killed the bad guys. Daddy protects me. From the basement, he protects me. It's my turn. I have to protect Daddy. I'll protect him from her. I'll protect him from the steel beasts. I'll protect him from the people on the porch. I'll protect him from the man on the radio. I have superhuman power. I eat misery and fear. I puke death. Nothing can stop me.

I look out the window. I see the graveyard. When the dead bodies come up, come at me, I won't run. I look out the other window. I see the stupid neighbors. They look at me. They cower. Pee their pants. No. Not yet. The stupid little girl is in bed. I see her through the window. The stupid mama sits and pats her head. The stupid girl might be crying. The stupid little girl points at me. The stupid mama stands up at the window. The stupid mama is wearing a bra and panties. They're called titties. Pussy. Travis told me everything. I see the stupid tattoo of a little kid. He's dead. Maybe I killed him. I need a weapon. I need a special potion. I fly through the windows and destroy them both. I throw the little girl through the roof. Throw her so high she never comes down. I squeeze the stupid mama's titties until they pop. She's a liar. They're all liars. I hate her. And her. And her.

Bitch. Liar. She wasn't there. She doesn't know. What you did. What you tried to do.

You beat her senseless. No. She got lucky. This time. You don't beat her. You never have. You're not lucky. Your head pounds. Somebody knocked on the door. There's dried blood in your scalp. You don't remember why. You watch the sex on the screen, but can't forget how unlucky you are. You smell shit. It might be yours. It's night up the stairs, outside. No matter what you do, dark creeps in. You're mad as hell. You're always mad, but this time it's different. You know what you're mad at. You're mad at her. For what she said. You tried to go to war. You tried to do it for her. Partly. You didn't ask to be assigned to the Laundry Corps. You couldn't help it that the blood, the bloody uniforms, they just kept coming. So much blood. You didn't want to see the faces and the bodies. You stopped knowing when they were real or not.

You're sweating. It drips in your eyes and stings. Your hands cramp from gripping Big Bertha so tightly. Where's the boy? Was he in the kitchen the whole time? Serves her right. You wanted to kill the bad guys. The recruiter said you could. You killed them all. The bad guys. You told the boy so. You didn't tell the boy the recruiter lied. He's an asshole like all the rest, wading around hip deep in the same bullshit as everybody else in this goddamn town. Bullshit that's run down off the mountain for generations. Bullshit that's pooled and stagnated in the pinched valleys and coves. Nobody who crawls up out of that muck and tries to get somewhere in the world stands a chance. The bullshit always wins. Bullshit about everything. About good and bad, right and wrong. Worthwhile. Not. Golf, for instance. All you wanted to do was play the stupid game. You figured, maybe, killing sand-niggers was a good second bet. It's possible to believe the bullshit forever. If you stay in the valley, it's the only bullshit you know. But, once you venture out of your mountainous cage you see there are other bullshits. Other bullshitters. Other believers. It takes a heavy toll.

There is so much blood. You never knew there was so much blood in the world. You never knew all the colors of spilled blood. You watched the TV shows, you watched the movies. The blood was different. False. The true blood stains. There is camouflage. The Army pretends. There is sand. Sand in your bed. Sand in your eyes. Sand in your breakfast, lunch, and dinner. Sand in your dreams. There are buttons and zippers and bootlaces; there are sheets and blankets; there are uniforms in so many different sizes; and it's all bloody. The bleach stings your eyes. You taste the detergent in the back of your throat. It's humid like some tropic island, in hell. Rinse, wash, dry. Rinse, wash, dry. There is never enough camouflage. There is always more blood.

Well, you know the fact is that we know that the wages of sin is death. That's the first thing we have to keep in mind. Those who enter into the Day of Judgment, and it will be almost seven billion people that will enter into the Day of Judgment, the first thing they are going to face is death. Maybe already on day one there will be millions who die, and on day two millions will die, and this will keep going until finally whoever is left alive on October 21, at the end of the five months, then they will be destroyed and the whole world is going to be annihilated and never be remembered or come into mind.

You kill her. You should have. Like you killed all the others. It's nasty work.

Hard, hot, nasty work, the killing. But you can do it. You are a soldier. A killing machine. A hero. What do you think about? Nothing but the death and suffering that passes through your hands. What does she know about suffering? Nothing. Who the fuck does she think she is? Nothing. Does she think her tears and her snot are gonna make some kind of difference? You've seen men and boys cry who had reason. You should've hit her. You ought to go upstairs and knock all that Jesus bullshit right out of her head. That's what she needs. It's what you need. The boy needs his mama. Peter Peter Pumpkin Eater. You had a wife and couldn't keep her.

Who is she to question? What you did, what happened to you? She knows nothing about what it takes to fight. You did the best you could. In your own ways. You wanted a rifle. You wanted grenades. You know how to use them. You know what they can do. You've seen it. You've touched that aftermath. What the fuck does she know? You ought to go upstairs and show her. You think about it. You think about every detail, in slow motion. You hold tight to Big Bertha. There's porn on the television. You're tired. Tired. Tired of the pills. Tired of the blood. Tired of pussy. Of cock. Of breath. It's dark somewhere outside. You should go. Up the stairs. You're the man. You're the hero. You think your way through the act. You see the carbon fiber head of the golf club as it travels the arc of your swing. You see it connect with her head, right at the hinge of her jaw. You hear the satisfying thwack. You see teeth fly out the other side. You see her eyes roll back. You raise the club again.

No. You cannot do it.

You hear the clock tower at the courthouse.

Sometimes you've got a crystal ball in your head. You can see forwards and backwards. You can see your daddy wheezing on a couch for the last ten years of his life. You see your own couch, your own years. You see no reprieve. You need your pills. There is a gun in the tackle box. You leave it there.

There was a man, once, touched a woman. Real gentle-like. On the cheek. He died.

You ought to go up. Stairs. You think your way up each step. You think of her face as she sat at the kitchen table while you shrieked and cursed at her. She cried and slobbered. Snot streamed from her nose. She is your wife. She looks helpless and pitiful. You sit on the couch, in the basement, in Joy, PA, and think of her choking sobs. Her eyes swollen, nose red and leaking. Pleading with you. She is your wife. And she is at your mercy. You think of these things. She begs. She pleads. You are the man. You are the hero. Warrior. The filthy details play in a loop through your electrified brain. And then it happens. You get hard. For the first time in years. Your cock pushes against your uniform, stands at attention.

I hate them all. I hate the man on the radio. I hear him. I hear his voice through the wall. His voice is like dark syrup. It catches all the flies. I hear him talk about Satan. Satan is in all the churches, preaching from all the pulpits. What does it mean, all the pulpits? At the same time? Like Santa Claus at Christmas? I want to ask Mama. She's dead. I hate her. She's not. I hate her more. I wonder how big Satan is. Does he wear a suit? I hate Satan. I am afraid. Of Satan. I am not afraid. The man talks about the end of the world. He sounds so happy. I hate him. I love when he tells me how everybody will die. I think about Satan in all the churches. If I go to the church down the street, I could find Satan and we could join together, and be a team, and fight the man on the radio.

I hear people call him and cry and ask him why, or when. I don't understand his answers. He talks about mercy. I don't know what that means. He makes it sound like a good thing. He makes it all sound good. I hear a woman call who's scared for her baby boy. I wish my mama would call. The man says we're all born sinners. Says we deserve to die.

I crawl under my bed.

I lie in the black.

She deserves to die.

They deserve to die.

I deserve to die.

I will not die.

We will fight.

the whole world is going to be annihilated

Abigail Augenbaugh takes solace in his voice. She lies in bed and tries to conceive of no more world. She knows there are roads that lead out of Joy. And railroad tracks. There must be airplanes overhead. And people and people and people. Do they hear the man? Are they listening? Do they understand that everything leads to desolation? Everything.

The man has explanations for all of it. She can't understand his theology. Numbers are involved. The man counts. The man adds and subtracts, divides and multiplies. Parsing out the past, present, and future. The man quantifies the whole universe. Abigail listens. Abigail is confused. Abigail prays. He talks about signs and symbols. She can't see them. There are prophecies and parables. The man speaks of demons and angels as if they're right outside on the bus-stop bench, or just behind in the grocery checkout line. There are God's chosen people. The *Elect*. There is God's *Salvation Plan* and God's *Judgment*. Abigail can't tell which is the act of love, or where the mercy dwells, but that's OK. The man explains, and though his reasoning confounds, Abby trusts. It's the voice, and the certainty that voice embodies.

It was the voice that first captured Abigail's attention, then laid claim, bit by intangible bit, to the rest of her until she was fully his, body and soul. The discovery of the man and his voice she owes to her son, Willie. They were in the car, months ago. The boy was angrily poking at the radio knobs, the tinny speakers spitting fragments of songs and speech. Then she heard it.

Because Holy God is so merciful, maybe he will have mercy on you.

That chamberous voice surges from the very belly of the earth, fills Abigail Augenbaugh's ears, spills out over her body. An ancient sound. Paternal. Wise at the sonic level. Distinct from, less terrifying than, the lifetime of televangelists and pulpit pounders she used to give her obeyance. Willie reached to change the channel. Abigail Augenbaugh wanted that mercy. Abby grabbed his wrist. Not long after, she noticed the several billboards around Joy, PA.

JUDGMENT DAY, May 21, 2011

Now, months later, a couple scant days from the end, Abigail still doesn't understand what the man on the radio means when he talks, but *how* he says those mystifying things suffices. Is enough.

Self-doubt, as a force, as a guiding principle, has shaped much of Abigail's life. But not, ever, doubt of authority, in all its forms. Insidious or otherwise. Too scary. Just beneath the surface of *belief* things get too muddy, too unclear. She finds it best, easiest, imagines it less painful, simply to obey. She hears the callers, the desperate or angry listeners who phone in to speak with the voice on the radio. Some weep. Some beg. Some smugly agree. And some mock. The man on the radio takes them all in and spits them all out. He is unflappable. He is impenetrable. How can Abigail not follow him? And how can she ever live up to his kingly standard? Even this night, so close to the finish, she worries that his God will hold those past doubts in judgment against her. The man on the radio says as much.

Now what God is simply teaching, He knows what's in our heart, He knows our situation, way better than we do, and the Holy Spirit here, of course, is God Himself, and so whatever it isn't, it isn't how loquacious we are or how erudite we are, that is how well we can speak and so on, and make any impact upon God at all. It's what's going on in our heart and God knows, exactly, exactly, better than we do, what's going on in our heart, and so this is a terrific assurance to us when we are so emotionally upset about something and either way, in joy or in terror or in whatever, we don't.

Does God know of her wickedness? Her greedy clutch on the lottery ticket? Does God know? Does he feel what she feels? Did God feel Darnell Younce's hot breath? Does he know the misery, the cruelty of the husband? Her unnamable quenchless yearning for the boy in the next room? Yes. The man on the radio says yes, God sees all. God knows all. Abigail is ashamed. She clings to the man's voice. She begs, as she was instructed. Beseeches. God sees all. All. Abigail looks up. Burns in the scrutiny. She looks, but can't find his eyes.

You are naked. You are hard. Years. It's been years. Bitch. Your pale bloated gut hangs low. You can't see your cock, but you grab it to make sure it's still hard. Who does she think she is? She is your wife. Goddamn it. You'll show her. You go through the kitchen but don't look at the mess. You stand at the bottom of the stairs. Has it been years? You think of the blubbering snotty face. You keep the picture in your mind and haul your heavy self up one step at a time. You stand at the closed door. You check again for the erection. You realize you left Big Bertha downstairs. It's OK. Come back to the picture. She's on her knees and sobbing. You open the door. She's lying on the bed. Still. Like she's dead or something.

A

Abigail hears footsteps. Maybe it's Jesus. Come early, and without the fanfare? On a covert mission? Maybe this is how the Rapture comes, with Christ as clandestine savior. She hopes. She doubts. She prays. Abigail wants the mercy. The footfalls are too heavy to be Willie. Graceless.

Abigail doesn't allow herself the luxury of lingering in hope. She is afraid, but no more or less afraid than she has been her entire life. There is, and always has been, trepidation every time someone comes to any door.

Abigail doesn't want to look. She wants only the comforting voice of the man on the radio. She wants to look up through the ceiling, through the rafters, through the shingles and the black sky, Heavenward. But try as she might, Abigail's vision fails her. There is nothing to see but cracked water-stained plaster. She lies motionless in her bed, in her unadorned bedroom, on the second floor of her steadily dilapidating house, and awaits instruction.

It's Burns. She's never seen him so heavy, so naked, but Abigail knows it is Burns standing in the doorway. He is backlit by some dim and distant light, so she cannot see his face. But even over the radio, she hears his laboring breath.

She ought to call out to him. She knows it. That's what a wife ought to do. Abigail doesn't.

She's not dead. Yet. You are the hero. The warrior. You can tell she's breathing. She is your wife. You recognize things. That damn granny-gown she's worn since before the boy. The bridge of her nose. The slight whistle of her constricted breath. You've been in this room before, but you can't remember when. Your head pounds. You are dizzy from the stairs. For a second you forget why you came. Then you check your dick. Still hard.

∀

Burns Augenbaugh galumphs the short span between the doorway and the bed. His flab is pale and loose. Abigail has seen this man before. Naked, before. He is her husband. Abigail thinks, for the briefest of seconds, of embrace. He's come to embrace her. To comfort. Abigail hopes. Then Abigail doubts. She knows this man. She has seen this man before.

There is his penis. He stands right at bedside. Abigail is embarrassed to be so close to his nakedness. Not always. They made the boy. Together. But now, she cannot tell what he means by this presence. Gift or threat? She wants to turn away, but can't. She hasn't been given permission.

It occurs to Abby that Burns may kill her. That she might die before the Rapture. She wonders, briefly, how God would handle the complication. Then Burns reaches out and grabs her. The touch brings Abigail back to temporality.

She is your wife. You went to war for her. Doesn't matter whether she thinks so or not. What you did. What you do. She owes you. You stand there, before her. You are ashamed of your fleshy body. What are you looking at! Even in the dark, you know she sees it. Who do you think you are! You flip this woman over. You let the shame consume you and blossom into a beautiful flower of rage. You can deal with the rage. Rage is a man's sport.

You flip her over, this woman, this wife. You don't want to see her face. You pull the granny-gown up, yank the white panties down just enough. You climb on the bed, straddle this woman, this wife. The mattress sags, the bedsprings squeak, the wood frame groans. Like a goddamn train whistle.

You have to lift your own fat gut to see the cheeks of her fat ass. You are a hero. A warrior. She owes you. They all do. You poke the tip of your dick into her business. It's dry. You try to get some spit but your mouth is just as dry. You just push harder. It finally goes in. You don't want to see her face. Not her real face. You scroll through the pictures in your brain. Find the one where she's blubbering like a baby. You hold onto that picture. You drive into her from behind.

Abigail Augenbaugh goes to Heaven.

She lies beneath the heavy man struggling behind her, struggling inside her, and tries to match her shallow, hard-won breaths with his thrusts. It lessens the pain. He is her husband. She knows she is obligated, complicit even, in what's happening. She was schooled in this knowledge, from before birth. He is the husband. He deserves this.

Abigail's face is in the pillow. She smells the unwashed bedclothes. She can't see anything. She hears the radio. She hears the man grunt each time he enters her. Each time the grunting man enters her, she claims the pain as her own. Turns the pain into a small door at the core of her being. Each time his penis goes in, it pushes the door of pain open a little farther.

Abigail imagines Heaven just on the other side of that door. She rides the Slinky float all the way. At Heaven's gate, the crown is bestowed upon her. Pure joy. Complete happiness. No more pain. The hope excites her. Just a little more of this earthly suffering, she thinks, and she'll be home. Will it be like this when she is the bride of Christ? Will the Lord's desire be so furious? Something almost animal inside Abigail stirs. She arches her back ever so slightly to meet her husband's onslaught.

You want it. You know you do. The snotty nose, the drooling mouth, the red and swollen eyes. The helplessness. This is what you want. You are the man. You are the warrior. And you will slay every last motherfucker who tries to tell you different.

You hear the clock tower at the courthouse. You time your stroke to the clapper's strike. One. Two. Three. Four. Five. Six. Seven. Eight. Nine. Ten. Eleven. Twelve. Thirteen. Fourteen. Etcetera. Too many bells, but you don't question. She likes it. She must. She is your wife. You have a right. Doesn't matter how fat you are. Doesn't matter how fat she is. You hear her call your name. You think so, anyway. You don't want to see the face. You've done this before, this in-and-out. You get distracted. Then the blood creeps into your brain. You're cock is raw and stinging, but you work harder, push deeper. Harder. Deeper. Like a good soldier. But your brain betrays you. Your dick betrays you. You feel it shriveling. Burning. You try to call up other images. Anything but the blood. You think of hitting her. You think of pulling her hair until her neck snaps. You think of all the mouths and pussies and assholes in every porn movie you've ever watched. You think of the pharmacist with the mole and the little titties. Your mind races, reels, desperate for something to hold to. But it can't outrun the blood. You can't outrun the blood.

Soon enough, the door of pain opens wide, and Abby, ushered in by the mad tintinnabulation of bells, passes through. Eagerly. Giddily. But she finds herself in a colorless and formless place. The words that have defined Heaven—throughout her childhood in her mother's church; and now from the man on the radio—the words remain cuneiform. They refuse to be anything other than consonants and vowels. Nothing more than thin black scribble in infinite white space. They are not ladders, nor stairs. The words will not sing. They will not shine in glorious golden beams. They are neither sweet nor bitter to the taste. They will not become robes. Nor wings. Abigail cannot even find a secure foothold amid the words.

Abigail does not like the Heaven she has stumbled into. The Hell. She doesn't want to be here. The man on top of her pounds away. Pounds away. She knows his face. She's never seen him before. The husband. Jesus. The man. The faces all become one. The body above, driving away at the body below. Penetrating. The body. The man. He may have finished what he came for; she can't tell. But still he pounds away. Abigail cannot block the images in her mind. Abigail needs assurance, blessed assurance. She wrestles her arm free, reaches over, and turns up the radio.

The blood usurps. A coup d'état of your psyche. You keep humping that ass, but your dick is shrunken and useless. You keep humping because you have to. She likes it. She's making noises. She likes it. You can tell. Except they don't sound like her. Whose voice is that? Somebody is talking. Talking to you? To her? Some asshole is in the room, watching. Watching as you fuck your wife. You'll kill the fucker. Get out of my fucking house, you say. Except that you can't see anybody. Hey, you say. Shut the fuck up, you say, trying to locate the voice. He keeps talking about Jesus. Then you realize she'd turned the radio on. While you were inside her. You start slamming into her crotch harder and harder. You don't need a cock. You'll split her wide open with your whole body. Every time you slam into her she grunts, the bed groans and squeaks and sags. Then the bed frame breaks. One leg snaps, the whole shebang tilts. The other legs follow suit. You both drop with a thud. Something else breaks. Ribs maybe. That voice on the radio babbles through it all. Yammering on and on about Jesus, about Judgment.

"Goddamn you!" you say. You grab the radio from the nightstand, yank the cord from the receptacle. It sparks. You can still hear his voice. "Goddamn you!" you say and raise the radio high, ready to smash it down.

"Burns," she says.

"Daddy," another voice says. "Daddy."

I didn't see anything. I didn't see anything. I didn't see anything.

The enemy is attacking. Inside and out. They come from all sides. They've taken Daddy. They have mind control. And Mama. And Mama. I have to be strong. I have to prepare myself. It's just me now. At the end of the world. The dead ride their giant Slinkys up out of Hell. It's just me now. I have to prepare. I slam the door. I go under my bed. My hideout. My lair is bulletproof. Bombproof. Whatever they use, I'll resist. Weapons. I need weapons. It's dark. They've taken the moon. I didn't see anything. I didn't see his nakedness. I didn't see her nakedness. I didn't see the raised fist. I am Super Boy. See my uniform? They're coming. I am fearless. I am not scared. I am not shaking. I am not crying. I didn't see anything.

Breath comes at a price for Abigail Augenbaugh. Each time she inhales, pain knifes a hot path up her spine and around her cranium. The breaths have to be shallow, or she'll surely faint. Enough oxygen filters in, but just. Broken rib. Ribs, maybe. When the bed gave way. When she crashed to the floor with Burns on top of her, Abby felt something surrender in her chest. Heard the crack.

Breath always comes at a price. She was prepared to die. When he raised the radio over her head, she expected it. Expected his heavy arms to come smashing down into her skull. She'd follow that voice in the radio right on up to Heaven.

But Burns didn't hit her. He smashed the radio against the wall. It shattered, went silent. Burns struggled to his feet. Abigail heard him on the stairs. The descent seemed to take hours.

Burns is her husband. She's seen him before. He didn't kill her. Abigail isn't brave enough to admit that death may have been preferable. She acquiesces to the easier path, the ancient illogic. The Lord has a different plan. Except that, without the wise and comforting voice of the preacher, how will she know what to do next? How will she know what the Lord wants from her?

Burns took her lifeline. Her compass. Left her with the calendar, the clock tower's unreliable tolling, and broken ribs. Banished her to the few remaining days that stretch out, vast, unmappable, desolate, with no compass, no warden.

The world is quiet. The eggy sulfur stink from the paper mill permeates the dark. Abigail turns over, pulls the stretched panties up and tries to sit, but the pressure on her ribcage is excruciating. She rolls back onto her stomach, pushes to her hands and knees. Stands, eventually. Burns is her husband. She is his wife. Everything hurts, *down there*. Abigail limps into the bathroom, holds the sink for balance with one hand, cleans herself as best she can with the other. Across the narrow way, she sees a light go off in the DeFonzie house.

Abigail stands, wobbly, unsure, in the hallway. The boy, Willie, their son, he saw things. He bore witness. She is his mother. Judgment Day is nigh. She has to do something. Abby musters the little maternal courage she has, braces against the wall and finds the way to his door. Finds him, in the foul-smelling room, smaller than she remembered, exhausted by the burden of the night's spectacle, curled up and asleep in his ill-fitting Superman pajamas.

The boy sleeps with his mouth open. His pillow is damp and crusted from crying. Abigail watches his eyeballs twitch and roll behind the lids. Abigail knows what he dreams. Abigail will never know what he dreams. She wishes she were braver. Brave enough to take the pillow, with its Hulk Hogan cover, and press it down over the boy's face. That's what a good mother would do. A good mother wouldn't leave her son to the merciless demons of the Apocalypse. But Abigail Augenbaugh would never be that good mother. She knows it. The very thought of the act makes her heart pound, her stomach heave.

She reaches to touch her son's face. Stops. Tries again. Can't. Abigail, desperate, has no recourse but prayer. A tool she's yet to master. It may be too late. Nevertheless, she offers him up to the merciful God. Abby gets to her knees, grimacing at the pain. She folds her hands together, puts her elbows on the edge of the bed. The broken rib hurts so bad, she weeps. But she accepts that pain. Feels good about it. Like she's doing her part. When she settles into the suffering, when it is time to open her mouth, Abigail's prayer stalls. What is she asking for? The boy's salvation? The boy's quick execution? Her own release? Abigail wracks her brain. What should she say? Abby wishes she could hear the man on the radio. She grows desperate. Light-headed. Casting about in her compromised memory, she begins to babble. But the words she speaks do not fly Heavenward. It is as if she can see them fall. As if she can see the words, the syllables she utters, roll off her tongue like ball bearings, clatter across the floor, down the stairs, into the street, into the gutter.

"Our Father," she says.

"Oh Holy God," she says.

"Lord and Savior," she says.

I sleep for a thousand years. My body is frozen in liquid nitrogen. Fueled and made strong by the people I serve. I am the Savior. All await my triumphant return. I have no memory, and I have no fear. When I wake I will decimate my enemies. I sleep for a thousand years, but they come at me in the dark. They roll down out of the graves. They float up from the ground into the fiery sky. Dead people flying all around. I hear crying. Weeping and wailing. I hear them call my name. They need a superhero. They need me. I command the New Heaven and the New Earth. I sleep for a thousand years. The boy. The boy will wake me. When I wake, the world will tremble at our coming.

Abigail prays with all her might. Or tries to. Abigail, whipped and beaten by her past (both distant and near), mauled by her future (moment by moment), can do little more than blubber and babble. A haphazard glossarist. She cries out to God. She calls out the boy's name.

"O Lord,"
"O Willie,"
"O Lord,"
"O Willie."

They call my name. The dead and the living. They want to worship me. They want to kill me. The dead are tricky. Evil. They have mind control. They have Mama. Mama is dead. I saw them kill Mama with Daddy's arm. Daddy is dead. I am frozen. I will not wake for a thousand years. They can't trick me. I'm too strong. Too powerful. They use Mama to trick me. They use her voice. *Willie,* they make her say. *Willie. Willie.* I cover my ears. I squeeze my eyes tight.

Willie, she says. Willie. And it seems so real that I wake up. I have to wake up. And when I wake up I am in my bed, and she's kneeling beside me.

"You're dead," I say. "You can't trick us."

"No honey," she says. "I'm not dead. I'm right here."

"I saw him kill you," I say. "I saw them kill you. You can't trick me. You're dead."

"Nobody killed me, Willie. Me and Daddy were just—, nobody killed me."

"No!" I say. I pull away. I am strong. I am brave. I press myself into the wall. I become the wall. I can strike without warning.

"Willie," she says. It sounds so real. I blink. I blink away all the other dead bodies in the room. I blink, and try to make her go away. She's still there. It's night. I can see through the window. There are no fires burning outside. No weeping or moaning. Just her, reaching toward me.

"No," I say. I will not give in. I will not crack. I will not cry.

"Willie."

"No," I say. I will not cry. I will not cry.

"Willie."

"Don't go," I say.

She doesn't speak.

"Don't go to Heaven without me," I say. I am crying. They have me. They have my mind. I can't help myself. I fall into the evil one's arms.

"I heard the man on the radio," I say. "Don't go to Heaven. Please, Mama! Please don't go to Heaven! Please! Please! Please stay with me, Mama."

She's not talking. I can hear breath whistling in her chest. She's crying too. Tears drip on my neck. But she's not talking.

"I'll pray again, Mama. I'll beseech the Lord, just like you told me. I don't want the world to end. I don't want to be here when the earthquakes—"

"It's," she says. "It's not my decision, it's the Lord's."

I pull back. I have to see her eyes. To see if they have her eyes too.

"Can I go with you?"

I beg and beg. I promise to be good in Heaven. I promise everything.

"Please take me to Heaven with you, Mama. I'm scared, Mama."

"OK," she says. Finally. But I'm looking right at her. I know she's lying. I know she'll go to Heaven and leave me behind.

"I'm scared, Mama."

"Everything is OK, Willie," she hisses softly. "It'll all be over soon."

DAY 3

One. Two. Three. Four. Five. Six. Seven. Eight. Nine. Ten. Eleven. Twelve. Thirteen. Fourteen. Fifteen. Sixteen. Seventeen. Eighteen. Nineteen. Twenty. Twenty-one. Twenty-two. Twenty-three. Twenty-four. Twenty-five.

This is how many times we stab her.

What remained of the battering night passed without further incident. The triumvirate of casualties, father, mother, and son, hunker alone in their respective foxholes and await daylight.

Abigail Augenbaugh wakes first, if she ever slept. The sun is just clawing its way up over Scald Mountain. Thick fog pools in the valleys, snags in the branches of the hickory, the walnut, and the buckeye trees. There is beauty there, to be seen. But the beauty is occluded by ugly pain. Merely breathing is endeavor enough. Abigail limps to the bathroom. She cannot lift her right arm. She tends to her ablutions as best she can, without looking in the mirror, dons her Slinky smock, and descends the stairs haltingly. She leaves the busted radio scattered on the bedroom floor.

Abigail leans against the kitchen counter, unseeing, clinging—without intention—to the few remaining moments of the organic grace that accompanies all trauma. That finite bubble of timelessness in which the body tries to take care of itself, free of the mind's nonsense. Soon enough she'll have to reconcile the ravaged household, her bruised groin and raw sex, betrayal's grimy veneer, the fractured bone, the rancid taste of deceit in her mouth.

Every breath hurts. Abigail thinks maybe she ought to eat something, but she's nauseated from the pain. She gags, and the retching seizure of her diaphragm hurts so badly Abigail nearly passes out. She thinks, maybe, she ought to go to the hospital. But in just a couple days Jesus will come, and she'll get a glorious new spiritual body. The man on the radio promises it. She just has to hold on a little longer.

The night's events begin to prick pinholes into her awareness. Memories of what happened, meteors of sensory detail, flash across Abby's brainpan. Slowly, at first, then in torrents. Her son. Her husband. Her savior. Her self.

It's a school day, and Willie is still up in his room. What's left to learn, she wonders, in these last few days? Let the boy sleep, or whatever it is he's doing. She needs to get out of the house. She needs to fill her day, to do her part. Abigail knows, without being able to articulate it, that misery and discomfort can be displaced. Squeezed out. What she lacks, though, is discernment. So, like most, Abby usually just swaps one sorrow for another. She sees the crumpled edge of a Rapture tract peeking from beneath the garbage can lid. She retrieves them all and tucks the whole damp stack under her useless arm. She closes the front door and hopes to leave the whole mess behind.

It's early. Too early for the mailman. But Abigail worries about being ambushed by the DeFonzies before she reaches the Celebrity. And hobbled as she is, can only move so fast. Each step brings a grimace, a throaty grunt. In the narrow passage between their houses she pauses, rests, gathering crumbs of strength. It's early, but Abigail hears movement in her neighbors' home. It's Tina DeFonzie. Laughing. Burns used to say (before he went into the basement) that the woman belonged on the Animal Channel, with that laugh.

This morning, as the day makes its incremental claim on Joy, the laugh, the laughter, confuses Abigail Augenbaugh, more than anything else. She locks the Chevy in her sight and tries to hurry down the skinny cracked sidewalk.

"Hey," she hears someone call. Abby doesn't look. She wants to quicken her pace. Can't. By the time she reaches the car, Abby is in agony. She weeps quietly, fumbles with the key. Drops it. Stoops to pick it up. Cries out. She hears the DeFonzies' back door open. Hears, again, the call. "Hey?"

It's Tina. Abigail can tell.

Abby sits heavily, bumping her ribcage against the steering wheel, cries out again, uncontrollably. Abigail pushes through the pain to slam the car door. She locks it, then braves a look. Tina DeFonzie, halfway across her yard, in a short white bathrobe held barely closed at her chest, approaches. She is naked beneath. Tan.

"Hey."

Tina DeFonzie leans her face close to the glass. Abigail struggles with the seat belt. Struggles with the agony.

"Are you—" the woman says.

"Can I—" the woman says.

"You've got to—" the woman says.

Abigail looks straight ahead. But she waits. Listening. What? Abigail wants the true completion of any of those half-spoken sentences. What? Abigail has her own answers, but is unable to offer them up. Abigail can only sit and wait. What?

Tina DeFonzie puts her fingertip on the window. Abigail cannot look—the broken rib, the shame, the confusion, rendering the pane of glass between them too vast to transgress. What? The reach to turn the key in the ignition is almost too excruciating to bear. Abigail Augenbaugh takes up that cross of pain and drives it down the road.

I open my eyes. No. I open one eye. The other is welded shut. Maybe they plucked it out. I am not afraid. I will conquer all with a single mighty eye. I peed again. In the bed, again. They took my eye. I'll piss in the empty socket. I'll piss on them. I can do what I want. No. Not plucked. Not welded, not stitched shut. Just crusted over. I remember crying. I remember my dead mama. She told me lies. She stroked my head. Daddy is dead in the basement. I know it. I have to be strong. I have to go see for myself. I will avenge his death. I will avenge her death, even against her body. Where is my Game Boy? I need to think. To plot. I stink. My smell is a weapon. No. I go to the bathroom, open the spigots. No hot water. I fill the tub with cold water. I climb in. I sit down. I shiver. I am so cold it hurts. I go inside the hurt. I go down down down to the bottom of the tub. I stay there forever.

∀

"Ma'am." Abigail Augenbaugh hears the call. There is more wheeze and grunt than celestial fanfare. But she hears the call nonetheless.

"Ma'am." The swirl of light and dark, the wracking waves of pain. Abigail just knows her soul, her spirit is about to leave its body behind.

"Ma'am," the voice says again. And Abby can't not hear the incessant rapping on the window. She opens her eyes.

Abigail sits in the Celebrity. At a traffic light. At an intersection with churches on three of its four corners (the fourth, a parking lot that the churches fight over from time to time).

"License and registration, ma'am." A policeman stands close, peering in at her. "Open the window, ma'am. Open it slowly."

It's like TV, Abigail thinks. Like one of those reality shows, or something about mistaken identity. Maybe she'll get shot, or handcuffed. The policeman sees her struggle to open the glove box, hears her groan in pain.

"Are you all right, ma'am?" he asks.

The moment is a gift—the second of the morning—to be accepted or rejected.

She looks at the policeman. He's younger than she. She sees herself, or at least the person he sees, reflected in his aviator glasses.

"Are you all right, ma'am?" he asks, with more authority.

Is she? Abigail grapples with the question. Is she all right?

These moments (of potential) crop up often enough in every life, but are difficult to see except through hindsight. Abigail Augenbaugh could answer him. She could open her mouth and say it all, out loud. And in doing so would change, to one degree or another, everything that followed. She almost knows this. She strains against everything that shackles her to a bleak, mute, blind past. Struggles frantically but briefly for a *different* kind of answer.

"Cramps," she mumbles, through clenched teeth. A lie tinged with both rare genius and utter embarrassment.

The officer leans into the car, looks at the Rapture tracts on the seat. He chastises her for something. She's not sure what. "Third-graders cross this street," he says. "Second-graders."

He gives her a form to sign. He says it's just a warning. It does not mean that she is a complete failure as a mother. As a wife. He tells her to go home.

"Next time you won't be so lucky," he says. "Go home," he says, again, as if it's just that easy. "Go to bed. You look like you need the rest."

Abigail drives away, cautiously, but the magnitude of the policeman's compassion overwhelms her. She wants to turn around. To run the light. To speed through the streets and sideswipe cars until she is back in his good grace. His judgment. Kind. Forgiving. Handsome. Her boy, Willie, could maybe be a policeman, if there were more time left. He'd be good at it.

And forever. Then my lungs explode. Lightning flashes inside my head. I drown. I rise up. I resurrect. Tornadoes spill from my open mouth. I have all the elements at my command. I am unstoppable. I am naked and shivering. I am brave. I'm a little teapot, short and stout. Here is my weapon of mass destruction. I go downstairs. The dead mama is gone. Daddy is not dead in the kitchen or the living room. I step carefully, avoiding the land mines scattered on the floor. I hear someone on the front porch. I yank open the door. The mail lady looks at me, looks up and down my brave naked body. I push against the screen door. She drops the mail at her feet, puts her hand on the can of mace at her belt, backs down the steps. I decide to let her live. She may be of use to me later. I take the mail. I push it deep into the trash can. Something pierces my palm, slices it open. The gash is pretty. I move my thumb, and the cut opens and closes, like a little mouth.

Abigail drives cautiously, despite the panicked mouse that is her heart hurling against its cracked cage, yearning for escape. There was something so delicious about her brush with the law that Abby entertains, for one mad moment, giving the last few days of her earthly life over to sin. Sin. But she wouldn't know how to start. No. Not true. Abigail knows all about sin. Abigail knows exactly where she would begin. Abigail hurts. All over. Adrenaline barely tempers the pain. Duty prevails.

Abby looks at the Rapture tracts in the passenger seat. She drives obediently down Wright Street, past the six-pack shop where, on a windowless side wall, a peeling mural of Colonel Bartholomew Joyner and his dog oversees everything. Abigail drives past the trophy shop; the outstretched arms of the faceless and sexless figurines in the window catch and hold the morning sun. She slows to let a pedestrian—man or woman, she can't tell—cross to the laundromat, bent nearly double under the massive bags balanced on their back. When the laundromat door opens, the stink of fabric softener and bleach fills the car. Abigail gags. The cracked rib throbs in her chest. It takes everything she has not to stomp the accelerator.

She has to get to work, has to get away from the policeman, the boy, the man, and all that happened last night, has to get through the day. To get through whatever is left of the days. But a block away, Abigail is impeded yet again. In an enclave of Section 8 housing an open-topped U-Haul trailer, jackknifed behind a rusty pickup, blocks the road. In the bed of the truck, the thin iron post of a floor lamp with a dented yellow shade leans against an old La-Z-Boy recliner. Cardboard boxes are scattered haphazardly on the weedy yard. In and around the trailer, half a dozen men grapple with the massive plaster fish strapped there. Trout? Bass? Abby doesn't know the difference, but the greenish thing is longer than her car, and almost as big around. Its toothy mouth gapes. Its white eyes big as plates. Abby hears a thump, and a tall, rail-thin man with wild red hair and beard curses loudly. The fat man standing opposite, with spiked gray hair and a too-small Grateful Dead T-shirt, laughs. Loudly. She can't tell if they're moving the fish in or out. Several onlookers gawk from the apartment windows. Kids and adults.

Abigail wants to scream at them all. "Stop!" she wants to yell. She can think of nothing else.

Why? Why is this happening? Why the obstacles in her path? Abigail knows that suffering is a favorite tool of God's. Everybody says so. God's true love is found deep within His wrath. The more He loves, the more you hurt. Right? Abby knows that God makes her suffer in order to teach her things. She's known this her whole life. She's never understood how it works, though. She's never, ever—not even once—been able to see the lesson clearly. She doesn't understand why Burns lives in the basement, or what she is supposed to learn from last night. Her boy, their son, an unsolvable puzzle. Maybe Burns is God.

Abigail is in Joy. There is no doubt about it. The streets, these people, these details, are all ancient and oppressive facts in her life. She just wants to get to work. She just wants to clock in once before Jesus returns. Abigail feels an obligation to the boxes. To Jinx, even. She will work. She will dream of riding the Slinky float one more day. She will work through the pain of broken ribs. She'll pack, with one arm if need be, and lay a ragged shard of memory from last night (from every night of her life) in the box with each toy. She'll seal them up, send them down the conveyor, and let those two boys on the loading dock ship the hurt far away. If she could only get past these men and their giant fake fish.

Abigail slumps against the steering wheel. The Celebrity's horn startles her more than anyone else. All the men wrestling the fish look at her.

"Yea though I walk through the valley of the shadow of death," Abigail prays.

Are they going to hurt her?

Are they God?

"I will fear no evil," Abigail prays.

Abigail prays without need. One of the men blows her a kiss, then they all go back to their struggle with the plaster behemoth; they leave her alone. It's just a broken rib, Abby thinks through the scrim of hurt. Her Lord suffered so much more. She can endure. She bumps the shifter into drive, works at the steering wheel with her good arm, turns and inches forward. Then reverse, then forward, and eventually she gets the car turned around.

But a block away, where Wright Street merges into Pulp Way, Abigail sees a train emerge from the tunnel, like some terrestrial black leviathan scuttling from the belly of Scald Mountain to wreak havoc. There is no way she can make the crossing in time. Abby knows this train. She's watched it unfurl forever, dragging its mile-long tail through Joy. The hoppers full of coal so black it sparkles, like they're hauling broken chunks of the starry night sky itself. The boxcars, nearly always empty; gaping doors on both sides play peekaboo as they pass. And the tankers, so many tankers full of sloshing chemicals on their way to or from the paper mill, with their warnings emblazoned seductively at both ends. Like the rest of humanity, Abigail feels the irresistible draw of toxicity. The crossing gate comes down clanging and herky-jerky. Abby puts the Celebrity in park. She smells diesel fuel and hydraulic fluid. Every time a train car rolls across the grade, its tonnage quakes the roadbed and rattles the Chevy's chassis, and Abigail suffers. Another lesson?

It's just a broken rib, Abby thinks, again. Burns didn't mean it. He loves her. Just like God. Her Lord suffered so much more, she thinks again. Can she endure? She wishes for some guidance. For aid. And then, even through the hurt and doubt, she sees it. The message, blinking in and out of view between the passing train cars. The billboard she's passed so often on the outskirts of Joy that she's stopped noticing it.

JUDGMENT DAY WILL OCCUR, MAY 21, 2011
"blow the trumpet . . . warn the people"
Details @ FamilyRadio.com

Abigail looks at the billboard. *Sees* it. She looks at the gospel tracts. She knows what to do now. She knows how little time is left. She understands her obligation. Her duty, her debt, is to her coworkers. Her neighbors. The townspeople. Her poor family, husband and son. The billboard states it, plain and clear. God put her here, in agony, put the train in her way, so that she could be still and see. The man on the radio is speaking directly to her. To Abigail Augenbaugh. Abby has the Rapture tracts, each a missive from God himself. The *Truth*. Abigail has the Truth scattered on the front seat of her Chevy Celebrity. More Truth than she can ever use. She knows what to do, at last. And inasmuch as conviction is an adequate balm, however temporary, with the train's passing, Abigail

Augenbaugh drives through the lingering and familiar stenches of diesel and hydraulic fluids (tinged now, ever so faintly, with the rare scent of glorious triumph), around the block and back up Wright Street.

We talk. I bleed a little bit. I lick my palm clean. I make a fist. It hurts, but I eat the pain. Someone knocks, on the door. Maybe it's the mail lady, come back to get what she deserves. Come back to join forces, with me. I'll take on all comers. I yank it open. The door. I don't know this enemy. I stand there naked, ready to attack.

"William," she says.

I don't know this enemy. I push my nakedness against the screen.

"William. It's Mrs. Onkst. From school."

She is strong, this one. Masks her fear well. She looks me straight in the eye. Her lies are perfect.

"Is your mother here, William? Are you OK, William?"

She knows the mother is dead. She helped kill the dead mother. I put the dead mother out of my mind.

"William, I need to speak to your mother or your father."

No, I think. I think I say. I say aloud. "No."

"William. Look at me, William. Do you know who I am?"

I cannot look into her eyes. That's how they get mind control. I see the butterfly tattoo on her anklebone. I recognize the tattoo. I chew it off. No. I don't. I grab my dick, like Travis taught me. But it hides from me. And she doesn't move. I think quick. I have to become one of them. If I want to survive, I have to play their evil games.

"They're not home," I say. The sentence feels too big for my mouth.

"I'm sick," I say. "Alone."

"You've been absent, William. Are you OK? Is that blood?"

I will not give her my eyes. Of course it's blood. What else would it be? She tries to look around me, into the house. I wish I had my cape. I wish I had my Hulk pajamas. My hurt fist throbs. Turns green. Swells. No, grows. Massive. Bigger than my head. I raise it high. My mighty fist comes down through the screen door and onto the head of my enemy. I smite her. I drive her, like a nail, through the floor of the porch. It happens so fast. She has no time to move. No time to speak. She can't even scream.

"William," a voice says. "Put some clothes on, William. I want to talk to you."

It's her voice. Cloned, or resurrected, or regenerated, she stands there again before me. I underestimated her powerful magic. I must plan my counterattack.

"No," I say. "I'm sick. I've been sick."

"I want you to come with me, William. I want you to put your clothes on and come with me."

I wish I had my cape. I wish I wasn't naked. I'm glad I am naked.

"Fear the beast," I say. Show her my weapon. She will not leave. She will not take her eyes away. They get you through the eyes.

"Where is your mother?"

"Not home," I say. Not *Dead*. Not *On her way to Heaven*.

"At work," I say. I can lie too.

I do know this enemy. She is tricky. She has captured me before, at the school, the enemy camp. She lies. I've been in her torture chamber before. It smells like girl, like lady. She makes me sit on her couch. Nothing to do but look at the stupid pictures of her stupid perfect family on her stupid desk. Stupid perfect freckles. She pretends to be nice, pretends to like me. I almost gave in once. I will not give in now. I will not tell her about my superpowers. I will not tell her about last night. I will not tell her about the end of the world.

"William, where's your father?"

And then, like a god or a wizard, he appears.

Back up Wright Street to the drive-thru at Joy Savings & Loan. She pulls into the far lane, serviced by a clear capsule pipeline, a small oval speaker, and a clunky camera. Abigail empties their meager bank account for cash. Between the harsh suck of the withdrawal slip making its way and the somewhat gentler return, she clings to the wheel, looks straight ahead; but her hands palsy as she removes the thin envelope. Abigail pauses before pulling away.

"Will there be anything else?" the teller asks.

Abigail hurts too much to twist her body, to crane her neck, in the direction of the window two lanes over. She looks up at the camera and the speaker.

"May I help you with anything else?" the teller asks.

Everybody deserves a chance, Abigail thinks. *Everybody deserves the Truth.* She tucks a Rapture tract into the clear shuttle and presses the button to send it back up the pneumatic tube.

Abby feels good. Almost.

Like a god. Like a storm trooper, he swoops in and destroys mine enemies. She is powerless, this Mrs. Onkst, against his force. Blood and guts splatter the porch. Her head bounces off the neighbors' roof. An arm and its flopping hand land in the road. I put the butterfly tattoo in my pocket. Up and down the street people close their blinds, lock their doors. He's here now, and there's no stopping him. They all know it. They all tremble in fear.

I'll put on my cape. I'll join him in battle. We will march down the street and lay waste the town. Any minute now he'll call me to his side.

"Willie," he'll say. And I'll go.

"Willie," he'll say. "Willie."

"Willie?" It's like the voice is right behind me. "Willie, what the hell are you doing?"

I open my eyes. The lady is driving away. There's no blood on the porch. Daddy stands behind me, in the door to the basement.

You wake up in the desert. No. It's damp. You wake up in the desert. No. It's damp. You keep trying to wake up in the desert, but it's always the goddamn basement. Your head pounds. It might be the sump pump. You wake up in the basement. Your mouth is full of sand. You wear the uniform. It proves something. Your dick hurts. It proves something. You lie on the couch. Daylight cuts a hard edge around the garbage bags you've taped to the window. Daylight. You should be asleep. Still. You reach for your pills, remember that you are out of pills. The sump pump rattles your skull, your ribcage. You sit up. Your fly is open, button and belt too. You scratch your swollen gut. Scratch your crotch. Everything is sore. Your cock hair is matted and crusty. What the hell? Oh. You remember. It's been a long time. You feel, a little bit, like a man. Like a husband. You puke, but nothing comes up.

You think about her, the wife. Her soft behind. She used to be pretty. You think so, anyway. You like her fat ass. You think so, anyway. You think about her a while, try to stir something up down there. You remember a rayon dress. No. It's gone. She shouldn't have said what she said. You did what you had to do. The sump pump pounds. On the door upstairs.

No. Someone is knocking. You hear voices. It's your boy. You're not sure what day it is. What month. Why he's up there. You feel like a man, like a husband. It makes you feel like a father. Almost. You put your sweats on, go upstairs. You'll take care of things. The boy stands at the door, naked. Someone drives away.

"Willie," you say. "Boy. Willie. Boy. Willie..."

Over and over, until, finally, he looks your way.

Good. Almost. Wright Street.

Abigail doesn't go to work like she is supposed to. She quits her job. Sort of. She just decides not to go back. Not to clock in. The decision makes her heart surge hard; blood roars in her eardrums like the beat of the box-and-tape machine she is abandoning. Schkkk-chick-chicka. Schkkk-chick-chicka. Schkkk-chick-chicka.

Andy, Mitch, Sue, Darnell. Even Jinx. Abigail knows she'll never see them again. Not even Sue, who'll surely be Raptured. Heaven's probably too big. She tried to warn them, tried to spread the gospel. But they mocked her. The man on the radio said it would happen. He said the True Believers would be mocked. He said prayer is the only weapon. But the man on the radio is stronger than Abigail. She feels, despite the momentary thrill of quitting Slinky, inadequate. She wishes she could hear his voice again. One more time before the end.

The bank envelope is propped against the tracts on her seat. Abigail realizes she could buy another radio and hide it from Burns. She pulls into the parking lot of a failed party supply concern, and counts the money.

Two hundred sixty-eight dollars. The whole of the Augenbaugh life savings amounts to this paltry sum. Much as she wants a new radio, Abigail knows there are other things to buy first. She has to take care of her family, to provide something for her husband and son, to help them into the last days. Soon Abby will be gone, called up, lifted out of the torrent, to be with Jesus. Burns and Willie will, surely, be left behind. The man on the radio explained that there will be four months between the moment of Rapture and the final destruction of the universe. Millions, billions of people will die that first day. But some will live on. Burns—her sad and hurtful husband—and Willie, their poor son, might get lucky. But they're not ready. Burns doesn't know. He doesn't believe, or care. And Willie.

Abby folds the money, puts it into the pocket of her Slinky smock, and drives, unhindered, to, where? Surplus City, maybe. She'll buy plastic bins, one for each of them. She'll buy flashlights and batteries, extra pairs of warm socks. Canned food. A couple chocolate bars. What else would they need at the end of time? What else?

She feels good. It is almost a plan.

She is almost a real wife.

Almost a real mother.

Almost a True Believer.

"What're you doing, boy?" you ask.

"Put some clothes on," you say.

You have to take charge. You are the father. The father takes charge. He doesn't move. The boy seems scared. Or stunned. Who was at the door? You ought to ask the boy who was at the door. You've seen her before. You think it was that bitch from school. What does she want? You ought to ask the boy what the hell she wanted. You know your red tape well. She shouldn't be here by herself. She's going to cause trouble. She's probably on her way to call Child Welfare. Who does she think she is? You are the father. You are the man of this house. You serve. You protect.

The boy slams the door, and a thought-bomb explodes in your head. You flash to last night. You and the mother, fucking. The rut. The boy in the doorway. Did you hit her? The mother? Did you kill her? You don't think so. But you can't ask the boy. Where is she? She might be upstairs. Dead. You did what you had to. You ought to go look. For the body. You don't know what you'll do when you find it. You've seen bodies before. You are a soldier. A warrior.

"Go upstairs," you say to the boy.

"Find your mama," you say to the boy.

"Put some clothes on," you say to the boy. And he looks at you. You look around the house. It's a shithole. What happened? He is your son. You are the father. Act like it. She'll come back, the woman from his school. She'll bring along a whole battalion of pencil-dick social workers. But you'll show her. You won't be here.

"Get ready," you say. "We're going out."

Like a storm trooper. A war hero. He takes charge. I am not afraid. I go to my room. I search and search and find my Evel Knievel shirt, the black pants. I put on boots, not shoes. No socks. I think my toes bleed. I pull the curtain back, snarl at the stupid neighbors' house, the graveyard, the whole outside world. I tuck the Game Boy in my waistband. Like a pistol. Daddy is downstairs, waiting on me.

I am not afraid. I will go with him. Anywhere.

Is she dead? you ask the boy. *Did you find the body?*
No, you don't.
"Get my club," you say.
You are the father. The boy does as he's told.

The basement scares me. It is the lair of the Dark One. But I serve the Dark One. I must be brave. I do as I am commanded. The club is on the floor by the couch. The Dark One sleeps on the couch. He takes my daddy. He gives back my daddy. The couch holds the shape of his body. The Dark One is disguised as a fat man. One day soon, he will rip off the fat suit, rise up in glorious rage, and reveal his true self. I pick up the club. It sizzles and crackles with fire. The club is the ultimate weapon. I bear it to my master. Together we will destroy the world.

"What are you wearing?" you ask. The boy doesn't seem to hear you. Dumbass pajamas. It's her fault. You close the only two buttons on your army jacket. You should've put a shirt on, but it's too late. There's a jelly jar with some pocket change by the busted telephone. It's not much. You take the jar, without counting. Under the phone book, in the junk drawer, an envelope holds your debit card and Visa. You pocket both and hope for the best.

"Open the door," you say to the boy. You don't have a plan. You are the father and the husband. You don't need a plan. You shoulder Big Bertha and let the boy go out first. You almost go back inside. Almost retreat. It's the sun. Too bright. Too many colors. You can barely see. In the desert, and in the basement, there aren't so many colors. But the boy steps off the porch, and you have no choice but to follow.

How long has it been since you left the house? Two days? A decade? It's all the same. You're the father. He's the son. You have to show the boy things. He's turning into a mama's boy. A pussy. You showed her; now you'll show him. She liked it. You could tell. He will too.

I don't need Travis. I don't need Mama. I don't need school. I don't need Heaven. I serve the Dark One. When the Rapture monsters come, we'll stand together and slay them. I am not afraid. I am not afraid of the stupid neighbors. Or that bitch from school. I am not afraid of the dead bodies that'll rise up out of the grave tomorrow. I am with my daddy. He wears his uniform. He has his club. He is a war hero. I wear my uniform. I am body and not body. I am the boy. The boy is me. There is sky. There are mountains. We are going for a walk. I don't know where to. I don't care.

You take the boy through the alley because the mountains are harder to see there. You don't want the boy to know that you fear the mountains. You see the toppled grotto in the neighbors' yard. You smile, sort of. At the end of the alley are two churches, one on either side. The boy walks too close to you.

"Move," you say. He does.

You have a son. One time you held his hand. You don't remember the day.

The church on the right has a big gold dome, shaped like an onion, topped with a cross. Simple. You've walked by this church your whole life. For most of it, you believed the rumors about satanic rituals. Whatever those are. Across the alley, a plain brick box with a thin steeple jutting into the afternoon sky. There may or may not be stained glass behind the thick, milky Plexiglas and the bars on all the windows. You don't care. The boy walks too close, still.

"Move, Goddamn it."

He does. The son. For God so loved the motherfucking world, you think. You might say it aloud. You don't know where you're going. It doesn't matter. You are prepared. You lead. You follow a higher order. Both church lawns are immaculate. The paint jobs, immaculate. The monkey bars and swing-sets, immaculate. The boy never had a swing set. You see the garden shed in the corner. There is a door; it may or may not be ajar. You've trained for this. You are ready for either scenario. You notice the trees in both yards. They're full of tent worms. The dense silk nests clot the branches.

"Come here," you say to the boy. "Here I am," you say. You take him beneath one of the trees. He's afraid. You can tell. You like that. You have things to teach.

"Here I am," you say, again. "Listen," you say. And you both lean close to the trunk.

"Listen," he says, and I do. I press my ear against the hard bark. It hurts. I'm scared of what I hear. But I do as I am commanded. The Dark One speaks sap and bark.

"No, dumbass," he says. "Listen at that."

The Dark One points right above my head to where the trunk splits in two. I see the nest. It's full of caterpillars. I know so, even though the white web is too thick to see through; the wormy shapes boil and squirm just beneath the surface.

"Listen," he says.

I listen. I shut out all other noise. I refuse to hear any sound except what spills out of the nest. It's like dry palms rubbing together. And faint clicks. Like crumbling leaves. I let the sounds fill my head, my body.

"Look up," he says. Points at the other nests in the tree. At the other trees with nests. All full of hairy black caterpillars fighting for space. The roar is so loud I fall to my knees and cover my ears.

"Get up, dumbass," he says. "Watch this."

The boy acts retarded. The boy is retarded. It's her fault. You're sorry you killed her. You're not sorry. You didn't kill her. You make him stand up. You take Big Bertha. You shove her titanium head right into the middle of the caterpillar nest. You dig it in deep and yank it free. It's like the nest is vomiting worms. They spill then dribble from the hole you gouged. They cling to the head of the club. You look at the boy. He has a spark in his eye. You feel like a father. You've shown him something.

Important. The tree is full of tent worm nests. You reach a little higher with the club, puncture another. The caterpillars fall, some tumbling in clumps to the ground. The caterpillars crawl across the face of the earth. The boy backs up, afraid. You stomp and stomp their yellow guts into the churchyard. You think you hear the boy laugh.

"I wish you could take that club to all of them," the boy says.

No. Not the boy. You turn. It's a man in a stark black shirt. He carries a plastic gasoline jug in one hand, a Weed Eater in the other.

"We're leaving now," you say. "No trouble."

When he puts the Weed Eater down and his hand out to shake, you see his collar.

"Pastor Mike," he says.

You could take him if you had to. With the club, or maybe with your hands. The boy could watch. You tighten your grip on Big Bertha. The man smiles. The man seems soft. Not weak, necessarily. Not flabby. Just not hard.

You don't take his hand. You don't trust the man. The three of you stand in the backyard of the church and wait for what comes next.

It's two against one. We wear our uniforms. Our enemy is in black. He smiles a black smile and the worms bristle in their cocoons. The worms are under his command. I am scared. I am not scared. Daddy has his club. The man in the black shirt wields a cruel weapon. It drips green blood. The man in the black shirt smiles when he talks. His teeth blind me. It's a trick. I want to yell to Daddy. It is us against this man and his world. Don't take the enemy's hand! I watch Daddy. Wait for orders. We stand in the grass for a long time without saying anything. Without doing anything. I can hear the caterpillars crawling.

"We're leaving now," you say to the preacher. "Don't want no trouble."

"They're bad this year," he says. Smiling. "I wish you'd stick around and stomp every last caterpillar for me. I might even be able to pay you."

We both look up into the trees. The boy, too.

The preacher stands close. You can't tell what he means to do. The sky is too blue. It makes you nervous. The grass is too green. The preacher's dandruff falls like snow. God of scalp and follicle. You push Big Bertha's head into a clump of caterpillars.

"You ought to douse them all with that gasoline," you say. "Set them on fire."

"Reckon that'd solve my problem?" the man says. Smiling. He looks at you and the boy. He looks you in the eyes, but you can tell he's trying to see it all.

This is the church and this is the steeple open the door and these are the people this is the church and this is the steeple open the door and these are the people this is the church and this is the steeple open the door and these are the people this is the church and this is the steeple open the door and these are the people this is the church and this is the steeple open the door and these are the people this is the church and this is the steeple open the door and these are the people this is the church and this is the steeple open the door and these are the people this is the church and this is the steeple open the door and these are the people this is the church and this is the steeple open the door and these are the people this is the church and this is the steeple open the door and these are the people this is the church and this is the steeple open the door and these are the people.

$$\ll$$

The boy fidgets. The boy is doing something with his hands. Is mumbling something, with his mouth. Stop it, you say. Maybe you don't.

"Listen," the man says. "It's about lunchtime. We've got soup in the church today. Y'all come on in."

"I don't think so," you say. The boy fidgets. Stop it, you say. Or not.

"It's free," the preacher says.

Fuck you. "Ain't nothing free about it," you say.

The preacher smiles.

"This can just be about the soup, friend," he says. "Nothing else," he says.

"Let's get the boy something good to eat. Maybe something to wear."

For God so loved the motherfucking world. You can't imagine it. What if? What if you let the boy go? What next? You think about it. Your brain hurts. There is no room for the possibility. No, you say.

"No."

The earth quakes. You feel it. The ground, the churchyard, shifts under your feet. You fall.

We win. With the Dark One, I conquer the church man. We march him into the garden shed. Lock him inside. It smells of dirt, moldy grass, and hot engines. We are not afraid to torture. But it's not necessary, this time. I follow him, Daddy, the Dark Lord, down the alley. He knows everything. He knows about fire and gasoline. I will always follow him. I hear the preacher screaming inside the shed. I hear the worms. They're close behind, and coming up fast.

I wish I could show him the hideout, under the train. I wish I could show him the things Travis showed me. I don't need Travis. I don't need Mama. I wish the Dark One would go to school with me, would take his mighty club, would avenge everything.

You fall. The man kneels beside you, offers his hand. Get the fuck away from me. You fall. You rise. You take the boy's hand. He trips. He falls. You pull him along anyway. Did you feel the earthquake? Did you? You take the boy away from the churchyard. You don't know what to say about the preacher so you don't say anything. You wish you had your pills. You wish the sun would quit shining so bright. You wonder why the boy isn't in school. You don't ask. You don't know where you're going. You might be leading the boy, but you might be following something too. Your coat is hot and itchy. You worry, but only for a minute, about people seeing you and the boy. You think you say something about keeping off the sidewalks. But you see the phone booth.

"Watch this," you say to the boy. You'll show him. You'll prove your power. You dig in your pocket for change, step inside. The boy follows, closes the door. The space is too small for you both. Something stinks. You think you hear wasps twitching their wings, getting ready. A cement truck rumbles by, and the whole damn booth quakes in its flimsy frame, like an elevator to hell, you think, beginning its descent.

Hold on. You can do it. Just pick up the phone. Say the word. Bomb.

You'll show him. He'll see how you control everything just by speaking.

You pick up the receiver. It's silent. Dead.

"Move," you say, and it takes the boy so long to get the hinged door open you think you might explode. Or push his head through the glass. You are the father. You have things to do, things to say. You go, without knowing where. You don't intend to go to Sheetz, but that's where you see the girl.

She comes out of the store with a bottle of suntan lotion. Her nails are perfect. You don't know the girl, but you know everything about her. Her name is Cheyenne. Her nametag says so. You've seen her before. Every day of your life. The short skirt and the stained white dress shirt say she's a waitress at the Scald Mountain Country Club. The handful of ass, flip-flops, the skull toe ring, the butterfly tattoo on her scrawny ankle, and everything else say cocktease.

You don't mean to step in front of her. You do mean to step in front of her. She backs against a steel cage full of propane tanks and looks at you, at the boy, back at you. There's fear in that look, but something else too. You can't tell what. Pity, you won't allow. Recognition, maybe. Does she know? What you've done. Who you are? You'd show her. You think quick. See the corner of the building. The brickwork is fancy, the mortar joints deep. You'll climb this. You'll show the bitch. The boy.

You step up to the wall. You know he's watching. You know she's watching. You watch yourself. In your mind, you scale the wall all the way up, do a backflip off the roof and land perfectly, inches from the girl. She smiles. You leave the boy. You take the girl. Life is good.

Truth is, you can't get your fat ass off the ground. You turn. She's walking around the store, down the path. You listen to the sound of the flip-flops slapping against her skinny feet. A mating call. The boy stands there, grinning, like you just did a magic trick. Abra-ca-Fucking-dabra.

"You see that," you say to him, pointing Bertha at the girl. "That there is the cause of it all, son."

You can't remember the last time you called him son. Conquer.

"Find a way to conquer that shit and you'll rule the world. Gospel truth, son. It's the gospel truth. There'll be nothing you can't do. Nothing can stop you."

He's watching her skinny ass walk away but you doubt the boy understands anything you've said. You don't care. You've done your job. It's hot. People are looking at you both. Walking wide berths around you. You see a lady with a cell phone. Another.

"Let's go," you say.

Somehow you end up near the river, on the weedy path to the golf course. It's just you and the boy and years of garbage. You recognize the place. It's probably noon. Did you miss the bells? You wonder what the hell you're doing.

The boy with you, he's yours. But what does that mean? It's just you and him and the trash, down by the river. The water is sluggish and shallow. Beetles skitter over its surface. You wish you could just walk right across it, up the other bank, and keep going. You could leave the boy behind. The boy walks too close to the muddy bank, slips, soaks his leg up to the knee. You could use Big Bertha and put him out of his misery. There's nobody around. One good swing would do it. Overhead, in the spilling leaves of a willow tree, a crow and a blue jay argue the point.

Gospel truth. Daddy told me the gospel truth. I'll follow him anywhere. That girl, that fraidy-cat. That slut, I've seen her before. Somewhere. I see her everywhere. The Dark One let her live. I'll follow him anywhere. Mama says the world is about to end. The man on the radio tells Mama the story over and over. I don't care. Me and Daddy will survive. He's shows me how. Nothing can stop me. The Beast is awake. I listen. I learn. We walk down through the woods. I know the path. Me and Travis walked it. I wish I could tell Daddy about Travis. I wish I could ask him about the Rapture. I wish we could've had some soup from the church. We keep walking. Maybe we'll walk forever.

I look at Daddy and try to keep up. I wish I had a club. I look at my arm. A caterpillar is climbing my sleeve. I don't like it. I brush at the worm and fall into the water. My boot fills. I almost get the Game Boy wet. Daddy stops, looks at me. I don't know if he's mad or not.

You leave him. You bash his sweet head in. You keep going. Together. They're all viable parenting options. All good in their own way.

"Get up, dumbass," you say. You reach out with Big Bertha. Your rod. Your staff. The boy takes the bulbous head of the club in his pitiful little hands, pulls himself back onto the path. That's when you see the ball.

You've been here before. The path skirts the golf course, following the dogleg of the seventh hole. Years ago, when you mowed fairways at the club, you walked this path to and from work. You know the place well. You know where you are. You've seen some things here. Tell him. Tell him about the pond and a sickle-shaped bunker where the fairway hooks left. You know the less skilled players drive hard from the tee box and overshoot the bunker. The rich bastards, the ones who don't mind cheating a little or a lot, the ones who can afford a new sleeve of balls every round, leave behind those that slice or hook deep into the weeds.

It's a Pinnacle you see half-buried in the black dirt. You dig around the ball with your finger and pluck it free. You wipe it clean on your pant leg. No cuts, no gouges. A perfectly good Pinnacle. You settle the ball onto a tuft of grass at the path's edge.

"Watch this," you say.

The boy steps back, waves a mosquito away from his face. You can see excitement in his eyes. You interlock your fingers on Bertha's rubber grip, plant your feet at shoulder width. Your gut is in the way, but it doesn't matter. You never told the boy this stuff. You're going to show him things he never knew.

Where do you aim? Doesn't matter. Somewhere back up on the course. Maybe you'll get lucky and hit somebody. You address the ball. It's been a long time. You flex your knees. It hurts more than you expect. The boy watches, looks like he's about to piss his pants. You center the ball on the clubface. You bring her head back. You'll show the boy what you're made of. You swing. You duff it. You dig a trench in the dirt, and the ball topples an inch or two away.

Fuck.

Did you say it aloud?

It's her fault. It always was. Original motherfucking sin.

It's been a decade or more since you've swung at an actual ball. Take your time. It's just you and the boy and the garbage. You're going to drive this ball into orbit. You have to. For the boy's sake.

You address the ball. You work hard to block the thought-bombs exploding in your brain. You focus. You shut out the basement, the desert. You shut out the pills. The garbage. The boy. The bloat. The blood. Everything becomes the swing. You swing and catch the ball with the toe of the clubface. The Pinnacle rockets wildly to the right. You grip Bertha tight. Who is failing here? Is it the club? You? The boy? He looks retarded standing there in his Evel Knievel pajamas. You see his mama in his face. You turn away. It's all you can do.

You jab at the underbrush with your club. You know what you're looking for, and it's there. "Get that ball," you say to the boy, and he wades into the weeds without hesitation, comes back with a muddy Top-Flite cupped in his palm like it's some kind of delicate egg. You snatch it away, shake your head in disgust, find another tuft of grass.

"What?" you bark, thinking the boy spoke. He looks confused, but doesn't reply.

You swing, and the ball slices up and out of sight.

Focus. Control. Focus. Control. You learned it in boot camp. Let the rage go. Let the fear go. Pay attention to the moment. You can't see another ball from where you stand. But you know beyond any doubt, with a certainty that tramples anything called *faith,* that there are other balls in the thicket of briars and thistles between the riverbank and the golf course.

You kick an opening in the dense, thorny weeds, use Bertha to widen the ersatz warren. Big enough for the boy to crawl in. You look at him. You hope he's smart enough to figure it out. You can't remember the last time you heard the boy speak. You can't remember if he actually can speak.

After a while, you tell him what to do. "There's balls in there," you say.

The boy gets on his hands and knees. He hesitates until you prod him with the club. The boy sticks his head into the thicket, wriggles his shoulders in, pulls back out with a mud-caked orange Titleist and two range balls with red stripes and deep nicks.

"More," you say. He goes back into the briars. When he pauses again, you push his ass with your boot. You are the father. You're teaching the boy lessons. About golf, about waste, about obedience.

Your son disappears fully into the dense patch of burdock, nettle, and beggar lice. You hear him thrashing around. You hear him stifle a cry. You wait. You wish you had some peanut butter crackers. Sometime later, maybe half an hour, maybe a decade, he emerges. The boy has made a little pouch by folding up the hem of his pajama shirt. You are proud of his resourcefulness. A thick briar stalk is tangled in the boy's hair; a jagged scratch marks his forehead. The boy's face and arms and bare belly bleed. His pajama pants are filthy. You are the father. He is the son. The boy kneels, pours his treasure at your feet.

A dozen balls. Good. Good boy.

"More," you say.

Through mysterious divination, or maybe just pain—the pain, transcendent, becomes paean—Abigail Augenbaugh finds her way to, her *self* in, the expansive Walmart parking lot, with its crisp orderly lines and abundant signage. She drove past her first destination, Surplus City, and its cramped gravel lot—even though her meager budget would go further there—because she didn't think she could face the narrow aisles of jumbled, precarious stacks of closeout items or the disarray of expired-date dry goods.

The Walmart is newish. It reeks of eternity. A vast windowless block that consumes acres of what used to be pastureland on the outskirts of Joy, where Homer's Gap allows the highway through the mountains. It's difficult to enter or leave Joy without passing it. Abby parked near a cart corral—mindlessly crushing the contents of a paper bag on the asphalt—and now leans on an empty shopping cart for support. She pauses. She can barely walk. Her ribcage feels as if it is caving in on her heart. Everything else aches. Her thighs, her buttocks, her belly, and her back tremble with each sluggish step toward the entrance. There are two sets of doors to choose from, quartering the broad storefront. Each a pair of vertical hydraulic mouths that hiss admittance or expulsion between plate glass lips.

Abby watches people come and go. An obese man in an electric wheelchair kicks at one door when it hesitates to open. Abigail follows him inside because it seems right.

She didn't make a list. She isn't exactly sure what her husband and son will need, post-Rapture. There in the cavernous narthex, she prays for guidance. But as soon as the second line of doors closes behind her, Abby doubts that any answer (Heaven-sent or not) can penetrate the sterile interior.

I am The Mole. I am blind. I need no sight. I feel no pain. Touch is my superpower. I burrow into the earth. My skin is one with the briars and rocks. I am on a mission for the Dark One. I am the son of the Dark One. I surrender the hurt. I will not cry. I will not bleed. I will not cry. I will not bleed. Nothing can stop me. I seek treasure for him and him alone.

The boy tunnels into the thicket three times. Your boy. Because you make him. Three trips into the underbrush, burrowing deeper each time. Returning, each time, looking more and more like he crawled from the grave. Bloody, filthy, stinking, he piles salvaged golf balls at your feet. Kneels there, waiting.

"That's enough," you say, sick of the whole thing. "Set them up."

You don't know what you're doing.

The boy squats by the mound of balls. Plucks one. Settles it onto a tuft of crabgrass. You line up and swing. You top the ball. It skips the surface of the river, hits a rock and thuds into the bank.

"Hurry," you say. The boy positions another ball. You shank it.

"Hurry up, goddamn it."

It'd be so easy to miss altogether. To slam Bertha's titanium head into the boy's skull. Mercy is bitter. Mercy is sweet.

You hit more balls. Poorly. You're out of breath. Wheezing. You sweat. The rolls of fat beneath your clothing are slick and wet. But you can't tell if it's really hot or your body is just fucking with you. You don't know what you're doing. In the distance, up on the fairway, you hear laughter. A foursome. Men and boys, you can tell. Fathers and sons, probably. Members of the Scald Mountain Country Club: assholes and assholes-in-training. You don't know what you're doing. Those men on the course, laughing with their sons, they confuse you. How does it work? What you ought to do is to march right up in their midst and start swinging. Teach them some lessons. Upend their goddamn tables. What you ought to do is knock heads all the way into the clubhouse. Take your boy with you. Teach them all some lessons. There are fifteen, maybe twenty balls left in the pile. The boy squats, ready. You turn and align your toes with an unseen, an un-seeable, target up over the bank, beyond the sumac and thistle. You aim for the fairway. You aim for the voices.

I watch. I wait. I bleed a little, for him. Daddy swings. The Dark One. He hits the balls. Some go high. Some scorch the earth. He's laying a trap.

We're laying traps for the enemy. When they get close, Daddy will unleash his full force. The sky is blue and empty. Empty except for the jet, too far up to hear. I see the smoke trail. It writes our names. Daddy swings the club. The jet explodes in midair. I see it all. I see all the way up into the nasty bowels of Heaven. I see the worms and the Slinkys, watch them eat the believers. I hear the enemies scream as they plummet to the ground.

"Hey!" they scream all the way down.

"Hey!"

"Hey!"

The inner doors close tight, with engineered precision, excising Abigail Augenbaugh from the outside world. She is welcomed by a greeter, almost ecclesiastical in his sincerity. The high white ceiling stretches into infinity. Row after row after row of bare fluorescent bulbs purge the environment of shadow and beat all color into dull submission. It's clean. So incredibly clean. Immaculate is the right word.

Stay. Abigail wants to just stay, there, in Walmart purity. Forever. There is air, but it is still. There are people all around. Shoppers, kids and adults, move in and out of the aisles, dwarfed by the wide, heavy shelves, guided and/or confounded by the ubiquitous advertising. Employees in blue smocks, wielding their price guns, transfer stock from wooden pallets, or manage the herds at the checkout. People everywhere, and they must be making noise. They must be talking; bemoaning prices, or relishing bargains. The kids, no doubt, are whining to get toys or treats. The cash registers have to blip and beep and churn out receipts. There is all this activity that warrants noise, but Abigail can't hear anything, save for a low-grade pulsing murmur. Like chanting in the distance.

Abby takes a shallow, painful breath. She doesn't know where to begin. She doesn't know if she can face this crowd, this place. This kind of piety. Maybe this is a version of Heaven, here on the shopping floor, where everything she could ever need is available. Maybe she doesn't belong in Heaven. Maybe God hangs just above the lofty ceiling tiles, passing judgment. Out of sight, like the ducts and cables and beams. She makes a plan. This is her plan.

≪

The bastards start shouting after the fourth or fifth ball. You must've hit one of them. You hope so. You laugh when they curse. The boy laughs too. You'll show them. You'll show him. "Line them up," you say.

The boy does as he's told. You swing, finally getting into the groove, and fire the golf balls up over the weed-choked bank, onto the fairway.

"Hey! Goddamn it!"

"Cut it out! Hey!"

They curse. You laugh. The boy laughs. You feel good. You are the father. You are in control. You command the chaos. You hear them knocking back the brush, looking for you.

"Run," you say to the boy.

He charges up the path, and you try to follow. Your body, sluggish and lumpy, won't cooperate. You lurch and stumble. When you finally get to top of the path, off the course, the boy waits by a dumpster swarming with flies. Blood pounds your eardrums, your whole fucking skull. Adrenaline so thick you can almost taste it. You almost feel good. You almost feel in control. You are the father. He is the boy. You are teaching him important things.

He rains death and destruction down upon all who stand in our way. He spares few. I am spared. I am with Daddy. He could kill me if he wanted. Squash me like a bug. He doesn't. I am with Daddy, and we rule the world. He says run, and I run. He doesn't have to run. He is the Dark One. He takes his time. No one stands in his way. No one can stop us. He doesn't kill me dead, like the rest. He has plans. He has reasons. I wait. I wait by the trash. I brush dirt from my uniform. I stand up tall. I hope to be seen. I serve the Dark One, and I am to be feared. Too.

You feel good. You feel like you might be having a heart attack. It's OK, then it's not. You come up on the boy. He looks wild and stupid. He has his mama's eyes. You gouge them out. No. You can't breathe. You showed him some things. Important things. He's looking at you like you're some kind of God. You are. A few minutes ago there was adrenaline. You feel it leak from the soles of your feet, fill up your boots. Or maybe it's piss. You can't tell. You felt good, just a few breaths back. Now there is sand in your eyes, blood in your mouth. Blood in your eyes and sand in your mouth. You hold tight to Bertha. You're in a parking lot, somewhere. You slump against the dumpster. The metal is cool to your cheek. Comforting. You could die here. Your mouth is so dry. A desert. Grit clots your esophagus. Your tongue shrivels and snags against your teeth. You want to speak, say something to the boy, to get him ready.

"Water." It's all you can manage. You finger the dollar bills from your pocket, crumple them, toss them at the boy's feet.

"Water," you say again. You hope he's smart enough to figure it out. The boy takes the money and runs toward the store. You hope he can find his way back. You hope you're still alive when he gets here. A school bus passes, its windows full of gawking eyes. You can see yourself reflected in all the eyes. You're dead already. You can tell. You lean against the dumpster. Wait.

∀

Her plan is simple. Abigail wants to get through the store. Just. Abigail wants to provide what she can, to help the husband and son she will leave behind. Two plastic bins, some canned goods, a flashlight. Maybe a couple magazines. Coloring books, for the boy. Does the boy still color? She can't remember. What else? She can't breathe. There is a wheezing, a sucking sound, in her chest.

It's late May, and the man on the radio says fire will destroy the Earth. They won't need coats or warm socks, unless they live into the winter. Abigail doubts they'll live into the winter. She'll get some burn ointment. A camp stove. Twine and duct tape.

These decisions, and the rare clarity that they arise out of, comfort Abby. Displace her despair. She feels brave, facing such difficult choices. The heavy blue plastic shopping cart bears her weight well enough. She enters the labyrinth of aisles with a labored confidence. Yes, she can do this. Yes, she is a mother, a mother who provides. She is a wife. She does what good wives do. Provides.

Abigail drops a socket set into the basket. She moves slowly, determinedly, deeper into Walmart. A dozen cans of Vienna Sausages. A case of powder Kool-Aid. Three thick packs of baby wipes. Abigail feels in control. Of her pain, and of the well-being of her family. She finds the bins, uses her foot to put them on the cart's bottom shelf.

Good. Abigail Augenbaugh feels good. Despite her broken rib. Despite what happened last night. But why? She tries, but can't put her finger on the reason. And it's not merely *good* she feels. There is something more. She runs some possibilities through her addled mind, to no avail. Abigail cannot name the thing, the feeling, the new, fanciful, and rough beast champing at the bit of her consciousness.

From an aisle endcap Abby plucks an American-flag pillow and a GI Joe blanket. Willie will like these. For Burns, an American-flag pocket knife and a box of 9/11 commemorative golf balls. See, she thinks. A good wife pays attention.

Purpose-driven, and fueled by the knowledge that God is on her side, Abby moves steadily, albeit slowly, through the aisles, decisively filling the basket of her cart. She will provide. She will. Provide.

Halfway into the store, on the far right, a wide lane separates Automotive and Pet Supplies from Sporting Goods. There, Abigail has a realization. She knows. It is *freedom* she's feeling. The awareness of the impending end of everything brings with it a feeling of liberation. Surprising. Delicious. Sustaining. Abigail remembers a television commercial from her childhood and wishes she could jump up and click her heels together. What she does instead is nudge a two-gallon jar of turkey jerky into the cart.

But conviction is fragile, and the mind behind it fickle. Abigail shops and shops and is practically giddy by the time she rounds the corner into Groceries. Her plan, her goal, is to fill the little space remaining with cans of beans and fruit cocktail, with boxes of assorted Helper meals. Then she hits the little girl.

The little girl, three, maybe four, lies at the base of a waist-high, open-topped freezer that runs nearly the depth of the store. The little girl wears a diaper and a Care Bears T-shirt. The little girl is playing with a Slinky, there on the Walmart floor.

Abigail doesn't see her. Abigail can't see her, small and tucked against the vast black base of the freezer. But when Abby's heavy cart rolls over the girl's foot, everybody hears the shriek.

Everybody.

Abigail slumps back in shock, bumps a display of Red Bull energy drinks. The blue-and- silver-and-red cans rattle across the floor. The enormous cardboard bull topples, bouncing off Abby's head, blocking—momentarily—her vision. When she can see again, everything has changed.

He is God. He is playing a God-trick. Laying a trap. Against the forces. The forces against us are powerful. Attacking from every side at once, and invisible. One minute the Dark Lord is standing strong; the next, he is down. I didn't see what hit him. Their weapons are mysterious. It is the God-trick. He bides His holy time. Ready to strike. Now, Daddy. Now. Get up, Daddy. God. I run back down the path. My toes bleed in my boots. I have to hold my pajama pants up. I am sweating. The sweat stings in my cuts and scratches. I am on a mission. I seek the potion. The magic salve. I have to save the Dark One. I wish I had a weapon too. I wish I had a club, like the Dark One. Like Daddy. Daddy needs me. I run. I run so fast. Nobody can catch me. Nobody can stop me.

∀

The piercing shrieks that spill out of that tiny gaping mouth fill all the available aural space, rend the prevailing murmur. The girl wails, and her mother, a low and very wide woman who is bent deeply into a Buy-One-Get-One-Free bin, struggles to right herself, cursing all the way. By the time she gets to her child, and Abigail Augenbaugh, who cowers between the freezer and shopping cart, they are all swarmed by Walmart employees.

"I'm, I didn't, it wasn't," Abby stammers.

The woman yanks the crying girl from the floor, clamps her between a fleshy tattooed biceps and pendulous breasts, jabs a cigar of a finger into Abigail's face, and begins a spewing of filth unlike any Abby has ever been the recipient—the victim—of.

Abby struggles to breathe. She has no recourse.

Somebody speaks.

"Poor little thing."

"Could've been killed."

Abigail wonders if someone shouldn't look at the little girl's foot.

The angry mother plucks a can of beans from Abby's cart, shakes it in her face, rages. Abby can't understand what she's saying, but feels sure the woman is about to throw the can at her. Abigail waits. She'll bear whatever pain comes her way. The Lord God will not give any more than she can stand. Everybody says so. Abigail waits for the impact. Waits for the rest of the mob to stone her to death in the aisle. It's OK. She deserves it. She closes her eyes, lifts her palms toward the ceiling, forgives them all.

I am brave. I am a stealth bomber. I am a warhead. I am a death ray. I am a lightning bolt. And I am a hero, just like my daddy. I run, and I will not stop. I will not surrender. I will show no mercy.

I hear the voices of the boys. Hundreds of them. I run down the path. The earth blisters behind me. I see the pond up ahead. I see the boys. I will not stop. Cannot. I jump. I jump so high. I block out the sun. I jump and the boys are piss-ants way below me. I jump and—

"Where you going, faggot?"

I land on my face. Hard. The. Breath. Knocked. From. My. Body. I curl tight. I am a stone. I do not move. I cannot be moved.

"Awww, what'd you do that for?" one boy says. "Let me help you up, little fellow."

I feel the fingers dig under my waistband. Yank. I bend like a hinge. I puke.

Any minute now I will unleash my fury.

"Look at this little pussy boy. Are you wearing your pj's, pussy boy?"

I get to my knees. I look around. There were hundreds. Most of them fled. Terrified. Any minute now.

"Look at the cute little Evel Knievel jammies! I wish I had me some Evel Knievel jammies."

"Jesus H. Christ, faggot! What the hell happened to you? How come you're all cut up and dirty?"

I know about these boys. Daddy told me. Golden boys. They are the spawn of country-club mothers and fathers. I am Captain Filth. I will destroy them. I use my superpowers to beckon the Dark One. Any minute now, he will explode on the scene. Together we will bring this army of golden boys to their knees.

But you don't die. Yet. Or maybe you did die. Maybe you've been dead for a long time. Who would know the difference? You feel a little cheated. This surprises you. No, not really. Your heart slows some. The lightning storm in your brainpan settles. Just enough breath gets through. You have a boy, you think. A son. You don't know what happened to him. You think you were together, earlier. Years ago, maybe. You do know what happened to him. He deserves better, you think, than to find you here dead, piss in your boots. Your mouth full of desert. Maybe you didn't have that son. Maybe you didn't have that wife. Maybe you don't have a house and a couch in the basement.

You wanted to do the right thing. You climbed the wall like you were supposed to. You wanted to kill the towelheads, like you were supposed to. You wanted to be brave for the boy you might have had. You didn't mean to drown in the blood. Resuscitate. You don't mean to drown in the blood, again and again.

The dumpster lid slams, jolts you to the core. You look up. A kid in a paper hat stands at your feet. He's filming you with a cell phone.

"I thought you were dead," the boy says.

"I might be," you answer.

You struggle to rise. The boy backs up just a little. But he never stops filming.

"Hey!" they say. "This is the fucker who was hitting golf balls at us earlier!"

I do not cry.

"Where's the old dude?" they say.

"The fat fuck in the Army costume?" they say.

"The freak—the perv—the cocksucker," they say.

I kill them all.

I do not cry when they take my money. I do not cry when they throw my Game Boy in the pond. I will not break.

"Pull his pants down," they say. "I want those jammies."

I do not cry.

"Give me your lighter," they say. "Let's burn the hair off his balls."

I do not cry.

"Hold him tight," they say. "Hey! Look! The little fucker is hairless!"

I do not cry.

"Look at that tiny worm-dick," they say.

"Get your phone," they say. "Take some pictures of this. Send them around."

I do not cry.

"Hey, take him to the water. Let the turtles bite his pecker off!"

I do not cry.

"Hold him still," they say. "Belly down! Belly down! Look at it dangle. Fish bait!"

The muddy water fills my mouth, my nose. I will not open my eyes. I will not cry. I will be strong and brave. I wish the Dark One would come. I will not cry.

"Hey!" they say. But the voice is different. "Hey!"

"What the hell are you doing?"

It is a girl's voice.

The boys drop me. I sink into the muck. I claw at the bank until I can stand. When I stand I see the girl in the bathing suit. No. Go away. I see three boys sitting on the path. Three boys. Dirty water soaks their dirty shorts. Dirty underwear. Streams down their stupid brown legs. She's yelling something. Her skin is slick and shiny. She jabs her finger into their faces. They smile. They don't smile. She is tan all over. I know this girl. I smell her. She smells like vanilla pudding. She makes me hungry. I want her to go away. I know this girl. I've seen her before. Every day. I want to bite into her. I don't look in her eyes. It's a trap. I see the butterfly tattoo. I see the flip-flops. The skull toe-ring. Her toenails are purple, like pieces of candy. Then it's quiet. Then the boys are laughing. I can't help it. The water is knee-deep. I have a hard-on. The Beast.

"Pull your pants up," the girl says, pointing at my crotch. "Go home."

I hear disgust in her voice. No. Go away. She smells like vanilla pudding. I crawl onto the path. The boys keep laughing. I see the butterfly tattoo. I wish the Dark One would come. I wish I had the club. I close my eyes and beat them all to death.

"Hurry up!" she says. "I have better things to do."

The boys say something about her titties. She cusses. She steps toward them. They laugh, then they run. Their laughter stays behind. I stoop and tug at my pants. They're full of water. Heavy. I fall down. I try again. The Beast. I tell her to shut up. I tell her to sex me. No. None of this. I get my pants up. I hold them tight at the waist. Cold water fills my boots. "Go," she says. It's all her fault. Her fault. I run back up the path. I trip. I can't help it. I cry. Just a little. I have failed. I failed the Dark One. I failed Daddy. A girl! I got rescued by a stupid girl. She saw me. My dick. She's not the hero; I'm the hero. Who the hell does she think she is! Stupid stupid girl. Stupid stupid me. Stupid Mama. Stupid end of the world. I run. My feet big and thick as cinderblocks. I want to find my daddy, to ask him about the gospel truth. I can't remember what Daddy said. Even if he's dead, there against the dumpster, I want to be with him. And when he's not there, dead or alive, I know they must've captured him, must've taken him away. He didn't die. He wouldn't die. He wouldn't leave me behind. I know he rose up, in triumph. I know he's fighting them even now. And looking over his shoulder for me. I don't care about the mud and the blood. I don't care who sees me cry. I know I will run until the world ends. I'll join the battle.

∀

"It's a damn miracle," somebody says.

Yes, Abigail thinks. She is ready. Ready for the miracle. Ready for the Savior to swoop down, sweep her up, take her up into the clouds. Maybe, even, Jesus will let her stop by the house en route to Heaven, to drop off the Rapture-ready boxes for her husband and son. She is a good wife, good mother. Jesus will understand. She wished, only, that she'd had time to change into her Rapture outfit. To look a little more presentable. Jesus will understand. Right?

But Jesus doesn't come, and Abigail wonders if she's waiting on the wrong miracle. She opens her eyes, looks into the face of the little girl who's whimpering now, not wailing. Abby looks at the congregants. Everybody is waiting to see what happens next.

Abigail grips the sticky handle of her shopping cart. She can't breathe. She can't think. There is a swelling roar. Abigail can't tell where it's coming from. The mob of shoppers and employees presses in on her, murmuring and agitated. Or, maybe not. It might just be the little girl's family, a few others. A security guard hovers on the edge of the crowd. He carries a bright-red first-aid kit. He wears an ironed white shirt. He has pepper spray in a holster and shiny handcuffs on his black belt. He looks about twelve years old. Abigail wants to pray, but can't think of how to start.

She wants to maneuver the cart between herself and her condemners, but lacks the strength. It will not roll. Abby looks down and sees the Slinky wound around the axle. Ruined.

"Look at her," somebody says. "Ain't she the cutest thing?"

Cute? Abigail is confused. She feels sick. Then she realizes they're talking about the little girl. The security guard is playfully shaking a box in the girl's face. It's a TV dinner, colorfully packaged: fish sticks, corn, and pudding. It's hard to know what's rattling around inside the box. The little girl smiles, a crooked snaggle-toothed grin, and the bubble of rage begins to deflate.

"She's going to be all right," the security guard proclaims confidently, holding the TV dinner overhead in triumph, and because everybody likes a good prophecy, an audible surge of gratitude washes over the crowd. One person claps. In the moment of reprieve that follows, a fragile grace supplants the anger. The little girl's mother does not hit Abigail with the can of beans. Instead she chucks it, with some force, back into Abby's cart, where the can knocks the Rapture tracts out of her purse.

"Dumbass old bitch," the woman hisses, then drags her limping daughter by the arm down the As-Seen-On-TV aisle.

"You look like you been rode hard and put up wet, hon," a barrel-shaped woman in a Walmart smock says, then lays her hand gently on Abigail's arm. And that's all it takes. Abby leans hard into her Samaritan's motherly bosom and sobs.

Abigail reads the employee's nametag. Marlene.

"Let's get you to a register," Marlene says, and shepherds Abby through the throng of onlookers who whisper and point as she passes. The air is thick with judgment. Condemnation greases their lips. But Marlene is there, by her side. Marlene will protect her. Marlene smells like White Rain hairspray and Dove soap. Abigail wants to fall into those aromas and never surface.

"What are they looking at?" Abby whispers. "What are they talking about?"

"Shhh," Marlene says, dabbing at Abigail's face with a wet wipe. "Folks are gonna do what they're gonna do, honey. Ain't much you can do to stop them. Don't you pay no mind. Let's get you in number twelve, here. Barely any line at all."

They wait. And wait. A skinny mom, smelling fresh from the beauty parlor—hair and nails in full glory—buys a buggy full of My Little Pony birthday party supplies, talking loudly on her cell phone all the while, and never, not once, looking at Abigail.

Abigail holds tight to the cart while Marlene unloads the basket onto the sleek stainless-steel counter. Abigail pretends it's just a normal day, pretends she's out shopping with—with her mother. They'll get fries and a milkshake later. Abigail pretends she can't hear the nasty whispers behind her back. Abigail focuses on the checkout clerk and steady heartbeat of the barcode reader. Focuses on the tiny window in the center of the checkout counter from which a geometric spider web of deep-red laser beams projects. Focuses. Focuses.

"That'll be three hundred seventy-six dollars and eighty-two cents," the clerk says, with absolute boredom.

"What?" Abby asks.

"That'll be three hundred seventy-six dollars and eighty-two cents," the clerk says, with an admixture of boredom and irritation.

Abby fumbles with her purse. Marlene stands at the ready. Abby finds her credit card and thrusts it, like a weapon, at the boy manning the register. Unfazed, he takes the card, swipes it, twice. Runs his pierced tongue across his lips while waiting.

"Declined, ma'am."

"What?" Abigail says. "What?" The word fires into the sudden quiet like a gunshot, ricocheting through the stillness. The credit card was canceled months ago.

"Declined, ma'am," the boy says, sucking air through his teeth. Clicks the tongue stud against his incisors.

"You got another card, honey?" Marlene asks.

Everybody awaits her answer. The whole store. Every shopper, every employee has gone quiet, has gathered behind Abigail Augenbaugh, ready. Ready to laugh. To mock. To ridicule.

"My boy needs these," Abigail says, choking back sobs. "My husband—"

"How about some cash?" Marlene says, reaching for the purse.

"No," Abigail says, clutching the purse to her chest. "No." Abigail grabs a handful of Rapture tracts. "No," she says. "No. No! NO!"

Abby holds the pamphlets at arm's length. She spins in a slow circle. "No no no! Stop! Who you are? You don't know me! I'm one of the Elect! The chosen. I don't know you! None of you."

Marlene tries to put a comforting hand on Abigail's shoulder.

"No! Don't. How, how can they do this? Don't they know?"

"Do what, sweetie? Let's get you over to the snack bar."

"They just go about their business like, like—"

"How about a hot pretzel with some mustard?"

Abigail Augenbaugh looks around, sees what feel like hundreds, thousands, of wide eyes staring at her. Unblinking. Ravenous. In what may be her bravest act ever, she scatters the Rapture tracts in the air. "Tomorrow!" she says. "The Lord Jesus Christ is coming back tomorrow to take the elect home to Heaven, tomorrow! And all of you act like—"

But it's too late. Abigail hears the laughter, and when she looks out again, all those eyes have closed or turned away.

"Lord have mercy, child," Marlene says, finally. Clucks her tongue.

"No!" Abigail cries, desperately. "Wait, don't go! Listen! Listen to me! I have something to say. I have things to tell!"

Abigail feels faint. The pain from her broken rib rides the full length of her skeleton. Does she see the security guard? Is he with the store manager?

"Please," Abby begs. "Just listen. I know things. I'm here, and I need to say. It's not too late for you. You have to listen to me. I've been chosen. You can't just ignore me!"

Abby sees the crowd thin, all but the cruelest voyeurs turning their attentions elsewhere. Some have their cell phones out, filming it all. What should she do? What would the man on the radio say? She tried to spread the gospel, tried to make them hear.

"He—" she starts.

He, who? What does she want to say?

"He, he said, he tried, he... he raped me. He raped me. He raped me!"

She says it. She says it aloud, and waits—hopefully—for the repercussions. But those few shoppers and Walmart employees who bear witness to her outburst are unmoved. For all they know she could be talking about the store manager, or God.

I am a traitor. I am a pussy boy. I am a worthless little faggot.
I am a traitor. I am a pussy boy. I am a worthless little faggot.
I am a traitor. I am a pussy boy. I am a worthless little faggot.
I am a traitor. I am a pussy boy. I am a worthless little faggot.
I am a traitor. I am a pussy boy. I am a worthless little faggot.
I am a traitor. I am a pussy boy. I am a worthless little faggot.
I am a traitor. I am a pussy boy. I am a worthless little faggot.
I am a traitor. I am a pussy boy. I am a worthless little faggot.
I am a traitor. I am a pussy boy. I am a worthless little faggot.
I am a traitor. I am a pussy boy. I am a worthless little faggot.
I am a traitor. I am a pussy boy. I am a worthless little faggot.
I am a traitor. I am a pussy boy. I am a worthless little faggot.
I am a traitor. I am a pussy boy. I am a worthless little faggot.
I deserve to die.

You stagger—a dead soldier—back through the desert, back down the alley, back toward the basement. You retreat. You're a coward. You've been dead all your life. You've got your club. You lean on Bertha. A Chinese woman in tight black pants jams an empty lettuce box into an overflowing trash can. Rotting leaves spill onto the asphalt. She might be a girl; you can't tell. *I've been dead my whole life,* you say to her. You think you do. Anyway, she runs back into the restaurant kitchen. The screen door slams shut, and the sound blinds you. You follow her inside, shove her head into the deep fat fryer, pull her black pants down to her ankles.

No, you don't. You keep moving. Your heart exploded years ago. You want your pills. You want to call the pharmacist. You want to call anybody. You want to bite the mole off her lip. No. Yes. You have a son. You don't know where he is. You have a wife. She cried. Her snot-covered face made you hard. No. Yes. You think about that face. Where's your goddamn wife? You want to be reborn. It's all her fault. No. Their fault. Where are you? You thought the boy was with you. Now he's not. You ought to care, but you don't. You can't. You pass the trophy shop. All the little golden faceless fuckers squirm and wriggle, break free from their shackles, jump down from their perches and run out the door after you. The chase exhausts you.

You're in a parking lot behind an eye doctor's office. Dr. What-the-fuck. Some goddamn towelhead name you can't pronounce, even after all these years in the sand. That must be his wife. Mrs. Dr. What-the-fuck. She's putting a bag of golf clubs into the trunk of a Lexus as black as her hair, her eyes. *I've been dead my whole life,* you say to her. You think you do. She backs against the car, drops her cell phone and several golf tees. You pick one up, lean in close enough to smell the goddamn nutmeg on her goddamn skin. You bite her throat, gently, right at the larynx, and shove the tee deep up into her nostril with your thumb.

No, you don't. She's driving away. And you, you've been dead your whole life.

Please don't die. Please don't die. Please don't die. Please don't die. Please don't die.

Please. Don't. Die.

You step off the curb and into the gaping mouth of the whale. It makes as much sense as anything else. Tires skid on asphalt. Someone curses. It swallows you, whole. You fall down down down into the fish's rank belly. It's full of bones. And bloody laundry. The boy is there. Your son. And your wife. You hear them scream. All the dead. It might be you. Screaming. No. It's you screaming. The massive fish looms and you are lying on the sidewalk beneath a bus-stop bench. A pickup truck and a U-Haul trailer block the road. A huge plaster trout tilts toward you. Half a dozen men hold tight to the straps. You scream, like a fucking girl.

"Watch where you're going, dumbass!"

It might be the fish talking. Jesus Saves! is written on the underside of the bench in red marker in cursive. You sit up, lean against the bench. You stare at the ad on the seatback. Some politician railing about high taxes. You might be bleeding. You may have bled to death years ago.

"Are you all right, fuckwad?" one of the men asks.

"Jesus saves," you say.

Abigail Augenbaugh leaves the store empty-handed and alone. But the sheer tonnage of her intangible goods will most likely crush her. Decades of shame yoke her shoulders. She lugs. She hauls. Generations of ignorance garland her flabby back. Abigail plows forward, each step of every day, dragging behind millennia of fear.

"I am the Slinky Queen," she says aloud. "All kneel."

Empty-handed, solitary, Abby, more dray horse than scapegoat, limps, and heaves, and slogs, and tows her mountainous burden all the way across the vast expanse of the Walmart parking lot to her car, where she finds the front tire on the driver's side airless. Flat.

And there he is, dead. The door stands wide open. I come through. I go into the basement. I hear the girl screaming outside. The stupid little neighbor girl. She screams because I kicked her. I stomped her into the ground. She got in my way. I had no choice. I go into the basement. She shouldn't have been there, on the sidewalk. She was putting Barbie Doll clothes on a bowling trophy. He's there on the couch. Dead. Daddy, I mean, not the man on top of the trophy. I see the club. I see the tackle box. I see Daddy. He's there on the couch. In the dark. Except for the TV. She's still yelling. He's dead. I know it. I just do.

Ɐ

Forsaken. Abigail Augenbaugh feels as if Jesus himself punctured the tire. But only for a fleeting moment. Then, as she has been conditioned to do, Abby takes the onus of guilt upon herself. It is *her* fault. She has sinned. Her faith is weak, her devotion insipid. False. The myriad of reasons why the good Lord may have deflated Abby's tire spin, dervish-like, round and round her weary mind. She doesn't know what to do. Her entire body hurts, so much. She is confused. She left her Rapture tracts scattered on the tile floor near the checkout. She has no supplies for her husband and child. She doesn't know how she's supposed to spend the next day or what she's supposed to do when the time comes. And she has no radio to listen to for guidance, for instructions.

Abby looks at the flat tire. Abby looks up. Even if she had the strength to change the tire, Abigail has no idea how. Heavenward. The deep-blue May sky offers nothing. She cannot walk home; she'd never make it. Abby scans the lot, with no idea of what she's looking for. But something does catch her eye. Scald Mountain rises just west of Walmart. The country club is on its far side. Abigail can barely make out the green fairways crisscrossing the slopes. On the east side, closer to her, the community college takes a small chunk out of the foot of the mountain. There, in a clearing hacked out of the laurel and sumac, on a patch of cleared ground looming high above the college's Vocational Trades building, a billboard stakes its claim.

JUDGMENT DAY IS COMING!
"cry mightily unto God"

So she does. Right there in the parking lot, between the cars. Abigail lowers herself to the pavement and begins to pray. Quietly at first, her forehead pressed against the Celebrity's front quarter-panel. Abby sees the torn paper bag near the flat tire, sees the crushed beer bottle it concealed before she ran it over. Sees the shard that penetrated her tire. The shard. The revelation makes her pray a little louder. Soon enough, in no time even, exhaustion overtakes her, and Abby lies down. The sun-warmed gritty asphalt against her cheek stinks of oil. There, lying in the Walmart lot, in front of God and all other passersby, Abigail Augenbaugh prays for all she is worth.

Willie? Willie?

Someone calls my name.

But I am alone.

Daddy is dead on the couch.

Mama is getting ready to go to Heaven.

Willie? Willie?

Maybe it's the girl. The one who smells like vanilla pudding.

I am wet. And cold. I am scared. I am not scared.

The sump pump sucks and whirs in the corner. The sump pump gurgles my name.

Willie. Willie.

I will not answer. I will not cry.

I am the boy. The boy will not cry.

I go to the couch.

I am a failure. I am a coward.

Mama is getting ready for Heaven.

Mama is in Heaven.

I stand by the couch.

I look at the dead Daddy.

Daddy is God.

I see the club. The mighty weapon.

I touch it. I pick it up. The power surges through me.

The dead Daddy is not real. The dead Daddy is fat and gray on the couch.

I raise the club high.

Prays like there is no tomorrow.

"Abby?"

"What?" Abigail Augenbaugh answers, as if she talks to angels every day; then she suddenly remembers her manners and hides her face. Heaven smells like brake fluid and rubber.

"Abby?"

She doesn't reply. Maybe it's a trick, the Devil trying to pull one over on her. Old Scratch monkeyshines. A satanic sly pokey. What else could it be? God, in all His glory, has never answered any of Abby's prayers so conspicuously. She doubts. She hopes. There in the parking lot, between the cars, with the cigarette butts and crumpled potato chip bags, alongside a sticky puddle of spilled red soda, Abigail lies as still death, holds tight to the breath she struggled so hard to catch, and waits for the messenger—seraph or specter—to pass, to move on down the line and find some more worthy soul to receive its gifts.

"Abby, what the hell are you doing down there?"

She recognizes the voice. Voices. There are two angels. "Are you from Jesus?" she asks.

"What?"

"Are you my savior?"

"I sure am, honey. In the right light, we're all saviors."

"Hush, Mitch," one of the angels says. "Are you all right, Abby?"

No. But she doesn't say it aloud. Abigail opens one eye. She recognizes the boots, too.

"What in the wigget-fuck are you doing laying there?"

It's Andy. It's Mitch. They smell like meat.

"Resting," Abigail says. There is some truth to her reply.

"I thought you were dead, girlfriend," Andy says.

"Could've been killed," Mitch adds.

The boys help her stand, help (with an unexpected decorum) wipe the dirt from her clothes, pluck a cigarette butt from her hair, then help her sit in the Chevy's passenger seat.

"I'm somebody too," Abigail says. It's all she can think of.

"You've got yourself a flat tire," Mitch says, then shrugs. "That's all."

A flat tire. It's a situation the boys understand, a problem they know how to solve. Mitch heads into the store.

"You got the list?" Andy calls out. Mitch waves it over his head.

"Buy this girl a drink!" Andy says. He digs through the Celebrity's trunk for the jack, lug wrench, and spare tire.

"You know we got fired," Andy says. "For climbing up that stupid tank. Or maybe for showing our asses. Either works."

"I didn't mean to—" Abigail says.

"Best goddamn thing that ever happened," Andy said. "And we owe it all to you."

"—to hit the little girl," Abigail says.

"Where's your lug wrench? It ought to be clipped right here," Andy says, but he's behind the open trunk. Abigail doesn't know where *here* is.

"It all went—things got all—I just need to get home," Abby says. "I have to get ready."

Mitch returns with his purchases. While Andy changes the tire, Mitch tells her, excitedly, about their new business venture.

"Jerky-Jenius!" he says. "We'll specialize in edgy, experimental jerky recipes."

Mitch waves something back and forth in front of Abigail's face. She can't focus, can't follow what he says. "Try it," he says. "Banana and jalapeño. Try it."

Mitch eases the strip of jerky into her mouth. Abigail lacks the wherewithal to chew, so it just hangs there.

"We got us a business plan and everything," Mitch says.

Everything. Mitch talks. Abigail closes her eyes, dozes. She wakes with the Celebrity bouncing each time Andy bears down on the jack to tighten the lug nuts. She wakes to the sounds of Mitch strumming the ukulele and singing.

"Poontang little and poontang small—"

"I have to go," Abby says, too weakly to be heard.

"Poontang stretches like a rubber ball," Mitch sings loudly, and off-key.

The bouncing car makes Abby queasy.

"I have to get home, to get ready—for tomorrow."

"Oh my babe, my salty thing."

Between stints at the jack, Mitch and Andy take turns eating from a massive plastic jug of generic cheese puffs. Their hands are greasy, black and orange. The colors of purgatory, no doubt.

"You're good to go," Andy says finally. He slams the trunk lid hard, then drums his dirty fingers across the roof. He stands at the window, smiling at Abigail.

"Hell's bells, girl," Mitch says. "I just had the best idea. Why don't you come to work for us! For Jerky-Jenius! You could be our bookkeeper and calendar girl."

Abigail looks at the boys. Abby wants to tell the boys about what happened in the store. About what happened last night. She doesn't.

"You look like shit, Abs," Andy says, with real concern. "Go home, smoke a fatty, and get some sleep. Come on over to our house tomorrow, and we'll discuss business."

Abigail watches her two angels, her liberators, her deliverers, wheelie their motorcycles through the lot. She tries to climb over the parking brake and shifter into the driver's seat, but it hurts too much. When she gets out to circumnavigate the Celebrity, Abby sees that the boys left behind the half-empty jug of cheese puffs sitting on the roof of her car, dead center. Its oil-flecked orange contents almost glowing in the late-May afternoon. Forever thinking of her boy and her man, what they're going to need and what they're going to have to endure in the coming days, Abigail Augenbaugh uses an old umbrella she got at a Slinky picnic to hook the jug off the roof. She nestles the fat plastic container into the passenger seat, takes the time to secure the safety belt across it. Heads for home.

What choice do I have? The enemy has captured Daddy's soul. Left behind this dirty brown bag of fat and bones. I will not cry. I will not surrender. I failed once. I will not fail again. The dead body is on the couch. Still. I have the mighty club raised high. I am ready to swing. I will bash the skull in. Knock the blind eyes from their sockets. I'll go out in the street and crush every person I see. I'll swing and swing my weapon until everything is dead and destroyed. My power, my bravery, in the face of the enemy will become legendary. Everybody will know my name. Everybody will talk about me. Everybody will worship at my feet. I'll be on TV. I'll be on the radio. What choice do I have but to remember the man on the radio? I will never be a legend. I will never be famous. The world is ending tomorrow. Nobody will ever know my name.

Willie.

The sump pump has learned to talk. The sump pump knows my name. It calls out to me.

Willie.

I wish Mama was home. I wish Mama wasn't going to Heaven without me. Willie.

I wish Daddy wasn't dead. I wish Mama was dead instead. I wish the man on the radio was dead. I saw Mama on her knees. The man on the radio says to pray. I don't know what *pray* means. I saw Mama on her knees. I put down the club. I get on my knees. The concrete is cold and hard. I saw Mama press her hands together. I press my hands together. I saw Mama move her lips. I move my lips. I want to touch him. Daddy. One last time. Before the end of the world. I reach out. I'm scared. I pull back. I move my lips. It might be praying. I lay my head down on his chest. And I feel it. And I hear it. The heart. Daddy's heart. Beating. Softly.

"Daddy?" I say. "Are you dead? Are you not dead?"

He doesn't answer, but I know right away. It's part of his plan. And I try hard but I can't help myself. I cry. I do. And I can't stop. I lay my head on his chest. I listen to his heart beat, and I feel the softest breath on the back of my head. I cry. My face is covered in wet snot. Daddy's shirt. I reach out. I put my arm around his belly. Daddy doesn't like that. To be touched. I can't help myself. I hug my daddy. My living daddy.

Any minute now, he'll wake up. He'll come to. He'll explain his strategy, all about how he tricked the enemy. All about how we'll stop the Apocalypse. I'll wait. I'll be here, ready, when he wakes. I stop crying by the power of my mind. Maybe I sleep. I don't know for sure. My eyes are closed, then they're open. And she's there. Maybe it's Mama. Except that she's naked and doing bad things. I close my eyes. I hold my living daddy tight. I open my eyes. She's still there. She's lying on her back. Even more naked. Even more disgusting. Or maybe it's the stupid neighbor lady. No. It's not Mama or the stupid neighbor lady and her stupid tattoo. It's the TV. It's a lady on the TV. She's naked. I don't understand what she's doing, and all of those men. But I do. Travis told me about it. It makes me feel sick, but I can't stop watching. Me and Travis used to watch the girls in their bathing suits. Travis taught me about camel toes. That's what we looked for. The woman on her back has so much hair. It's gross, but I can't stop watching. I don't know how long she's been there. I don't know how long I've been watching. I get up onto the couch with Daddy so I can see better. Willie. What? What are you looking at, Willie? It's her. She's calling my name. From the TV. She's looking at me. I see her lips move. What are you looking at, Willie? Daddy's not dead, I say. I know, she says. Hit him, she says. No. Want to see my thing? And I say yes. She shows me. Daddy's not dead, she says. I know, I say. Hit him. Can I see your thing? And she shows me. I never saw one like this before. And I'm so happy Daddy isn't dead. I wish he'd wake up. I bet he'd like to see it too. Me and Travis watched the girls. He showed me about jacking off. Don't watch me, he said. Look at them. Eventually, I got it right. Want to see what it can do? she asks. I nod. Yes. I can't believe the tricks she makes her thing do. I'm so happy Daddy isn't dead. My Evel Knievel pajamas are still wet and cold. I take them off. Here's another trick for you, she says. Travis showed me what to do. He moved away. Travis called it spooging. Travis said spooging is the best feeling in the whole world. When you spooge, everything stops, Travis said. Everything explodes. We looked for camel toes. Travis spooged. I almost did it. I almost spooged. Willie, she says, watch this. And she makes her thing whisper my name. Willie, it says, her thing whispers, and I'm pulling and pulling. Willie, it says. I watch her lips move. Whispering my name. Willie. And I'm about to do it. To spooge. Willie! She's talking too loud. Willie! She coughs. I'm almost there. Willie!

"Willie! Get off me!"

No. Not, what's, no. I look at the TV. She won't answer.

"Willie! Get off! I can't breathe—what in the fuck are you doing? You sick little shit!"

I fall to the floor. I grab my pants. I run. Up the stairs. Daddy is not dead.

"Willie! Goddamn it, Willie!"

Abigail Augenbaugh, clutches the half-empty jug of cheese puffs to her breast with due suffering; Jesus dragged his own cross, for the good of all mankind; the least she could do is bear the weight of this last sustenance for her family. She rounds the corner of her house in time to bear witness. But no prophecy could have prepared her for the vision of her naked son charging through the front door and into the woman he hadn't expected to be standing on the porch. Willie bounces off the guidance counselor and falls to the stoop. The woman stumbles backwards into the arms of the police officer standing behind her.

"Willie?" Abby says, dropping the jar. The powdery orange balls spill all over the sidewalk.

"W-W-William!" the guidance counselor stutters as she struggles for balance.

"Goddamn it, boy!" Burns yells, coming into view with Big Bertha raised and ready.

Willie cowers, clutches the balled up pants to his groin.

"I didn't, it wasn't, I don't, can't—"

I don't know what's happening. I don't know what to do. I curl into a ball on the porch. I don't know who these people are. I don't know what to say. What to think. I curl tighter and tighter. I am the Incredible Marble Boy. I shrink, I shrink, I am a ball bearing, a steelie; I roll away. I disappear. I am gone. Nobody can catch me now.

"Goddamn it, boy!" you shout. You go through the front door. You think you do. The world is brighter than you remember. Greener. You might be dead. Everything pulses. Throbs. Everything is loud. You might be alive.

"Put the weapon down now!"

What? What the fuck? How'd you get here? You see your wife. She's on her knees, on the sidewalk, raking cheese puffs into a pile.

"Put the weapon down now!"

What? Who keeps saying that? It's the two-headed lady. You see the tattoo on her ankle. You've seen it before. Cunt. Bend over. Who is yelling? Why is there so much yelling?

"Drop the weapon and put your hands over your head."

There is a cop behind a lady. Two bodies and two heads. A monster. The cop steps out. No monster. You are the monster.

"Don't you have anything better to do?" you ask the cop. You think so anyway.

"Bend over," you say to the woman. Your tongue is glued to the roof of your mouth. The cop looks like a robot, in his Kevlar vest and his belt full of kickass. You see your wife. She is on fire. No. Who is your wife? Where's the boy? Things move fast and slow at the same time.

"What the fuck are you looking at?"

You say it to your asshole neighbors. They stand in the grass, showing their tattoos and tans. He's made of plastic, or gold. Her bathrobe is so white it hurts your eyes. Bend over, you say. You feel good. Horny. For the first time in your whole life. To hell with your wife and the cheese puffs. Fuck the police. Then you remember the boy, and the basement, and the couch. Then things move slower and faster, at the same time.

You see him, hunched, practically naked, against the wall like a dog. Bootlicker. You start to kick him. The wife screams. It comes out like a cartoon bubble. It floats over all the heads. It snags in a tree and pops. The cop reaches for something. A train whistle rattles your teeth. The cop pulls a train whistle from his holster. The boy scrabbles across the porch. You kick. You miss. The boy starts to run, looking over his shoulder. Looking at you. Then the little bastard is airborne. You didn't know he could fly. It makes you proud. Really proud. All of a sudden, like. To think your boy is something special.

It's a miracle, you say. But you're lying. You don't believe in miracles.

"Stop. Please stop," Abigail Augenbaugh begs. But the scale of her cry does not equal the scope of her plea. She wants it all to stop. She wants her boy to stop running, naked, from the house. She wants her husband to stop the trajectory of the past few years. She wants her own weary body to stop hurting. She wants the police officer to recognize her from earlier in the day, and to say he's come to take care of things. She wants something from her God that she cannot articulate.

"Mrs. Augenbaugh. Mrs. Augenbaugh. Mrs. Augenbaugh—"

She wants to talk. To talk about Willie. To talk about the man on the radio and the end of the world. But she wants Willie's guidance counselor to stop talking, to move away from the policeman, to go back to wherever she came from. She wants to hold on just one more day.

"Stop—"

Your boy doesn't fly. Your boy hits the cop midbelly, bounces to the ground. The boy is a fuck-up. You wanted him to fly. You wanted a miracle. You got a fuck-up. The wife is a fuck-up. She birthed a fuck-up. It's not your fault. You are a fuck-up. It is your fault. You have things to teach him. It's not too late. It is too late. The cop grabs him. Grabs your boy. Your son. Grabs him hard. You think you hear the boy cry out.

"Take your goddamn hands off my son," you say.

You are the father. The son cries out. You are the father. The hero. The warrior.

"Put your hands over your head, now!"

For God so loved the motherfucking world. Your son.

The cop. He looks like a goddamn movie star in those shades. In those shades you see the whole world reflected. Except for you. You have no reflection.

Abby, on her dirty knees and in the grass now, watches it all. When her son runs, naked, stumbling, from the porch, and hits the officer, Abby, fearing a host of bad outcomes, cries out, louder than she's ever cried out before. "No!"

The officer, holding tight to the squirming boy, turns to look, and Abigail is blinded by the May sun bouncing off the mirrored lenses of his glasses. Abigail blinks, looks again, and in that ruptured moment, sees a bifurcated eternity play out on those two ovoid screens. Heaven on one side, Hell on the other. Past, present, and future. She's there in the front yard with her whole family, a day before the Rapture. Maybe the officer is her savior. Their savior. But as quickly as the divine visitation comes, it fizzles.

Burns takes a step forward.

"Take your goddamn hands off my son!" you say.

"Don't you have anything better to do?" you say.

"Taser! Taser! Taser!" the cop says.

You want ask *what,* but there is no time. Bertha clatters to the floor. There is body, and there is mind. You are in Joy. It is spring. Your body is rigid, on the porch. There is pain. Thorough and sudden hurt. You cannot move. It's not so bad, you think. This agony. This agony brings with it a clarity of mind so delicious you want to eat it forever. The cop lets off the trigger. You take a swing.

I scream. I am Scream. My howl is a shotgun blast to the sky. The sun curls up and dies. The clouds bleed. And still, and still, they will not set my daddy free.

<<

It's OK. You want to tell the boy that it's OK. This hot current that's surging through your body, you like it. You think dying might be like this. This might be dying. You like it. You think. An endless hallway of doors slamming open as you pass. You want to tell him about it, but you can't move. You'd like to see him. Maybe tell him to take care of his mom.

A rock bounces off the porch. Then another. You hear the cop yelling.

"Lady, get that boy now, or I'll take him down too!"

You hear the woman, the boy's mother. "Willie, please! Willie!"

You hear the other woman. The one with the butterfly tattoo. "Mrs. Augenbaugh—"

The cop releases the trigger. The Taser charge leaves your body, instantly. Instantly, you want it back. But. Can't. Find. The. Strength. To. Fight.

You try to breathe. He presses a kneecap into your spine. Cuffs your wrists tight.

"I know you, asshole," you say. Gasping. "I know who you are."

You don't mean it, though.

"We went to school together, Burns," the cop says. He means it. "You played on the golf team, didn't you?"

The boy runs. A school bus passes slowly. You refuse to look.

"Want me to go after him?" you hear your neighbor ask.

"No, Tim! No!" you hear his wife say.

Sweat trickles from your armpit and runs down your gut. You wonder what color her panties are.

"Go back inside," the cop says. "Mind your own business."

I run. Across the street. I run into the graveyard. I am not scared of the dead. I jump headstones. I stomp the grass beds of the sleeping dead. Wake up, you bastards, I say. A day early. Wake up. I am not afraid of the dead. I am afraid of the living. Their words, their chopped-up sentences, chase me all the way through the graveyard, to the top of the hill. I hear them now, just behind me, biting at my heels.

"Willie,"

"Boy—"

"—it'll take a miracle—"

"What if—"

"—squad car—"

"—he never comes back—"

You are in the backseat. You lie down. The vinyl is cool against your cheek. Your heart explodes. You hear the explosion. Maybe it's your head. You hear the explosion again and again. The back seat smells institutional. Like Army. You can't tell if this makes you feel better or worse. You lie down. The vinyl is cool against your cheek. Something is crushing you. It's your own bloated body. You think you might be on TV. You think there are cameras everywhere. There's a blood spot on your chest and one on your belly where the Taser probes went in. They might hurt, but you can't tell. You want a drink of water. The cop's radio chatters away. Squawks. Just like TV. You remember something about a boy.

A son, maybe? You'll ask the cop later. He's talking a lot. He tells you a story about high school. Something about a girl and an egg. You couldn't care less. It's the greatest story ever told.

∀

"Come on, honey. Let me help you up."

What? Someone is speaking to Abby, but she is too busy scooping the spilled cheese puffs back into the jug to look up.

"My name is Carole," she says. "Carole Onkst. I work for the school. I'm William's guidance counselor."

"I have to get these. These are for Willie and Burns. For, for after—"

"Let's get you inside, hon. We'll talk about it there. We'll talk all about it. About it all."

The woman lays a hand on Abigail's shoulder. Softly.

"After, after I'm gone, after Jesus, after the Judgment—"

"Just lean against me," she says. "We'll get you there."

Though she has to pry Abby's fingers apart—spilling out the crumbled snack food—the guidance counselor does so gently, and is at last able to help her stand. As if leading a cautious waltz, the woman nudges, steers, directs Abigail up the steps, across the porch, and into the house. Abigail looks back over her own shoulder all the way.

Carole Onkst guides Abby to the kitchen. Carole Onkst clears some space. They both sit at the table. No one mentions the squalor. They sit quietly for a moment. Abby cannot face those unrelenting, albeit kind, eyes.

"Can I get you some water?" the guest asks, as if it's her home.

No.

The guidance counselor mentions a doctor. Mentions the emergency room.

No.

"It's hard," the woman says. "Raising kids, these days. So hard. Isn't it?"

The guidance counselor puts a stack of papers between herself and Abigail. She has a lot of papers. She talks to Abby, quietly, but insistently. She talks about William. Willie. Her son. She uses words like "at risk" and "best interest."

"I just cross my fingers and pray every time my own girl leaves the house," she says.

Abigail Augenbaugh wonders if Burns will be home for supper.

Carole Onkst talks and talks. Says "child welfare." Says "social services."

Abigail wonders if Jesus will notice the earrings she's planning to wear.

"Willie?" Abigail says.

"They'll find him," Carole says. "They'll find William. They'll keep him safe."

Abigail wants to believe. Wants to have faith. Unshakable faith.

"It's very important that you read these over, Mrs. Augenbaugh. And sign them."

She talks still more, but eventually Abby nods her head.

"Get some rest, then," the guidance counselor says. "I'll make the phone calls and get back in touch with you tomorrow."

Abigail hears the door close. She wonders if that's Burns coming home for supper. Willie? She has a son. His name is Willie. She wonders where Willie is. Decides he must be out playing with friends. They're probably playing Army. He always gets so dirty playing Army. Abigail struggles to her feet. She holds on to the table's edge. She wishes she knew why her side hurt so much. There are some papers on the kitchen table. Abigail stuffs them deeply into the trash can. She smells something. A perfume. Some earthy oily scent, like patchouli. For a fraction of second she thinks she remembers someone being in the house just now. Abigail looks in the refrigerator. There's nothing inside. She steps gingerly over and around the mess on the floor. She opens a cabinet. Then another. There is something she's supposed to do, but for the life of her Abigail can't remember what it is.

"Hello?" she calls out.

It's called a holding cell. It holds you. You can't go anywhere. There are four walls. Cold tile. There's a bench and a toilet and a sink, stainless steel. There is too much light. There is a door. One skinny window with thick dirty glass. Wire mesh. You hear talking. Somebody is crying nearby. Dumbass. You forgive them. You wonder how you got here. You remember the electricity. You want more. You bang your head against the dirty window. You flush the toilet. It's so loud you go deaf. You flush it again and again. Each time the vacuum sucks you deeper and deeper. No. You're too big. You hear talking. Maybe yelling. Crying, too. There are four tiled walls. Graffiti in the grout. So and so sux cocks. I didn't do it. Jesus Saves. You touch one side. You feel something surging through the tile, through the grout. You reach out and touch the other side. So and so is a whore. I love Lucky. You stand there with both arms out, palms pressed against the walls. You feel something. You face the door. You feel a surge. You complete the circuit. You hear the voices. Every dumb son of a bitch that's ever been locked up here speaks. You press your hands to the tiles. There are nails. You don't know where the nails come from. Blood pours from your palms. *Look at me,* you say. *I'm crucified.* The floor buckles. The walls cave in. The sky boils, red then black. *Look at me,* you say. *I'm crucified.*

But they do, they do wake. All the dead. They rise up, teeth and bones loose and rattling, and they come. They come after me. No, I say. Go back, I say. Not today, I say. Tomorrow. But the dead won't listen. They come and they come. I know what to do. I know where to go. I go to the bridge. I scurry along the track. I climb down to the concrete trestle. And the dead can't follow. I wait. The dead keep coming, and the dead keep falling down between the railroad ties. They hit the water without a sound. The dead come after me. They fall, endlessly, into the river. I look down, see them writhing underwater. Reaching up. Calling out. The dead keep coming. The dead keep drowning. I wait. I'll wait until the cows come home.

The last night on earth finds Abigail Augenbaugh alone in the house, in Joy, for the first time in months. Years, maybe. The last night on earth comes skipping down the sidewalk, up the steps, through the squalid living room, into the wrack and ruin of the kitchen, and sits right down at the table. Where Abby sits, still, waiting upon her Lord.

Abigail takes her shoes off, digs her toes into the filth on the floor. Her ribcage hurts. She is hungry. She is weary. The man on the radio says we're supposed to come to the Lord broken. Abigail has never felt more broken. All she's ever wanted was to belong. Somewhere. Anywhere. And to feel sure about her place. She wishes it wasn't so hard, this being a *True Believer*. This business of *faith*. She's never understood. She's never felt smart enough to figure it out. The man on the radio says not to question.

Says to question is a sin. Abigail wishes she could pick up *sin,* wishes she could pluck a piece of sin from the floor and hold it, smell it, lick it, so that she might know for sure what it is.

But the mysteries of her Lord are not so easily fathomed. All her life, she's heard talk of a grand plan. Of God's everlasting wisdom. Of God's finger in every pie, thumb on every scale, eye on every sparrow. Of God's mercy, God's love, God's wrath. All her life, she's heard talk of her own fallibility, her own weakness. Of unworthiness. Of wickedness. Of immorality. Transgression. Trespass.

All her life, she's never been able to keep the stories straight. How did it start? Whose fault is it? And why? The floods of Genesis drown her still. The plagues of Moses torment. All her life she's endeavored to understand, but no one could ever, would ever, help her untangle the knots. All her life, loaves and fishes, the jawbone of an ass, the slaughter of the firstborn. All her life, Abigail Augenbaugh has tripped over parables, choked on beatitudes. And now her life is coming to an end. One more day. Tomorrow. She hopes. She waits. She hopes.

It is dark. I am hungry. I eat the dark. When the dark is gone, I eat the emptiness. I strike a match, then eat the light. I eat the box of matches. When I speak, buildings erupt into flames. The river gurgles below me. I eat the river. Overhead, the railroad ties gouge the sky. I eat the railroad ties. Creosote drips from my chin. I eat railroad spikes and concrete. When the train crawls by, just above my head, within reach, I open my mouth and suck its roar deep into my lungs.

I eat the moon, from the bottom up. It is dark. I am not cold. I am not scared. Night is here. It will not be eaten.

But her hope, there in the dark, is bilious. Emetic. When Jesus returns, when he plucks Abby from the face of the Earth and carries her up to Heaven, it means the earthquakes will have started. It means that death and destruction will roll like a tidal wave across the town, the county, the state, the country, the whole world. When Jesus comes to get the True Believers, everybody else will be left behind. To suffer. To die. That's what the man on the radio says. Her husband and her son will be left behind to suffer and die. And the True Believers will watch it all from up there. In Heaven. Abigail wonders if there will be seats, or benches. Or will she spend eternity standing, in worship? Will she be too busy worshiping God to care about the torment down below? The man on the radio doesn't speak about that. The man on the radio says it's all part of God's Salvation Plan. That He knows the end from the beginning. That He has it all mapped out. That He knew, that He chose the True Believers before He made them.

Abigail has a son. His named is Willie. He's gone. She doesn't know where he is. Abigail has a husband. Burns. The police took him away earlier. She doesn't know why. Abigail had a job, at the Slinky plant, but she quit. She's supposed to choose God over them all. She thinks it was God's will. But why? Why would God do these things to her husband? To her son? Or is she just being greedy? God sacrificed his own son, right? Begotten. What makes Abigail Augenbaugh so special that she thinks she ought to keep her son to herself?

One time, beneath the aluminum roof of the picnic shelter behind the Slinky plant, while eating lunch, Darnell Younce asked a question that Abby never forgot. "So, Sue," Darnell said, biting into a dill spear. "If Jesus started out up in Heaven, and ended up back there, after the donkey ride and the cross, what exactly did God sacrifice?"

Abigail remembers the pickle juice dripping from Darnell's chin.

Abigail never forgot the question. She wants to call the man on the radio and ask it of him. She wants to ask the man on the radio what she's supposed to do about Willie and Burns. How she's supposed to endure this ache in her heart for the remaining hours. Why God would create a world so cruel and hard. Why God needed so much worship. Why. Why. Why. What if the man on the radio is wrong? What if everything she's been taught is wrong? What if her whole life has been a mistake? The questions roil (with rare clarity) in Abby's mind. Hobble her. Blind and deafen her. She wants to get up, to march over to the phone, to call the man on the radio and demand some answers. But there is no phone in the house. And she can't remember the number anyway. She'll have to ask God himself.

Abigail Augenbaugh—worried mother; beleaguered wife; pitiful, worthless sinner—gets to her knees, plants her elbows wide on the seat of her chair, and tries to find the right words.

Then comes the knock.

It is night. I am night. All the world's darkness lives in my belly. I lie on the concrete pylon and dwell in my own pitch-black. I shiver. I eat the cold. The cold becomes a stone around my neck. I roll off into the Juniata River, sink down, drown without waking. I bob along the riverbed. I spill out into the salty bay. The black drums, the sturgeons, the stargazers, the carp and catfish—the bottom-feeders—welcome me home. No. I hear the moon roll by overhead. I hear the river surge below. I hear the thump thump thump of the earth's wretched heart. No. What is it? A thumping full of dread. I get to my knees. I lean over, look into the water. Look upstream, and there, bumping off stones, logs, tacking in fits and starts, back and forth down the river, toward me, toward the boy, comes the fish. No. Not a fish. More than a fish. The Leviathan. Its green skin dull and hard as armor. Its eyes—big as hubcaps—stare down all comers. Its mouth gapes. Beckons. I fall. I fall in. Into the open mouth of the gigantic fish. Into its gullet. I am swallowed. I am swallowed.

∀

Then comes the knock.

Then comes the fear.

Then comes the crushing guilt. Who is she to question the will of God?

Then comes the knock.

Could it be the Lord Himself? A day early?

No. No. Please no.

The knock continues. Jinx? Sue Grebb? The Walmart security guard? What if it's the neighbors? What if it's the police? The knock persists. Maybe it's Burns. Maybe it's Willie! Willie, come home to his mama!

"Willie!" Abby says, struggling to her feet. "I'm coming, Willie!"

Abby, unstable, staggers into the doorjamb, careens into the wall, but refuses to let the pain stop her. "I'm coming, Willie!" she says. "I'm coming!"

Abigail opens the front door. "Willie!" she cries out.

"Good evening, ma'am," the Mormon boy says. "I'm Elder Kevin, and this is Elder Brad."

"Willie?" Abigail says. "What happened, Willie?"

"I'm Elder Kevin," the taller boy says. "And this is Elder Brad."

"Good evening," the shorter boy says.

"Willie?" Abigail says, again.

They're so clean, these two Mormon boys. And slim, and handsome. Abigail has never seen such beauty in her whole life.

"Have you heard the good news?" Elder Kevin asks.

"About Jesus Christ," Elder Brad adds.

Their white shirts are immaculate. Goodness, peace, and contentment emanate from their clean-shaven faces.

Both boys hold Bibles in their strong, capable hands.

"OK," Abigail says. She looks at both the boys. Looks them in the eyes, back and forth. And in their tender gaze, she feels accepted. Seen. "OK."

Elder Kevin starts talking. Abigail doesn't pay much attention, just watches his mouth move. A car passes. Abby, standing in the door, feels lit up by, illuminated by, the purity and the love and the white shirts.

"What do you think?" Elder Brad asks.

"What?" Abby says. She missed the question. The Lord works in mysterious ways. Speaks in parables. Abby tries to unravel the puzzle. She sees Elder Brad look at Elder David. There is something in the look that troubles her. Some shard of doubt. Some slight retreat. The Lord gives, the Lord takes.

"No," Abigail says. Meaning *Don't stop.* Meaning *Come back.* Meaning *I want to bathe forever in your pure goodness.*

"Maybe there's a better time for us to come visit?" Elder Brad says, backing ever so slightly away.

What is it that God wants from her, in this moment? Abigail feels the threads of faith pulled taut. Give and take; offering and sacrifice.

"No," Abigail says. Meaning *There is no more time.* Meaning *I want you to stay.*

The boys clutch their Bibles a little tighter, confer quietly. Beautifully. The boys glow, radiant in their unblemished beliefs. Abigail yearns for that glow, for something other than her own stained past.

"Maybe there's a better time," Elder Kevin says.

Her dirty house, her dirty husband, dirty son. Her filthy soul.

"No," Abby says. "Jesus is coming."

The man on the radio proclaims it. And Abigail will be the Bride of Christ, forever. She wants to be at the Wedding Feast of the Lamb. Wants to be, forever, in the arms of her Savior. What is it that the Lord is asking of her? What does He demand of His bride? Abigail searches the eyes, the faces, the bodies of the two young men. She will do whatever it takes.

"We'll come back another day," Elder Kevin says.

"No," Abby says. "Jesus is coming tomorrow. Don't go."

And in a moment that surprises even her, Abby pulls her shirt up over her breasts, pulls her workpants and her underwear down to her knees.

"Don't leave me," she says.

But the two Mormon boys are already backing carefully down the stairs. Backing away and looking straight into Abigail's face, her pleading eyes.

"We'll be going now," Elder Kevin says.

Elder Brad says something about the Lord Jesus.

Elder Kevin says something about the weather.

Abigail Augenbaugh says what she means. "Will you just look at me?" she begs. "Please. Look at me."

Abby stands on the porch, exposed, listening to the rhythmic squeak as the Mormon boys pedal away on their mountain bikes. She can hear the beautiful elders even after the night has taken them from her sight. A school bus goes by, the marching band on its way home from some event. Even in the dark Abby can see the faces pressed against the windows. Can see the huge bells of the tubas, the feathered plumes on the hats.

"Take that skank-hole back in the house and cover it up!" some kid yells.

Abigail does as she is told.

Get up.

What? I open my eyes. It is not yet day. The stars rage overhead. I am cold, hungry. I am covered in bile. Where am I?

Retched up out of the belly of the whale.

Why?

Get up. Now.

What? Who said that? I stay still, my backbone fused with the concrete. Something crawls across my chest.

Get up. You know what you have to do.

Who is this? Who are you?

Who is this? Who are you?

I am a worthless little faggot. I am a pussy boy.

No. Who are you?

I am nothing. I am nobody.

No. Where is Daddy?

They took him away.

Where is Mama?

Going to Heaven.

Who are you?

I am scared. I am hungry. I am by myself.

No. Not yet. Get up. Put the river in your pocket. The railroad track is your belt.

I do as I am told.

When you walk, the earth groans. You spit tornadoes. You piss tsunamis.

I do as I am told. Millions drown.

Who are you?

I don't know.

You are as old as salt. You are as pure as the maggot in your heart.

I don't know.

It is time to go home.

I do as I am told. I walk the alleys. Scald Mountain trembles as I pass. The clock in the courthouse tower spins, faster and faster, backwards. Backwards. The clappers in the church bells shrivel and fall to the ground.

Who are you?

I am Willie.

What do you remember?

Everything.

You are Willie. Go home. You know what to do.

But it is cold. It is dark. I am in the churchyard. I think. A nighthawk screeches. I yank it from the sky and bite its heart out. I am lost. I say this aloud. I am lost.

You are Willie. You know what to do.

No. I don't.

Where is Mama?

Getting ready for Heaven.

No. Where is Daddy?

In jail.

You know what to do. Daddy told you. Daddy told you everything you need to know.

A police car drives slowly down the alley; the moon reflects in the rooftop bubble lights. I dive into the bushes. Roots surge over me. Beetles crawl in and out of my mouth, my nose, my ears. It happens so fast. I look up. I can see all the way to Heaven. It's busy up there, what with the coming Rapture and all. The man on the radio talks about God's complicated plan. I look for God, but don't see him. I lie still. I wait to be instructed. I am older than stone. I am older than orbits. I know everything. I wait. I wait a thousand years in the churchyard. Who am I? I am the Abomination of Desolation. I speak it.

I am Willie, I say. Aloud. I am Willie.

∀

The sleep that finds Abigail Augenbaugh is merciless. Night is a bootblack, predestinated. Night is a gyroscopic scapegoat. Night, devout as a dumbwaiter. Night sweeps over the land like a mad dowser. Night barrels over the horizon, sweeps the land like a mad dowser. And the lunatic moon, that clabbered albino, homes in on a bottomless well of fear.

Abigail dreams a vast nothingness, and falling and falling and falling. She dreams she is in the belly of Scald Mountain, and everything she has ever said, everything she has ever thought, is spelled out in bituminous black veins of coal. In Joy, PA, Abigail Augenbaugh dreams a lifetime of want and need, about to come to an end. Abigail Augenbaugh dreams the hymnbook. Sings. The sleep that finds Abigail Augenbaugh is merciful. But she is no prophet. She does not dream, she cannot dream, the day to come.

I know what to do. I don't know what to do.

Listen.

I can't hear. I can't hear you. Anything.

Listen.

I am. I listen. I wait. I listen. Please, I say. Come back, I say. Help me, I say.

Shhh!

Please, I say.

Listen.

Nothing.

And then, something.

Willie.

What?

Willie. Willie.

I'm here. I'm Willie.

Willie. Willie. Willie.

What, I say. Where are you? I say. Can I see you? I say.

Willie. Willie. Willie. Willie. Willie. Willie.

Stop it, I say. It's too loud!

Willie. Willie. Willie. Willie. Willie. Willie. Willie. Willie. Willie. Willie. Willie. Willie.

But it doesn't stop. Who's calling me? Who are you? Who's calling my name?

Willie. Willie.

Stop! I can't make it stop. It's too loud. I don't know where it comes from. It comes from everywhere. I lie in the churchyard. I cover my ears. I look up. I can't see Heaven. I see only the nests, the tent worm clouds in all the trees. I see the black-headed caterpillars writhing inside. Then I know. It's them. They whisper my name. All of them.

Willie. Willie.

No, I say. Stop it, I say. I jump up. I run. I see the shed in the corner of the churchyard. I run. I go inside. They chase me with their cries. My name clicks against their worm-teeth.

Willie. Willie.

Willie. Willie. Willie. Willie. Willie. Willie. Willie. Willie. Willie. Willie.
Willie. Willie. Willie. Willie. Willie. Willie. Willie. Willie. Willie.

I cover my ears, but it doesn't help. I close the shed door, squat against the wall. Their cries eat away at the wood, at my skull. I cry. Nobody can hear. Then I smell it, the gasoline. Then I remember. What Daddy said. Daddy told you what to do. I drag the gas can out of the shed. I have a lighter in my pocket. It has boobs and a naked butt. No head. I take the lid off the gas can. I go to the trees. I splash the nests. All of them. The whole world stinks of gasoline.

Willie. Willie. Willie. Willie. Willie. Willie. Willie. Willie. Willie. Willie.
Willie. Willie. Willie. Willie. Willie. Willie. Willie. Willie. Willie. Willie. Willie. Willie. Willie. Willie. Willie. Willie. Willie. Willie. Willie. Willie.
Willie. Willie. Willie. Willie. Willie. Willie. Willie. Willie. Willie. Willie.
Willie. Willie. Willie. Willie. Willie. Willie. Willie. Willie. Willie. Willie.

One by one, I ignite the nests of caterpillars. Each one offers a beautiful *fwooomph* to the night. I walk the line of trees, leave destruction in my wake. The night burns and burns. And I am triumphant. I have burned the tongue from my enemy's mouth. Scorched the throat. Seared the larynx. The nests sizzle, crackle, pop, as the bodies of the writhing tent worms swell and explode. I am victorious.

Willie.

No.

Willie. You know what to do. Willie.

They are screaming now. Enraged. In pain. Insistent.

Willie. Willie. You know what you have to do, Willie. You know what to do. Willie.

The churchyard is ringed in fire. I close my eyes. The blaze burns through my lids. My hands are torches.

Willie. You know what to do. You know what to do.

Leave me alone! Leave me alone!

You have to do it, Willie. It's the only way. You have to kill her, Willie.

No! No! No! No!

The only way, Willie. The only way is to kill her, Willie. You have to. Kill her. Willie.

The trees burn and whisper. Whisper and burn. The flaming caterpillars drop to the earth, passing their sentence all the way down.

You have to, kill her, Willie. Kill her Willie. Kill her, Willie.

I can't! I can't do that.

It's the only way, Willie. Daddy says so. You have to kill her. Kill her, Willie. Kill her.

OK, I say. OK.

I hear sirens. I hear a door slam. I run. I know where to go.

I am Burns Augenbaugh. You say it aloud. It's the only thing you know with any certainty, right now. You are in bed. In a hospital. You can tell this much. Your hands are cuffed to the bedrail. You don't mind. You wonder what day it is. What month. What year. The door opens. A nurse stands there for a minute, looking in. She's backlit. She glows like an angel. There may be wings. A halo. I am Burns Augenbaugh, you say.

I am Willie. I know what to do. I go home. It is the end, Willie. The end of the world. Whole. I alone can stop it. We know what to do. No. There are sirens. In the distance. I wonder why. I go home. The streets are empty. The streets are dark. Light spills from my body. I may be on fire. The house is dark. I know why. My coming was foretold. I enter the house. The house barely contains me. I am Super Willie. I listen. I sniff. I taste the air. I puke in the corner. I know what I have to do. I puke in the other corner.

I need a weapon. I need *the* weapon. I go to the basement. To find Daddy's club. With Daddy's club, nothing can stop me. There is no club. The enemy confiscated the club. I know what I have to do. Daddy told me. The house is dark. The basement is dark. In the dark basement I find the tackle box. In the tackle box I find the fillet knife. I pull it from the leather sheath. All of Heaven is reflected in the skinny blade. I don't question. It blinds me. This is a good weapon. This is the weapon for what I have to do. I know what to do. I slide it back into the sheath. It fits perfectly.

I know where to go.

I know the banister. I know the creak of every stair. I know the door-knob. I know the ray of moonlight cut into thin strips by the blinds. I know the blue blanket with red flowers. I know the body beneath the blanket. I know the nightgown. The one with puppy dogs. I know the breath in those lungs.

She lies on her back. The traitor. I know the smell of her.

Be brave.

I know. I know the feel of the knife's handle. The hush of the blade sliding out of the sheath. I know. I am Willie.

You are Willie.

Willie holds the knife tight. In both hands. Willie can see her heart beating beneath the nightgown. Willie lowers the tip of the blade to that heart.

Be brave. Be strong. You are Willie. The Great Willie.

Willie watches her breathe. Watches her heart beat. Willie knows what to do. How to stop it. Willie knows what to do. Daddy told him. She's breathing. Her eyes are closed. Her skin is so pale it's almost blue. Willie hates her blue skin. Willie hates her breath. Willie hates her puppy-dog nightgown. Willie hates her heartbeat.

Who are you?

You are Willie.

Who is she?

She is a traitor. She is going to Heaven. She is leaving us behind.

Behind her closed lids the eyes flit back and forth. Willie watches.

Breath and heartbeat. He puts the knife to her chest. He pushes. But just a little bit, just enough for the tip of the blade to penetrate the thin cotton gown. Leans his weight into the moment just enough for the steel knife tip to pierce her skin.

She winces, the traitor. A tiny bark, the bark of a catfish flopping in a bucket, escapes her mouth. She does not open her eyes. But the eyeballs roll wild in their bony cups. She cries, the traitor. Willie hesitates. Watches breath and heartbeat. Watches a tear roll down her cheek. Stupid cheek. Willie hates it. Watches the blood-red moon rise between her boobs. Stupid boobs. Willie pauses.

Abigail Augenbaugh, bride of Christ.

Abigail Augenbaugh, wife of Burns.

Abigail Augenbaugh, mother of Willie.

Bleeds with all the devotion she can muster.

Kill her they said. The caterpillars told me to. Said Daddy said. I tried. I am a failure. I am a little faggot. I am a pussy boy. I run into the burning sky. I run into the last sunrise on earth. I failed. I tried. I failed. I came to the pond. I waded in. I went under. Underwater I heard them, still, hissing and burning and screaming. Kill her kill her kill her.

But I tried. I couldn't. I am not that big. That strong. That anything. I am only Willie. I am wet. I am hungry. I am at the bottom of the pond. I want to stay here until the Rapture has come and gone. I dig at the mud, hold tight to the roots, suck the nasty water deep into my lungs. I die. No. I don't. I fail. I am a coward. I crawl onto the bank. I puke. My puke is green. I hear the boys with their golf clubs. I want to lie there and let them beat me to death. No. I fail. I am a pussy boy. I crawl into the bushes. I hide. I cry. Just a little. And quietly.

I hear sirens. The sun is bright and hot. I don't know what to do. You do know what to do. No. I close my ears, close my eyes, close my mouth. I don't want the Rapture. I don't want Mama to go. To Heaven. I don't want Daddy in jail. But I am only Willie. I am Willie, only. I am hungry and too little to stop the world from ending.

No. Kill her.

No. I want to stop them. The tent worms. They're in my head. They crawled into my ears. Their feet, by the tiny hundreds, scritch and scratch inside my skull. Their little black heads bump against my eardrums. Whispering whispering whispering: Kill her.

No. Stop, I say. It's too loud, I say.

Where's the knife? I say. I'm here. By your side. The whole time. The handle fits perfectly. I pull the blade from the soggy sheath. The blade is thin and bends easily. There is a fish scale stuck in the blood groove. I sit in the grass, on the bank of the pond. With the skinny blade I dig the caterpillars out of my ears, one at a time, and toss them, one by one, to the carp floating at the surface with their mouths gaping. The blood trickles from my ears, down my neck, makes a pretty necklace at my throat. My fingers are bloody. The caterpillars, bloody, squirm. The fish don't seem to mind. They're beautiful, the carp. Floating like fat balloons. Catching caterpillars in their open mouths. Catching the sun in their orange scales, they burn and burn. Kill her.

What?

I can't hear you. What? I can't hear. You.

What?

Kill her.

No. Stop it. I can't. You can.

You are Willie.

Stop. It.

You can. Kill her. You can.

And then.

I smell.

Vanilla pudding.

And remember.

The gospel truth.

"Mrs. Augenbaugh, we're looking for your son, William."

Abby stands in the doorway, unclear how long she's been there or who these people are. Maybe they're familiar faces, maybe not. She feels naked. She checks. She's not.

"It's too late," Abby says.

"What? Excuse me?"

They shuffle papers. Shuffle furtive glances.

"I need to sit down," Abby says. And she does. There in the doorway.

"What do you mean, *It's too late?*" a woman asks.

There's something in her tone that Abby dislikes. She looks at all the knees. She wishes she had some tracts.

"The Rapture," Abby says. "Today is the day. It's too late. For Willie. For all of you."

"We're coming inside, Missus Augenbaugh, to look for your son, William. And you seem—you're bleeding. We have to get you some help."

"No," Abby says.

They look through the whole house. Abby waits in the living room. They return. They surround her. They say a lot of things. They leave behind warnings and judgments and instructions and a whole stack of papers. They leave empty-handed.

Abby wonders if any of her work friends will be in Heaven with her.

"Sign here, Mr. Augenbaugh."

What?

"Note the court date, and don't forget it. Do you have a ride?"

You're free to go. Not to stay. They say so. They know your name. They don't know what you are capable of. It's not true. You are not free to go.

"Where?" you ask.

"Home," they say. "Go home."

"I'll walk," you say. "I can walk. It's not far."

You lie. There's no map to anything you could call home. You want to ask for your club back, for Big Bertha, but you don't. You feel the pills. They burn in your belly and your esophagus. But it's good. You feel them in your head too. It's good. The pain brings focus, clarity. It's been a long time. You don't know how long. You put your hand in your pocket, grip the pill bottle, make sure it's still there. You don't know how long.

You sign your name. It feels almost true.

You'll walk home. You'll walk all the way. You'll walk slow, and think about stuff. It's a new day. There's some space in your brain. You'll walk home, and think about stuff. When you get there, you'll have things to say.

Do you smell it?

What?

Vanilla. Vanilla pudding.

So?

Now I know.

Know?

What to do.

How?

I just know.

You are Willie.

You are the Truth. The Gospel Truth.

It's the end, right?

Yes.

The Day of Judgment. Right?

Yes.

And who can stop it?

You. Only you.

And how do you know?

Daddy said so.

And who are you?

I am Willie. I rise up, out of the muck, and follow my nose. I know what to do. I know because I know. I say so.

You are wet and hungry. Are you sure?

Shut up!

Who is she?

I don't care.

Why, then?

I know what to do. Daddy told me. He told me what to do, there at the store. She's the cause of it all, he said. Conquer that and you'll rule the world, he said.

Who said?

Daddy said.

He's in jail. He's dead. He's nobody.

Shut up! Daddy's a hero. A war hero. He told me what to do. I'll do what I have to do.

You're a pussy boy. You're a faggot. You're a failure.

I am Willie, I say.

I walk around the dumpster, and there she is. Lying in a patch of weedy grass on a Hello Kitty towel. She wears a bathing suit the color of cantaloupe, with tiny hearts, white and red. She is beautiful. Her skin is perfect. Her butterfly tattoo is perfect. Her skull toe-ring is perfect. Her camel-toe is perfect. Her eyes are closed. The lids, perfect little upturned scoops. There is a Game Boy beside her head. No. It's a phone, with ear-buds plugged in and leading to her most perfect ears. Her foot sways to music I can't hear. I want it. I want to go inside her beautiful head.

Stop it, Willie.

She can't hear me.

I step to the edge of her Hello Kitty towel. I look closer. There's a robe bunched under her head for a pillow. Dirty green flip-flops peek from beneath a thick yellow book, *Biology for Dummies*. A bottle of Naked-Shake stands in the grass, surrounded by a baggie of celery and carrot sticks, a Little Debbie Swiss Cake Roll, and a bottle of tanning lotion. The stink of vanilla clots in the back of my throat.

Every time she breathes her perfect boobies rise up in their orange cups. I am Willie. I know what to do. I step up. I stab her. One. In the booby. The blade goes in so easily. So deep.

"Hey!" she says. Her eyes wide. "Quit that!"

Like I pinched her or something. She starts to sit up. I stab her again. Two. In the belly. The blade almost disappears.

She looks confused. Beautifully confused.

"You're that kid," she says.

I am Willie. I don't want to hear her talk. I stab her again. Three. In the throat. A giant redbird unfurls its wing. Feathers brush my face. She puts her hands up to her throat. Her mouth works like she's chewing something. Like she's eating. She rolls from side to side. I sit on her belly. Be still. I know what to do. I stab her again. Four. She bleeds. I didn't know there was so much. I wonder what her nipples look like, but it doesn't seem right to peek. I stab her again. Five. Six.

I'll tell Daddy. Look, Daddy, I'm conquering the world.

I keep stabbing. Seven. Eight. Nine. Ten. Eleven. Because Daddy would want me to. Because it's what I have to do. She squirms some. Wiggles. Her eyes go in and out of focus. They're pretty. They're green. I almost kiss her, but then I realize it's a trick, one of her evil ploys. Thirteen. Fourteen. Fifteen. Sixteen. Seventeen. I stab her again. I am Willie. I will not be deceived. I look up, out of her gaze, out of her spell. I see the back of the apartment building, all the little balconies. I see the windows and the sliding glass doors and all the faces of all the people there cheering me on. Eighteen. Nineteen. Twenty. Twenty-one. Twenty-two. Twenty-three. Twenty-four. Twenty-five. Go Willie! Go Willie! Willie go! Twenty-six. Twenty-seven. Twenty-eight. Twenty-nine. Thirty. I am the champion. I am the victor. Thirty-one. Thirty-two. Thirty-three. You can do it, Willie! Thirty-four. Thirty-five. Thirty-six. Thirty-seven. Perfect. I stop there. There's no good reason. I hold my knife aloft; blood drips down my arm. Everybody claps and hollers. My pant legs are soaked with blood. I bounce a couple times, sitting on her slack belly. Little geysers of blood erupt from her holes. The crowd goes wild.

I can do anything. I know the Truth, the Gospel Truth.

Get up, I say. I can do anything. Get up; go tell them all what happened. Tell them all who rules the world.

She doesn't move, though. Except for twitching. And something like a hiccup.

You're making me mad, I say. I am Willie. I can do anything. Get up.

But of course she can't. I'm still sitting on her.

I don't move. I am hungry. I am tired. Ruling the world is hard work. I see the Little Debbie Swiss Cake Rolls. My fingers are slick. It's hard to tear the plastic. But I finally get it open. They taste like blood. I don't care.

Don't move, I say, and she listens. I sit, triumphant, on top of the stabbed girl. I eat all her snacks. I pick up her cell phone. It's playing music. I can't hear it. I stand up. I look down at her. She's perfect. Beautiful. Don't move, I say. I want you to stay like that forever. I have an idea. I use her phone. I take the picture. I wish I could call Travis. I wish Travis could see. I ought to call somebody. I have an idea. I open her phone, tap on the screen. See *Mom/Work*. I call.

"Good afternoon, Joy Area Middle School Guidance Office. May I help you?"

"Oh," I say. I know that voice. "I know who you are," I say.

Now I get it. Your mom is that lady. In the office. With the tattoo. Like yours. Now I see how the evil plot thickens.

"Who's this? May I help you?"

"I am Willie," I say. "Oh," I say again, then, quick-thinking. "There's a bomb."

"William? Where are you, William?"

"There's a bomb," I say again.

She's not listening.

"Where are you, William? Are you OK? Is everything OK?"

I am a genius, I say, to the stabbed girl. Then I have another idea.

I tap her cell phone screen another time. See *Mom/Cell*. I find the picture of the beautiful girl, stabbed. I press *send*. I lick my fingertip clean. I tap at the small keyboard.

One. Two. Three. Four. Five. Six. Seven. Eight. Nine. Ten. Eleven. Twelve. Thirteen. Fourteen. Fifteen. Sixteen. Seventeen. Eighteen. Nineteen. Twenty. Twenty-one. Twenty-two. Twenty-three. Twenty-four. Twenty-five. Twenty-six. Twenty-seven. Twenty-eight. Twenty-nine. Thirty. Thirty-one. Thirty-two. Thirty-three. Thirty-four. Thirty-five. Thirty-six. Thirty-seven. This is how many times we stab her.

I press *send*. I am a genius, I say again. She doesn't disagree. I am a mess, I say. It's your fault, I say. She doesn't disagree. I have an idea. I take the robe from beneath her head. Gently. It is pure and white. Spotless. Stainless. A miracle, no doubt. I put it on. The robe fits me. Perfectly. Covers me. Completely. I want to do something nice for her. I plug the earphones back into her cell. I snug them, gently, back into her ears. I wipe the knife in the grass, sheath it, hide it inside the robe. I walk. Toward home. I put my hand in the robe's pocket. I find something there. Small. Plastic. Rectangular. I wrap my fingers around the find, pull it out, look at it there in my open palm. It's her nametag.

Remember what Daddy said. "Conquer that shit and you'll rule the world. Nothing can stop you." I did it, Daddy. We did it. Me, the boy, you, the Dark One, we conquered that shit. I can do anything. We can do anything. Anything. You'll rise, full of life, come out of the basement, uniform spotless. Jesus will stay up in his clouds. Mama will make dinner. I did it. Just like you said to.

Her nametag says *Cheyenne,* and *Property of Scald Mountain Country Club.*

I am Willie, I say. Property of no one. I toss the nametag into a weedy ditch. In the distance, on the ridge of Scald Mountain, the windmills stand ready. Spin, I say, and they do. The massive blades chop the afternoon sky into brilliant blue bits. I walk down the alley toward home. I'll walk right past the graveyard, tell the boys there to settle their bones. I'll tell them what I did. I'll tell them how I fixed everything. Made everything all right.

You are Burns Augenbaugh. You are walking the streets of Joy, PA. The hills and cracked sidewalks are, mercifully, familiar. You pass the Toyota dealership. Over it the biggest flag you've ever seen whips in a wind you can't feel. Sounds like machine-gun fire, but it's not. You say it out loud: It's just a big flag and some wind. You keep walking. You are out of breath. You rest at a bus-stop bench. You look up. You think about Scald Mountain throwing its hump against this sky for millions and millions of years, and you know you'll make it home. For good measure, you squeeze the pill bottle in your pocket. Head down the street, toward a rented house, where you sleep on a moldy couch in the basement. You don't own anything real. You had a wife and a son, a while ago. No. Stay clear. Hold on to the clarity. You had a wife and a son just yesterday. You have them today. Is there any reason to believe you won't have a wife and a son tomorrow? You see the courthouse clock tower. It mindlessly claims the moments as they pass. You hear sirens. This time you know they're not coming for you.

Abigail Augenbaugh fidgets. She fusses. She holds a pair of clip-on earrings up to her face, then another. She lays out a skirt and a blouse. She lays out a dress. She rifles through her underwear drawer. Modesty is key. What about makeup? she wonders. Maybe just a little lipstick. But she can't find the old tube. Abigail wants to be ready. Abigail wants to be pretty. To be perfect. For Jesus. In Heaven, Abby expects nothing less than perfection. She paces. She looks at the clock. She looks at the clock. She looks at the clock. There are sirens in the distance. Is it the Apocalypse come early? She's been listening, waiting. But still is caught off guard. Abigail makes an anxious little bark. She hurries. She's leaving for Heaven today, and nothing in Joy is going to stop her. Not a broken rib. Not the deep bruise it bears to the skin's surface. Not a stack of confusing forms. Not her raw, stinging sex. Nor the penetration. Not filth. Not memories. Not regrets. Nothing. She looks at the clock. She looks at the clock. The Rapture is hours away, and every minute yawns—eonian. The house is a shambles. She can't let Jesus see such a mess. Abby has to decide whether to stand in the backyard or in the front yard to await the Rapture.

"Daddy," I say, when I see him. "Daddy!"

Back from the dead. Back to life. I did it. I brought him back. There's nothing I can't do.

"It's me, Daddy. Willie. I'm Willie."

He's standing in the front yard. He's looking down the street toward me as I approach. He's proud. I can tell. I can feel it. My glory washes over all. Everything shines.

"It's me, Daddy. It's Willie. I did it. I made it right. I did what you said. I did everything you told me to do. And now you're back! You died. You were dead and I brought you back. You know what that means, Daddy?"

See how happy he looks, how glad to see me. My power overwhelms him. Daddy backs up, just a little, to make room for my awesome presence.

"Do you know, Daddy? Do you know what it means? It means I stopped the Rapture too! I listened to what you said, Daddy. I am the conqueror. I did exactly what you told me to do, and I brought you back to me, I stopped Mama from going to Heaven without us, and I stopped the world from ending. I stopped the end of the whole world, Daddy! I am Willie. I rule the world now."

I open the white robe of purity. I open my arms. I embrace him.

∀

"Are you from the Rapture?" Abigail Augenbaugh asks.

In rushing for the door she had missed buttons on her blouse, left a shoe behind, hurried too much with the lipstick. She'd hoped for Jesus himself, would forgive him for being early.

"Are you from the Rapture?" she asks again, confused and disappointed by the suit-clad representatives. "Is that why you're here? Are you with the Apocalypse?"

"Every day is the Apocalypse for somebody, lady," one of the two plainclothes police officers says.

The other tells her they're here to arrest her son, William Augenbaugh.

Abigail looks at them. Tries to focus. Tries to concentrate.

"Willie?" she calls into the kitchen. "Your friends are here to play."

"Willie!" she calls again, even louder. The boy probably can't hear her over the washing machine. Her husband, Burns, is in the basement doing a load of laundry. That old washing machine gets off balance easily, thumps and bumps the wall, and practically jumps across the floor.

⋈

One. Two. Three. Four. Five. Six. Seven. Eight. Nine. Ten. Eleven. Twelve. Thirteen. Fourteen. Fifteen. Sixteen. Seventeen. Eighteen. Nineteen. Twenty. Twenty-one. Twenty-two. Twenty-three. Twenty-four. Twenty-five. Twenty-six. Twenty-seven. Twenty-eight. Twenty-nine. Thirty. Thirty-one. Thirty-two. Thirty-three. Thirty-four. Thirty-five. Thirty-six. Thirty-seven.

This is how many times we stab her.

∀

Aftermath. In the end, there is no mystery. There is no conspiracy. In the end, as in the beginning, there are only humans, mucking about in the slough. Abigail Augenbaugh stands in the yard, in her Sunday best, awaiting the Rapture. Her Rapture. Stands there through a light rain, through the spasms in her back, the cramping calves. Abigail stands, enduring in her penance the gawkers, the chiders, awaiting her Rapture.

"Jesus?" she says, mistaking the empty Coke bottle tossed from a passing car. "Are you there?"

No. In the end, Abigail Augenbaugh just goes back into the house. Just. The same house. In the end, there is Burns Augenbaugh, crying down in the basement after Pastor Mike left some soup on the doorstep. The tribulation—of local news, of courtrooms, of doctors, lawyers, and expert witnesses—is immediate and hellish. No other way to say it. But soon (predictably, inevitably) peters out. And before the summer is over, there is Tim DeFonzie, who mows the weedy patch of Augenbaugh yard, who takes his Weed Eater and trims around the house. Because it needs to be done.

No. In the end, the rooms of the Augenbaugh house are no more or less empty than before. The boy's absence is as immense as his presence was. In the basement there is the sump pump's obscene suck and the comforting roar (though subdued) of the crowd on the PGA Masters Historic Edition game.

One day, because it had to be done, Abby picks up Burn's prescription from the pharmacy. At the register, she avoids eye contact. Looks instead at a display of Med-Minders, buys a blue one, a seven-day dispenser. That afternoon she organizes her husband's pills for the week. Then, because it had to be done, she continues the practice.

In the end, Abigail Augenbaugh will go back to the Slinky plant, back to the blessed schkkk-chick-chicka of the box-and-tape machine. Some of the Slinky employees talk to her; some don't. She doesn't drive anymore, and in walking she passes the ad hoc shrine of candles and artificial flowers and photographs behind the apartments, near the dumpster, where Cheyenne Onkst died. Was killed.

In the end, Abigail will not know that one of the other waiters at the country club where Cheyenne worked will hang a strand of origami butterflies in her locker in the employee bathroom. Nor that many of her classmates in Bio 101, at the community college, will not notice her absence. Kids drop classes all the time. Abigail will not know these things. They will happen anyway.

In the end, there will be Carole Onkst and her estranged husband, fighting because he thinks cremation is "wrong." Carole's wishes will hold sway, but she'll make concessions she'll regret for the rest of her life. The father will have Cheyenne's face tattooed over his heart. Carole will take a few weeks off as guidance counselor at Joy Area Middle School. She just isn't capable of guiding. Abigail will not know these things.

The Rapture billboard will be plastered over with a Lite Beer advertisement featuring a girl in a really small bikini holding a hockey stick. Everybody will see the change. And the benign hump of Scald Mountain will press down upon Joy, PA, for the foreseeable future.

One day, Carole Onkst sits at a red light, thinking about (mercifully) nothing. It is May. Or June. Or July. It doesn't matter. A bus pulls up in the next lane. Carole Onkst looks out of her window into the scowling face of a pink princess the size of her car: A Disney ad covers the length of the bus. Carole blinks, looks up, because she has to. Looks into the window, into another face, the face of the passenger looking back at her. Abigail Augenbaugh is on her way home from her weekly visit with Willie. The women see each other. Abigail looks away, because she has to.

The bus's air conditioner is broken. Abigail struggles to catch her breath in the stifling heat. Because visiting hours are right after work, Abby wears her Slinky smock. The polyester fabric is hot and sticky. Abigail knows this intersection. She cranes her neck, looking between the rows of seats and through the windshield for something she couldn't name. Carole Onkst means to flick on the turn signal, but her hands tremble and miss the mark. The windshield wipers flap madly. It is May. Or it is not. Scald Mountain doesn't care. Abigail Augenbaugh can't breathe, and in that airless, choking moment, does the bravest thing she's ever done. She looks back, into the face of Carole Onkst. The face of Carole Onkst is there. Maybe it never left. The Bradford pear trees offer up their petals. The mountain, its shadow. Abigail looks and sees Carole Onkst lift her hand, slowly, and press her palm to the window. And Abigail Augenbaugh breathes in the gesture. And it is good.

Abigail Augenbaugh reaches toward her own thin pane. The traffic light turns green. The bus veers left, leaving a cloud of diesel smoke in its wake. Carole goes straight. And it is good.

I am Willie. Do you know me?

ACKNOWLEDGMENTS

I would like to thank the following for their expertise and generous support (and one of them for her very existence): Officer Kermit Alwine; Matt and Dalia Evans; Officer H. T. Fownes; Michael Griffith; Simon Lipskar; Michael "The Jerky Jenius" Lowery; Thomas Metzger; Lee Peterson; Marci Rowland, PhD; G. C. Waldrep; Gary James "Xavier" Weisel; and Jerry "The Godfather" Zolten.

CPSIA information can be obtained at www.ICGtesting.com
Printed in the USA
BVOW02s1339120415

395705BV00002B/17/P